Beowulf For Cretins

a love story

ANN MCMAN

Bywater
BOOKS

Ann Arbor

Print ISBN: 978-1-61294-117-2

Bywater Books First Edition: June 2018

Printed in the United States of America on acid-free paper.

Cover designer: Ann McMan, TreeHouse Studio

This novel reimagines and expands on
"Falling From Grace,"
which was first published in the short story collection,
Sidecar by Ann McMan.

Sidecar was originally published by Nuance Books, a division of
Bedazzled Ink Publishing Company, Fairfield, California in 2012.

Bywater Books
PO Box 3671
Ann Arbor MI 48106-3671
www.bywaterbooks.com

For Domina and HB.
This book would not exist without the warm
welcome you always provide—whether I deserve it or not.

This book also is dedicated to dear Father Jimmy
(and his Sister Adorers of the Divine Wrath).
Thank you for showing by example that God has a sense of humor.

"For the vision is yet for an appointed time,
but at the end it shall speak, and not lie: though it tarry,
wait for it; because it will surely come . . ."

—Habukkuk 2:3

Chapter One

Going to a party was the last thing she felt like doing.

Well. Maybe having her fingernails pulled out with rusty pliers would actually be the *last* thing. But going to a party—any kind of party—had to be next in line right after that.

And a damn costume party?

Even worse.

Who in the hell besides Annette Funicello threw a costume party to celebrate their sixtieth birthday?

Rizzo, that's who. Born on Friday the 13th, Rizzo was famous for her macabre masked balls. And this year, she promised to make it one for the record books.

Yippee.

Grace looked out the tiny window beside her seat. She hadn't been anyplace in months. And this damn trip was costing her a fortune. But Rizzo was her best friend, and she had been planning this shindig for nearly a year—long before Grace's relationship with Denise had hit the skids.

Hit the skids? Hell. Roared off a damn cliff was more like it. You had to hand it to Denise. She didn't mess around. When she decided it was over, it was *over*. Capital *O*.

That had been ten months ago. And those had been an agonizing ten months for Grace. Ten months of trying to fit the broken shards of her life together into something that halfway resembled a human shape.

1

It was amazing. If you used enough duct tape and baling twine, you could patch yourself up well enough to walk around without a limp. It was the ego that was harder to fix. And this time, it was a toss-up to determine which part of her had taken the biggest hit—her ego or her heart.

It had been a classic setup. An old standby. A golden oldie. A Blue Plate Special. One Number Six.

She got dumped for a younger woman.

And it got even better. She got dumped for a younger woman with an indifferent IQ, a head full of hair product, and a perky set of store-bought boobs.

But those were the breaks, right? The universe giveth, and the universe taketh away. The Ten Thousand Things rose and fell. And that was mostly okay—unless, of course, you happened to be the poor schmuck standing in the crosshairs when all Ten Thousand of the damn Things came crashing down to earth and nailed your ass.

There was a ding, and above her head, the "fasten seatbelt" light illuminated. They were coming into Phoenix. They had a very short time on the ground before the flight would continue to San Francisco. She glanced at her watch. It wasn't worth deplaning, and since she didn't have to change seats, she decided just to stay put and enjoy the solitude.

For once, the landing was uneventful. The flight wasn't completely full, so it didn't take long for the rest of the passengers to collect their bags and head out into the heat. Grace leaned her head against the window frame and watched the bored-looking baggage handlers toss suitcases onto the conveyor like they were sacks of mulch.

It could always be worse, she thought. *I could have to do that for a living.*

Suddenly her job teaching English literature to bratty, self-important Gen-Z-ers seemed like more of a gift than a curse.

"Excuse me. Would you mind if I took this seat?"

Grace looked up to see a tallish woman wearing a tailored business suit standing in the aisle next to her row. She was holding a book and a briefcase.

Grace stared at her stupidly for a moment before she realized that the woman was politely waiting for her to move her shit off the seat.

"God, I'm sorry," she said, collecting her notebooks and lesson plans. "Life at the center of the universe, you know?"

The woman smiled and sat down. "I apologize for disturbing you. I really wanted an exit row seat for the extra leg room, and all the other ones look taken." She gestured toward the seats across the aisle. They were all tagged with magazines and empty barf bags. "I thought I'd try to move up before they boarded the passengers for the next flight." She stowed her black leather briefcase under the seat ahead of her. It was a nice one. Monogrammed. Grace didn't have time to make out the initials. "I guess we had the same idea," she added.

"What idea?" Grace asked.

"Staying on the plane during the layover?"

"Oh, that." Grace shrugged. "Ever been to Phoenix?"

The woman laughed. "Once—under duress. I swore I'd never do it again voluntarily."

"Wise woman. Unless, of course, you're into video gambling, in which case, you're missing a golden opportunity."

The woman pulled a small pair of reading glasses out of a sleeve on the outside of her briefcase. "To do what?"

"I dunno. Win lots and lots of tokens that you can redeem for oddly colored stuffed animals?"

"Unfortunately, I'm not much into stuffed animals. Nor am I very lucky, as a rule."

"That makes two of us."

The woman looked at her for a moment, and then extended her hand. "I'm Abbie."

Grace shook it. "Grace. Also unlucky at games." *And love,* she thought.

"Where are you headed?"

Grace smiled at her. "Same place as you, I'd imagine."

"San Francisco?"

Grace nodded.

"Do you live there?"

Grace shook her head. "Nope. Never been there, in fact."

"Really? Is this a business trip?"

"No. Pleasure. I'm visiting an old friend."

"Same here."

"Small world."

"Sometimes it is." Abbie put on a pair of wire-framed glasses. Somehow, they made her look even more attractive. She glanced down at Grace's pile of papers. "Are you a teacher?"

Grace shrugged. "So they tell me."

"What do you teach?"

Grace sighed. "Right now, I'm teaching four sections of '*Beowulf* for Cretins.'"

Abbie laughed out loud. "I guess that's code for Freshman English?"

"You might say that."

"I think I just did."

"Oh really?" She tapped her fingers against her ear. "I must have a trace of tinnitus."

"From flying?"

"No, from straining to hear myself think."

Abbie smiled. "Are you sure you're not a nightclub comic?"

"Trust me," Grace replied. "No one would pay to listen to anything I have to say."

"Except maybe the parents of your cretins?"

"Oh, they don't really have a choice."

"They don't?"

Grace shook her head. "Nope. For their kids, it's either college, or forced internment in a gulag."

Abbie raised an eyebrow. "Just where do you teach—Siberia?"

"Close. New England."

"Ah." Abbie glanced down at her feet. "That would explain the crampons."

Grace laughed. "Yes. I was amazed that TSA didn't confiscate them."

"Well, things have grown slack since the first decade following 9/11."

"So true." Grace looked more closely at her. *Damn.* Dark hair. Intelligent blue-gray eyes. Killer smile. This woman was truly gorgeous. She was probably in her late forties. Classy, stylish. A great set of legs.

And totally out of her league.

Probably married.

When she could, she stole a glance at the woman's ring finger. *Fuck.* There it was—the inevitable band of gold.

It figured.

"Well," she said. "I suppose I should let you do whatever it was you intended to do when you decided to remain on the plane."

Abbie looked down at the book on her lap.

Grace followed her gaze. It was a parallel translation of Boccaccio's *De Mulieribus Claris.* Of course, she'd be brilliant, too. Why was the universe so unkind?

"I suppose so." Abbie sounded almost disappointed. "I'm sorry. I'm not normally such a chatterbox."

"Oh, please." Grace extended a hand. "Don't apologize. I thought I was distracting you."

"Well, if you were, it was a distraction I welcomed."

They smiled at each other a little awkwardly. Like teenagers who had just been introduced at a sock hop.

A flight attendant who was making her way up the aisle from the rear of the aircraft stopped next to their row.

"Would either of you ladies like something to drink?"

Grace looked up at her in surprise. "Can you do that?"

The flight attendant made a grand display of looking over both shoulders. "As long as you don't tell anyone," she whispered.

Grace looked at Abbie. "Do you drink?"

Abbie nodded. "Whenever possible."

"Okay," Grace said. "Bring us two of your most indifferent, overpriced wines."

The attendant smiled and nodded. "Red or white?"

"Red," they replied simultaneously.

The attendant moved on toward the front galley of the airplane.

"Wow." Grace shook her head. "I think my tinnitus is worse. I'm hearing echoes now."

"That wasn't an echo, it was an affirmation."

"Oh. No wonder I didn't recognize it."

"Really? I guess it's contagious."

"You, too?"

Abbie nodded. "It hasn't been one of my better years. But I think things are looking up."

"Short term, or long term?"

"If I'm lucky, maybe both."

"I thought you said you weren't lucky?" Grace smiled at her.

"I figure that sooner or later, the law of averages has to catch up with me."

"True," Grace said. "And failing that, there are rumored to be certain drug therapies that are efficacious."

"You mean, at producing medically induced delusions?"

Grace nodded. "Of course. It's all the rage."

Abbie sighed. "Nobody tells me anything."

"Maybe you need to get out more?"

"Maybe I do."

Grace was about to reply when the flight attendant approached them with a tray containing two plastic cups of wine.

"Here you go, ladies. On the house." She handed them each a cup.

Grace looked up at her in surprise. "Really?"

"Yep. It looks like we're gonna be stuck here for a bit longer than forty-five minutes. There are some storms rolling through the Bay Area, and they've pushed our departure back."

Abbie looked concerned. "Do we need to get off the airplane?"

The flight attendant shook her head. "Not unless you get drunk and start swinging from the overhead bins." She smiled at them. "Enjoy the wine." She walked off.

Grace looked at Abbie. "I love JetBlue."

Abbie held up her cup, and they clinked rims. "Me too."

Grace discreetly looked her beautiful companion up and down. *Might as well torture myself a little more.* "So, if it's not too personal, why have you had such a bad year?"

Abbie flexed the fingers on her left hand and stared at her lap for a moment without answering.

"I'm sorry," Grace apologized. "I didn't mean to make you uncomfortable."

Abbie met her eyes. "No. It's okay. I'm not uncomfortable because of your question, I'm uncomfortable because of my answer."

"That's intriguing."

"Is it? Funny. From where I sit, it just feels pathetic."

"Well, why not just put it out there and let me judge for myself?"

Abbie seemed to think about that.

"All right. Why not?" Abbie set her cup of wine down on the tray table and half turned in her seat so she could cross her legs. Grace had to fight not to stare at them. They really were things of beauty.

"I lost my husband to heart disease eighteen months ago, and I've been struggling with how his death should change the way I live. That's really what this trip is about for me—figuring things out. Making choices."

Grace was stunned, and moved, by Abbie's honesty. She struggled with how to respond. "I can't imagine why you'd find that pathetic."

"Ah. That's because you don't know what the choices are."

"Fair enough." Grace shook her head. "And I thought *I* was on God's shit list because I have to go to a damn costume party."

Abbie smiled at her. "West-Coasters tend to have more eclectic tastes."

"Ain't that the truth."

"What's your costume?"

Grace raised an eyebrow. "You don't really expect me to tell you, do you?"

Abbie shrugged. "I don't see why not. I more or less just showed you what's lurking behind mine."

"You're wearing a costume?"

"Of course. That's why my choices are complicated."

"I begin to see now why you wanted to be seated in the exit row."

"Do you?"

Grace felt her pulse rate accelerate. "I'm not really sure what we're talking about."

"Choices. Costumes." Abbie smiled. "And emergency exits."

Grace was beginning to feel like she needed to make use of one, before she made a fool of herself.

"Right. Okay. I'm going as a Greek philosopher."

"Which one?"

Grace held up her hands. "Take your pick."

"They're really not interchangeable."

"They are when you shop at Party City."

Abbie laughed.

"But since you asked, I was thinking about Demosthenes."

"An interesting choice. Why?"

"Because to pull it off, I only need a toga and a mouthful of pebbles. It greatly simplified packing for this trip."

"But won't the pebbles make it difficult to talk?"

Grace nodded with enthusiasm. "See? I knew you'd get it."

Abbie rolled her eyes. "Cheater."

"Not really. I hate talking to strangers."

Abbie sucked in her cheeks.

Grace blushed. "I mean, generally."

Abbie took a sip from her cup of wine. "Lucky me."

Grace felt her pulse rate take off again.

They both looked up when the flight attendant appeared again.

"Drink up, ladies. It looks like there was a break in the weather action, and we're going to start boarding in a few minutes. I'll be back shortly to collect your cups." She walked on toward the rear of the aircraft.

Grace and Abbie looked at each other.

Grace held up her cup. "How about a toast?"

"Okay." Abbie followed suit.

"To having what we *do* become one with who we *are*."

Abbie stared at her for a moment before slowly clinking plastic rims.

"You really are eloquent—pebbles notwithstanding."

"Only on Mondays and Wednesdays, from nine-ten to ten-fifteen."

Abbie looked at her watch. "It's ten-thirty, and today is Friday."

"It is?" Grace looked at her own watch. "Well, holy Grendel's Mother."

"I guess nobody tells you anything, either?"

"You got that right, sister."

They finished their wine just as the first passengers started to board. As she fastened her seatbelt, Grace decided that maybe flying out for this party wasn't such a bad idea, after all.

Rizzo's birthday shindig was being held at the South End Rowing Club on Jefferson Street—a landmark in the Fisherman's Wharf neighborhood and a stone's throw from the Fort Mason cultural arts complex. It was a perfect venue for a party, with beautiful views of the Golden Gate and Bay Bridges and a cavernous, wind-sheltered sundeck.

Rizzo promised that the guest list would be small—only twenty or thirty people—and she further insisted that Grace wouldn't have to worry about blending in because everyone would be in costume.

Right.

But when Rizzo insisted, it was best just to capitulate and go along. Grace had learned that one the hard way. Rizzo was hardcore. A tough-talking, straight-shooting, don't-blow-smoke-up-my-ass truth-teller who had survived more personal horrors than the combined casts of a dozen Brian De Palma movies.

You didn't say "no" to Rizzo. Not without a good goddamn

reason—and, in this case, Grace didn't have one. A candy-ass case of ennui just didn't count.

So here she was, feeling short and ridiculous in her blue-trimmed toga and sandals.

At least the damn outfit was uncomplicated. Some of the other ensembles on display were fantastic, jaw-dropping creations right out of an Edith Head catalog. Rizzo, herself, was unadorned. She insisted that, as the hostess and guest of honor, she had the prerogative to appear however she fucking well chose.

Nobody argued with her.

Rizzo worked the room like a pro, making certain that everyone felt welcome and that every empty hand was quickly filled with a fresh drink or a plate of hot food. And she kept a watchful eye on Grace, making certain that she didn't drift off to any dark corners to brood or to hide from the rest of the crowd.

She knew Grace pretty well.

"Warner," she'd demand. "Get over here. I want you to meet some people."

So, she did. Countless people. A slew of names without faces, since most of them were wearing masks or sporting so much cheap makeup it would be impossible to pick them out of a police lineup.

Maybe that was the point. Rizzo's guest lists tended to be rather eclectic.

Later on, when the live music started, Grace seized the opportunity to sneak off the sundeck and meander down toward the water, where a flotilla of long boats was tied up in the small marina and sea lions lazed about on the piers. The sun was setting, and the air rolling in across the bay was growing a lot colder. She knew she wouldn't be able to stay out here for very long. Her cheesy toga was too lightweight to offer much protection from the night air.

It really was beautiful. She could understand why Rizzo loved it here. Maybe she needed to make a change—get the hell out of Vermont and start over someplace new? Why not? There was nothing holding her there. Not now. Especially not her career. She liked her teaching job well enough. But colleges like St. Albans were a dime a dozen—self-important bastions of the liberal arts that offered upper-middle class white kids ivy-covered halls, small classes, and boutique majors—all for an annual tuition bill that would dwarf the sticker price on any new Lexus.

Change? Change could be a good thing. Why not move on and try to reinvent herself? She was still young enough to make a fresh start. She was . . .

Wasn't she?

"I thought that was you."

Grace was so startled by the voice coming from just behind her that she nearly dropped her glass of wine. It sloshed all over her hand and splattered across the front of her toga.

"Shit!" She shook her hand off to try and disperse the red liquid.

"Oh, god, I'm sorry." The voice was closer now.

Grace turned around to see that it was coming from . . . Bonnie Parker?

At least, she thought it was Bonnie Parker. The toy tommy gun, the tweed suit, and the black beret were pretty big clues.

She looked lethal. And she looked hot as hell. In fact, she looked a lot like . . . *Abbie.*

"No way," Grace said, looking her up and down. "Is that really you?"

Abbie smiled. "I think so. Small world, isn't it?"

"You know Rizzo?" Grace was stunned.

Abbie nodded. "We met in grad school at Chicago, about a hundred years ago. But we've always stayed in touch. I wouldn't miss a big event in her life like this one—not for the world."

"I think I'm in shock."

"I know what you mean. I saw you about thirty minutes ago, shortly after I arrived, and I've been trying to make my way over to you to say hello. But by the time I finally broke free from some other college pals, you had disappeared. I came outside to see the view, and saw you down here." She gestured back toward the cook shack. "Frankly, I was also trying to escape the music."

Strains of "Now That I Found You" drifted toward them.

Grace struggled to avoid seeing the irony. "Not a big fan of bluegrass?" she asked, with a smile.

Abbie shrugged. "I can tolerate the instrumental parts, but the vocals make my teeth hurt."

Grace stared at her for a moment, then shook her head. "I just can't believe we're both standing here at the same damn party. What are the odds?"

"I don't know." Abbie looked smug. "I think I told you that the law of averages would catch up with me sooner or later."

"I thought you were talking about wanting your luck to change?"

Abbie smiled at her. "That's exactly what I was talking about."

"I'm not trying to be dense, but how on earth does this qualify?"

"Do you always underestimate yourself?"

Grace was completely flustered. She had no idea how to respond, so she didn't make any response. She just stood there. Stupidly.

Abbie gestured toward the front of her toga. "I'm so sorry I startled you, now you've got red wine stains all over the front of your costume."

Grace looked down at it. "That's okay. If anyone asks, I'll just tell them I'm Julius Caesar."

Abbie laughed. "Beware the Ides of March?"

Grace nodded. "Maybe my luck will change, too?"

"Maybe it already has."

They stared at each other again.

"I'm not sure if . . . are you . . ." Grace didn't know how to finish her sentence.

"Am I what?"

How was it possible for Abbie to be so damn calm? "Just exactly what kind of life changes are you talking about making?"

Abbie hefted the barrel of her tommy gun before resting it against her shoulder. "I don't know. Maybe I'll embrace a life of crime."

"That's one way to blaze a trail."

"Or maybe I'll embrace something else."

"Such as?"

Abbie shrugged.

"Losing your courage?" Grace asked.

"On the contrary," Abbie replied. "I think I'm finding it."

Grace could feel her pulse rate going haywire again.

"What are we really talking about, Abbie?"

"You're a friend of Rizzo's. You shouldn't have to ask me that."

"Rizzo isn't gay."

"No. But you are."

Grace narrowed her eyes. "Does my toga zip on the wrong side or something?"

"Not that I can tell," Abbie replied, looking her over.

"Then how in the hell would you know something like that about me?"

"Am I wrong?"

"I didn't say that."

Abbie smiled. "Maybe I asked."

"You asked about me?"

Abbie nodded.

"Why?"

Abbie rolled her eyes.

"No. Come on . . . you said you were married."

"I was married."

Grace still didn't get it. "And now?"

"Now, I'm not married."

"But you're curious?"

"Not exactly."

"You're not curious?"

"Well, curious about you, maybe. But not about this."

Grace sighed. "I think I need another drink."

Abbie smiled. "I can take care of that. Wait right here."

Grace touched her on the arm. "Gimme the gun. I'll cover you."

Abbie laughed and handed it over to her. "I didn't know this was hostile territory."

"You can't be too careful."

Abbie met her eyes. "Believe me when I tell you that you can."

"Is that what this is about?"

"No. This is about getting you some more wine." Abbie laid a hand on Grace's forearm. "And maybe a jacket. You're freezing. Stay put. I'll be right back."

Grace watched her walk back toward the cook shack. She was wearing a knit sweater and a tight tweed skirt. She looked a lot more like Faye Dunaway than Bonnie Parker.

Not that anyone would complain about that. The woman was hot.

Holy shit. This is so not happening. The last thing I need right now is to become somebody's goddamn science experiment.

Abbie reached the steps that led up to the sundeck and turned around and waved.

On the other hand, why the hell not? It's not like we'll ever run into each other again.

They spent the next hour sitting on a bench overlooking the water, watching the flicker of lights on the two bridges.

Grace learned a little bit more about Abbie. A very little bit. She lived in North Carolina, and had been married for six years before her husband died. They had no kids. For the last two years, she'd worked as the executive director of a nonprofit, philanthropic foundation. She liked the work, but felt that she was ready for something different.

Grace wondered if her desire for something different helped explain why she was spending the better part of the evening sitting on a bench in the cold and trading witticisms with a stranger.

It was clear to her by now that Abbie was flirting with her—testing the waters. Hell. There was enough electricity flying back and forth between them to light up one of those fucking bridges.

So, what was she going to do about it? It couldn't go anyplace. That much was clear. They lived in different parts of the country, and for all practical purposes, she knew next to nothing about her.

But none of that mattered. That wasn't what this was about. This was about something that Grace rarely did, and hadn't done in more than ten years. This was about what Rizzo liked to call "an overnight rental," or at least it could be, if she played her cards right and didn't lose her nerve.

She shivered. The breeze off the water was like a blast from an open freezer door.

"You're cold." Abbie shifted closer to her on the bench. Grace didn't mind.

"It's my own fault for picking such a ridiculous costume. I should've gone with my first choice."

"Which was?" Abbie asked.

Grace looked at her. "Scooby Doo."

Abbie laughed.

"You find that amusing?"

She nodded. "It's hard to imagine you dressed up like a giant dog."

"I don't see why. It would have had several advantages."

"Like?"

Grace held up her hand and commenced ticking the advantages off on her fingers. "Well, first, there's the fur coat."

Abbie nodded. "I can see where that would have been beneficial."

"Second, there's the flea collar. Very useful when you're traveling in warmer climates."

Abbie looked dubious. "Okaaayyy."

"Third, it would have allowed me to do things that I could never do dressed like this."

Abbie looked intrigued . . . and suspicious. "Is that a fact?"

"Oh, yes. Absolutely."

"What kinds of things, exactly?"

"Oh, you know . . . dog kinds of things."

"Dog kinds of things?"

"Yeah."

"And what might those be?"

Grace had no idea where her newfound bravado was coming from, but she decided to run with it. "Do you need me to show you?"

Abbie took a long, slow breath.

God, the woman was sexy as hell.

"I'll probably live to regret this, but, yes. Show me."

Grace took hold of Abbie's face with both hands. Her skin felt soft and warm. With the small part of her brain that was thinking rationally, she wondered how it was possible for Abbie to be so damn warm when she was fighting to keep her own hands from shaking. As slowly as she could, she leaned forward until their faces were nearly touching. Abbie remained completely still and made no effort to pull away. Their breath mingled on the night air as Grace hovered there. Then, in a flash, she stuck out her tongue and licked the tip of Abbie's nose. Just as quickly, she dropped her hands and sat back against the bench.

"That kind of thing," she said.

Abbie looked incredulous. "Did you just lick me on the nose?"

Grace nodded.

"I can't believe you did that," Abbie said.

"Why not? You asked me to show you."

Abbie shook her head. "All I can say is, thank god you didn't get the Scooby Doo costume."

"That bad, huh?"

"I'll say."

"I guess it was a lame joke." Grace touched her on the arm. "I'm really sorry."

Abbie looked at her. In the half-light, her eyes glowed like hot coals. "I'm not." Her voice sounded husky.

Grace's head was starting to spin. "I'm confused again. You're not sorry?"

"Not at all. If you were dressed like a dog, I couldn't do this."

Before Grace knew what was happening, Abbie closed the distance between them and kissed her. Hard.

Grace had been kissed before, but never quite like this. There was something raw and uncontrolled in the way they came together. The kiss went on and on. Grace was practically in Abbie's lap by the time they finally broke apart.

"Woof," she said when she could find her voice.

Abbie laughed softly against her hair.

"As soon as I can manage to stand up, I want you to push me into the bay."

Abbie drew back. "Why on earth would I do that?"

"To cool my ass off," Grace said.

"I thought you were already cold?"

Grace shook her head. "Not anymore."

Abbie pulled her closer. "Maybe I like having you hot."

Okay. There was that pulse rate thing again. "I think we should talk about this."

Abbie kissed across her forehead. "Really? Talking is what you want to do right now?"

Grace swallowed hard and forced herself to draw back. "Of course not. What I want is a whole lot more related to . . . nonverbal communication."

Abbie smiled and reached for her again. "Me, too."

Grace held up a hand. "Wait. I haven't done this in a really long time." She paused. "Well . . . I mean . . . I haven't done *this*. Not in this way."

Abbie looked confused. "I know I've been out of circulation for a while, but how many ways are there to do it?"

"That isn't what I meant."

"All right. What did you mean?"

Grace took a deep breath. "How about I ask you a question instead?"

"Okay." Abbie sat back and folded her arms.

"You've been with women before?"

Abbie thought about that. "Define 'been with.'"

"You're really going to make me work for this, aren't you?"

Abbie gave her a shy smile. "I'm sorry. I don't mean to be obtuse. This isn't something I have much experience talking about."

Grace nodded. "Well, here's your opportunity to practice."

"Funny you should say that. I thought that's exactly what I *was* doing."

Grace laughed. "Honey, if that's what you call practice, then you're a shoo-in for a reserved seat at the head of the class."

Abbie smiled. "I've always been an overachiever."

Grace smiled, too. "Lucky me."

They stared at each other for a moment without speaking. Behind them, the band's spirited rendition of Willie Nelson's "I Gotta Get Drunk" finished with a flourish, and a wave of applause rolled out across the small marina. Grace heard the bandleader thank the audience. It seemed clear that the entertainment portion of the party was over. That meant that Rizzo would be making her rounds again. They probably didn't have much more time to sit here, alone in the dark.

Fuck me, and my damn scruples for wasting it. Women like Abbie sure as shit didn't come her way very often.

What the hell was she thinking? Women like Abbie never came her way.

She sighed and nodded toward the lighted patio behind them. "I think we just ran out of time."

Abbie followed her gaze, then looked back at Grace. "Maybe not."

Grace raised an eyebrow.

"Where are you staying?"

Something fluttered inside her chest. "The Fairmont in Ghirardelli Square."

Abbie smiled. "Me, too."

"I had a coupon," Grace explained.

Abbie shook her head. "Are you walking?"

Grace nodded.

"Me, too." She glanced at her watch. "Want to meet me out front in about thirty minutes?"

Grace nodded again.

"Are you okay?" Abbie touched her hand.

"I honestly don't know. I feel like I'm sleepwalking."

"Funny. I feel like I'm finally starting to wake up."

"What the hell are you two doing out here?" Rizzo's voice cut through the darkness. "Get back up here. We're getting ready to do the cake."

Grace turned around to see their hostess leaning over the railing of the sundeck. She was framed by the backlight of a hundred Japanese lanterns. Her shape was unmistakable, and so was her air of authority.

"Save me a corner piece," Grace called out to her.

"Fuck you. Come get it yourself." Rizzo turned around and disappeared into the crowd.

Grace looked at Abbie and sighed. "She has such a way with words."

Abbie agreed. "I know. It's a useful skill for a poet."

They shared a laugh, then stood up and slowly made their way back to the party. They reached the wooden steps to the sundeck, and Abbie linked her pinkie finger with Grace's. For some reason, it felt like the most erotic thing she'd ever experienced.

She looked at Abbie. "Did you say thirty minutes?"

Abbie nodded and smiled.

"I'll eat fast."

Abbie gave her finger a short squeeze, and then released it when they reached the top step. They separated and rejoined the party.

Three-hundred-and-twenty-four bucks was the most she'd ever spent on a hotel room—especially one she never used.

Grace unlocked the door with her keycard and stepped inside. It was freezing. The AC was blasting. She forgot that she'd set it so low before she left for the party last night.

She leaned against the back of the big door and closed her eyes.

Good god. Did any of that really happen?

It was so not who she was.

But wasn't that what they'd both talked about wanting to do? Change who they were?

Right. Who they were, but not how they lived. Today, they were each headed back to their real lives. Alone. Abbie was already on her way to the airport. Her flight for Charlotte was leaving in two hours.

They had made no promises, and no offers to stay in touch. Abbie never suggested it, and Grace didn't have the courage to offer first. So, they both remained silent.

It was a missed opportunity. She knew it. One she'd probably keep on missing for the rest of her life.

She didn't even know Abbie's last name.

So now, she'd collect her shit and head back to Vermont with nothing more than a memory.

Unless . . . She could always ask Rizzo about Abbie?

No. If Abbie had wanted to stay in touch, she'd have said so. They would have exchanged names and phone numbers. They'd have talked about finding ways to try and meet again in one place or the other.

But Abbie had said nothing, so Grace said nothing.

Fuck it. Grow up. You knew what you were doing. Don't weep about it now. There are no victims in this little drama.

She sighed, walked to the bed, and flopped down on it. She had six hours to kill until her flight left. Might as well try to get a little sleep, since she hadn't gotten any last night.

She closed her eyes, but all she could see were visions of Abbie.

Jeez. The woman sure made up for lost time. They both had. It was fantastic. *Incredible.* Without a doubt, it was the most erotic and exciting thing she'd ever done. What Abbie seemed to lack in experience, she made up for in enthusiasm—and determination. And she hadn't been kidding. She was one hell of a fast learner. In fact, Grace had felt like the novice. *What a great problem to have.*

She rolled over and stared at the bedside clock.

This was a colossal waste of time. She was too keyed-up to sleep. Only one thing could help her now.

She got up to head for the bathroom and a cold shower.

Chapter Two

Back at St. Albans, things soon settled into a normal routine.

Memories of her "overnight rental" didn't exactly fade, but they gradually became easier to think about without an accompanying attack of angst. Or regret. She resolved to chalk the entire experience up to a growth spurt—an exponential leap forward in her recovery from the Disaster-That-Was-Denise.

Classes were spiraling toward the long, Labor Day weekend. All four sections of her English Lit survey had papers due. She'd be up to her ass in reams of bad prose by Wednesday afternoon. She knew better than to waste her time holding classes on Thursday. The students would all have decamped for exotic end-of-summer destinations long before then.

Fall break would roll around next, followed shortly by midterms. Then finals. It was hard to believe how fast the semester was advancing. At least the long Christmas break would give her a chance to work on her book. That was how she filled up the empty spaces in her life right now—by continuing her halting attempts at writing the next Great American Novel.

She called it her GAN.

In fact, her GAN wasn't really living up to the *G* part of its acronym. At least, not yet. But hammering away on *The Disappearance of Ochre* kept her busy through the succession of dull and interminable nights that kicked in after Denise moved out.

Grace had been an undergraduate at Haverford when she first

heard about how the famous "Woman-Ochre" painting by Willem de Kooning had been slashed from its frame and stolen from the University of Arizona Museum of Art in 1985. Two unassuming, albeit oddly dressed, patrons had walked in at 9 a.m. on the Friday after Thanksgiving, tarried in the gallery for about ten minutes, then departed in a hurry with the de Kooning rolled up and hidden beneath an overcoat. They were never identified or caught and more than three decades later, the painting's whereabouts remained a mystery.

It wasn't until graduate school at Vanderbilt—and a fiction writing seminar with novelist Ann Patchett—that Grace cobbled together her fledgling idea for a fictionalized story about the subject of the painting, an artist's model she called "Ochre." She was writing the novel as a series of short stories, each detailing Ochre's first-person accounts of her sojourns with quirky and wildly divergent sets of captors. Part of the appeal of this narrative approach was that it allowed her to work in shorter, more episodic bursts.

She liked to think of this enterprise as a homage to her literary idol, Italo Calvino.

At least, that was the idea.

When she wasn't working on her GAN, she filled her lonely days by making protracted progress on an endless series of renovations to her small, Craftsman-style bungalow.

Grace had purchased the place six years ago when she first started teaching at St. Albans. It was a small, unremarkable house in a line of other small, unremarkable houses that occupied a block several streets back from the main quad. That appealed to her. The campus, with its ivy-covered Georgian halls and manicured grounds, had a storybook kind of beauty—but she liked not having to stare at the bleakest aspects of its classroom buildings when she looked out her windows at home.

Of course, these days, that wasn't much of an issue. Most of the front windows on her house were obscured by heavy plastic sheathing while the asbestos shingles were being removed. She and Denise had shared grand prospects for restoring the vintage house to its original glory. It was only after their renovations commenced that they uncovered a sequence of numbers stamped at regular intervals on exposed joists and rafters that identified their bungalow as a bona fide, circa 1936 Sears "Vallonia"—one of the 370 varieties of kit homes that people of modest means could order up right out of the same fat catalog that brought overcoats, rubber galoshes, longline corsets, Bakelite toasters and Hercules boilers right to their doorsteps.

The lion's share of the renovation work was being carried out on weekends by Grace's brother, Dean, who ran his own business restoring historic homes—and operating a hugely successful regional chain of home improvement stores.

He was the rock star of the Warner family.

Unfortunately, Denise had decided to decamp long before the restorations were completed, and Grace now lived with the consequences. Every room of the house was in some state of disrepair. It didn't escape her notice that the level of disruption in her home paralleled the mess of her interior life. It was like an object lesson writ large. When she stopped to think about it—which seemed to be more often lately—she understood the irony that restoring order to the disarray of her fractured soul probably proceeded along the same timetable as setting the house to rights.

She sat down in front of her office computer to check her email one last time before packing up and heading for home.

There were several messages from students offering creative excuses for why their papers would be late. She archived those for later. There were also two messages marked "high priority" from the Presidential Search Committee. One suggested that an announcement from the Trustees would be forthcoming soon.

Grace rolled her eyes.

Yeah, that one promised to be a real nail-biter—*not*. They were all persuaded that the board would make a "traditional" choice—which meant another musty, dried-up non-academic with an indifferent resume, deep ties to the Catholic church, and even deeper pockets.

It was a small college no-brainer.

Especially for a place like St. Albans.

Pre-Law, Pre-Med and Pre-Menstrual. That's how Grace characterized most of her students.

St. Allie's, as they called it, was sixty-three percent female. And it showed. Even though the admission staff worked hard to level the playing field and recruit more males, the balance stayed the same. Or rather, the imbalance stayed the same. The lopsided enrollment both helped and hurt the small, northern Vermont college. Grace found that classes more heavily weighted toward females tended to have more—*gravitas.* She supposed that was because a classroom full of girls was more inclined to focus on the content of the course, and less inclined to primp and preen for any males plopped in their midst.

Well. With certain exceptions . . .

St. Allie's was gaining a reputation for *that* characteristic, too. Numerous dour and tight-lipped trustees would scowl and cluck their tongues when the annual *U.S. News & World Report Guide to America's Best Colleges* awarded St. Allie's a consistent top-ten ranking for "Most Lesbian Friendly" small college.

Yeah. Great for academics and field hockey—not so great for growing the endowment. Or so they said. For her part, Grace thought the tiny place should embrace and capitalize on its burgeoning mark of distinction rather than work so hard to paper it over and will it to fade into obscurity.

She recalled her own tenure as a plaid-skirted coed at Bishop Hoban High School in Wilkes-Barre. In "health class"—a benign euphemism for the dark and murky netherland that encompassed anything related to female sexuality—Sister Mary Lawrence (they all called her Sister Merry Larry) instructed the pockmarked, ragtag group of alternately amused or embarrassed teens about what to do if a boy became "overexcited" on a date.

In Nun-Speak™, "overexcited" meant "erect."

Sister Merry Larry lowered her alto voice to a near whisper. "You slap it hard to make it go down."

Slap it? Hard?

Grace found that to be a curiously . . . *intimate* . . . response to an uninvited consequence. More than once, she wondered about Sister Merry Larry's familiarity with the predicament. Unlike the other nuns at Bishop Hoban, Sister Merry Larry was more . . . clued-in. For one thing, she was younger by decades than most of the other Sisters. And she had come to Wilkes-Barre from a more progressive order in Philadelphia where the nuns lived in off-campus apartments, versus the crumbling convents that typically sagged off the back walls of parochial school gymnasiums. She also wore a short habit and black Reeboks. That distinction alone gave her street cred.

Still, Sister Merry Larry's visceral advice about how to respond to presumed unwanted outcomes was, in Grace's view, a decidedly *Catholic* innovation.

Create the world. Invite the people in. And don't hesitate to slap them down—hard—if they get overexcited.

Grace felt fortunate that she never had to test that last part of the dating equation. None of her half-hearted fumbles in the back seat of Jamie Zook's '69 Maverick ever escalated to the "slap down" stage. That was probably because Jamie was a lot more interested in Grace's brother, Dean, who smoked hard-pack Camels and rode a Kawasaki KZ1000. That was okay with Grace because *she* was more interested in Jamie's sister, Amy. Amy didn't smoke or ride anything—not unless you believed those stories about Sister Merry Larry catching the head cheerleader behind the bleachers, occupying a compromising position atop the Argents' quarterback, Nick Szeptak.

Those rumors didn't hurt Amy's reputation a bit.

And they didn't diminish Grace's appreciation for the popular blonde's . . . charms.

But that was all ancient history. Grace scrolled past a newer slew of *mea culpa* emails from her missing-in-action students to read a message from the board chair—inviting the entire community to an all-campus meeting at two o'clock that afternoon.

She looked at her watch.

There was a follow-up email from her department chair that

required all members of the English faculty who were still on campus to attend the announcement.

Not that she would want to miss it. An event like this one was a big deal in the life of a small college. The last two presidents of St. Allie's had been pulled from business backgrounds. This time, the faculty dared to hope they'd at least get a real academic at the helm—someone who would take a greater interest in curricular development and scholarship, rather than shaking the money tree.

She sighed. *Fat chance*. It was all about raising money these days. Still . . . it would be interesting to see which one of their dried-up old clones the big boys flushed out this go-round.

She shut down her computer and picked up her messenger bag. She'd have just enough time to run home and grab a sandwich before the meeting. She got outside and saw, with a sinking feeling, that it had started to rain. *Great*. She had plans to spend the weekend out on Butler Island and had been hoping the calls for rain would all be wrong—the way they usually were.

One thing you could always count on in Vermont was how the weather forecasts were moving targets. If what was predicted wasn't to your liking, you didn't have to worry much or wait very long for it to change.

But this wasn't looking like the kind of rain that was just passing through on its way to greener pastures in New Hampshire. This was the slow, lazy, I'm-gonna-hang-out-on-your-porch-and-drink-up-all-your-beer-before-moving-on kind of rain.

She looked up at the sky. It was the color of dull pewter. *Crap*.

A boat ride in the rain was sure to be a real blast.

The auditorium was packed.

And things were definitely looking up. Grace exchanged surprised glances with Grady Shepard as Mitchell Ware, the board chair, finished talking about the methodology used by the search committee and finally shared details from the Chosen One's curriculum vitae.

It slowly became clear that, this time, the committee had apparently listened to the faculty. The new president was an academic with a solid background in research and scholarly publication—a teacher and a thinker with stellar credentials, including a master's degree from the University of Chicago and a Ph.D. in Classics from Princeton. The winning candidate had authored a list of books and articles a half-mile long, and had spent eight years teaching literature and philology at Princeton, before taking the helm as director of the prestigious Duke Endowment—one of the largest philanthropic foundations in the country.

It was a slam dunk, and the board chair knew it. The normally unimpressed members of the St. Allie's faculty were literally sitting on the edges of their seats, waiting for the big reveal. You could've heard a pin drop in that joint.

He made them wait.

"When she joins our community, we will begin a new chapter in the life of this exceptional institution of higher learning," he said.

Grady and Grace looked at each other in shock. *She?*

A titter of conversation spread throughout the hall.

The board chair smiled. "No, that wasn't a mistake. I said 'she.'"

The hall erupted in applause. People got to their feet.

The chair shouted over the din, "It gives me great pleasure to introduce the fifteenth President of St. Albans College, Élisabeth Abbot Williams."

The applause in the hall was deafening. People were whooping and cheering. Grace got to her feet and strained to see around the bobbing rows of heads in front of her.

The cheers and the applause went on and on. This was a seminal event in the life of the college—the first female president in its one-hundred-and-sixty-five-year history.

Grace finally took a step out into the aisle so she could get a glimpse of their new leader, who had taken the stage and now stood towering over the board chair, smiling and waving at the audience. Grace stared, stunned, and dropped back into her seat.

Jesus H. Christ.

Her hands were shaking. She felt light-headed and feared she might pass out. She knew that Grady was looking at her strangely.

This was not happening.

It was Abbie.

Grace's mother had been pissed when Grace called her to say she'd decided to spend the long holiday weekend on Butler Island instead of making the trek to Wilkes-Barre.

"I'll try coming down over fall break," she said. But she knew she probably wouldn't. Not now. Not after seeing Abbie.

Correction. Not after seeing the new president of St. Albans . . . her boss.

God.

This mess was like the plot of a twisted Eugene O'Neill play. A ludicrous joke—and she was the punchline. These things didn't happen in real life. These things only happened in literature to characters like Oedipus—or in movies that starred Deborah Kerr.

What the hell was she supposed to do now? Pack up and move to Idaho?

She scoffed and took another big swig from the Grey Goose bottle. It had been part of a thank-you goodie basket sent to her from members of the curriculum committee she'd chaired last semester.

Pear-flavored vodka. How . . . *inventive.* It was only a pint bottle, but right now, it was getting the job done just fine.

She was sitting on the back steps of her small house. The rain was still coming down. Big, fat drops that exploded on every surface—including her. She knew that her jacket and her hair were soaked, but she didn't really care. Maybe if she sat here long enough, she'd melt right into the landscape, and never have to worry about how Abbie would react when she finally realized Grace was one of her newest . . . *employees.*

"What the hell is the matter with you?" Grady Shepard had asked earlier, when he caught up with her outside the auditorium after the announcement. "And why are you walking so goddamn fast?"

Grace just shook him off. "I don't feel so well. I think it must've been those hot dogs I ate at the Commons."

He looked skeptical. "You ate hot dogs at the St. Allie's cafeteria? Is this some new self-flagellation technique?"

"Could be." She didn't want to prolong the conversation. "Look, Grady, I really feel sick." It wasn't far from the truth.

"Oh, man." He ran a hand through his short Afro. "I really wanted to talk about this. Call me later?"

She shrugged. "Maybe."

"I hope we're still on for the island this weekend."

Grace had been headed for the solitude of her office—until she saw her love-struck student stalker, Brittney McDaniel, making a beeline toward Ames Hall. It never failed. Brittney seemed to have a homing beacon where Grace was concerned.

She nodded at Grady and abruptly veered off on a brick sidewalk that led away from the building that housed the English department offices. "Talk to you later, okay?"

He continued to stand there as she walked away. "Hey, Grace?"

She stopped and turned around.

"She's pretty hot, isn't she?" He grinned at her. "Just your type, too."

Grace hadn't eaten any hot dogs that day, but right then, she really did feel like throwing up.

"Yeah," she said, turning away. Rain was pelting her in the face. "She's *just* my type."

God. She took another drink. Once the vodka was gone she knew she'd start feeling how fucking soaked she was.

The Nine O'Clock Dog was barking.

Every twelve hours at precisely nine o'clock, her neighbor's dog barked. Without fail. In rain, sleet, or snow—on the brightest of days, or the darkest of nights—at the crack of nine, Grendel barked. Grace really had no idea what the dog's actual name was. She had bestowed the moniker because something about the dog's persistent aura of suspicion and menace reminded her of the infamous literary antagonist.

The Nine O'Clock Dog was one of the constants in her life—just like grading papers, watching reruns of *Frasier*, or meeting the wrong goddamn women.

She checked her watch. *Yep.* Nine o'clock. Straight up. She felt sorry for the dog—it seemed like she was left alone over there most of the time. The tenants hadn't been around much for the past couple of weeks. Their cars seemed to be gone more than parked in their rutted driveway.

She raised the bottle in a toast. "More power to ya, Grendel. If I had the chops, I'd be barking, too."

But Grendel wasn't paying any attention to her. Grendel was frantically pacing back and forth along the fence that flanked her yard. This was a much more vigilant display than usual, and she was barking well beyond the requirements of her customary alert. Clearly, someone was coming to kill them all, and Grendel didn't understand why no one else seemed to care.

Grace didn't have the patience to try, either. She'd just about decided to get up and go inside when she caught sight of someone coming around the corner of the house.

Shit. Company was the last thing she needed. And who the hell would show up now, during a driving rainstorm?

A person wearing a long black cloak with a hood stood there a moment before advancing toward the porch. Grace felt a moment of panic. *Maybe Grendel was right?* Then the figure tossed back its hood.

The warm buzz she'd been feeling from the vodka evaporated in a nanosecond. It was Abbie. *Again.*

"Jesus Christ," she blurted. "You scared the shit out of me."

Abbie stopped in front of her. Her expression was ominous—like a reflection of the storm. "Now . . . or earlier today?"

Grace shrugged. "Take your pick."

"May I sit down?"

"Can I stop you?"

Abbie sighed. "You can if you want to."

Grace hesitated.

"I guess showing up here was a bad idea," Abbie said.

"Now—or earlier today?" Grace quoted.

"Very funny."

"I do try," Grace replied.

"I remember."

"How did you find me?" Grace asked.

Abbie shrugged.

Grace gave a bitter laugh. "I guess rank has its privileges."

"I saw you from the stage."

"You did?"

Abbie nodded. "I was stunned."

"That makes two of us."

Grendel was still barking.

"You might as well come inside," Grace said. "She'll never stop if we stay out here."

"Would that be okay? My feet are soaked."

Grace looked down at her shoes. "You walked here in those?"

"I didn't exactly plan on hiking through a monsoon when I got dressed this morning."

Grace nodded. "Shit happens."

"That's true."

Abbie stared over her shoulder at the barking dog, which was standing up on its hind legs and leaning against the fence. She looked back at Grace. "Its tail is wagging."

"She's conflicted." Grace shrugged. "It's going around."

Abbie actually smiled. She gestured at the bottle Grace was holding. "What are you drinking?"

"This?" Grace held it up. "It's pear-flavored vodka."

Abbie made a face. "I think I'll pass."

"Wise decision."

"Got anything else?"

Grace stood up and opened the door so Abbie could enter the house. "Only one way to find out."

31

They went inside. Grace kicked off her shoes, then removed her soggy jacket and hung it up on a peg near the door. She turned to Abbie. "May I take your shroud?"

Abbie rolled her eyes. "Sure." She shrugged out of her long cloak and handed it to Grace.

They were standing in a small, screened porch that overlooked Grace's back yard. It was simply furnished with several distressed-looking Adirondack chairs painted in bold colors and a faded outdoor rug. A tower of papers sat on a table beside one of the chairs.

"This is a great porch," Abbie said. "You must spend a lot of time out here."

Grace nodded. "I try to. It takes some of the sting out of all the hours I spend grading papers."

"I can imagine."

"That's right. You've done your time in the classroom, too, haven't you?"

Abbie shrugged.

"Don't be so modest, Dr. Williams."

Abbie looked at her. "You seem determined to make this harder than it already is."

"Define 'this.'" Grace made air quotes with her fingers.

"Our . . . predicament."

Grace folded her arms. "We have a predicament?"

"I'd say so."

Grace knew that she was acting like a bitch, and she needed to snap out of it. This mess wasn't Abbie's fault. It wasn't any-body's fault.

She took a deep breath. "I'm sorry. Take off your wet shoes and come on into the house where it's drier."

Abbie kicked off her shoes and followed Grace into the kitchen. It was small, but cozy and well appointed.

"Have a seat." Grace indicated a small table and two chairs in the corner of the room. She walked to a tall cabinet and with-drew two glasses and a fat brown bottle. "Like cognac?"

Abbie nodded. "Got any coffee to go with it?"

"At nine o'clock at night?"

Abbie shrugged. "I don't think I need to worry about it keeping me awake."

"I see your point. I'll make us a fresh pot."

Abbie sat down and looked around the kitchen while Grace made the coffee. "This is an incredible house. How long have you been here?"

"Do you mean in this house, or at St. Albans?"

Abbie smiled at her. "Yes."

Grace carried the bottle and the two glasses to the table and sat down across from her. "Six years. I'm up for tenure this year."

"Think you'll get it?"

"It was looking good before this afternoon." She gave them each a generous pour of cognac. "Now there appears to be a monster-sized fly in the ointment."

"On the other hand," Abbie picked up her glass, "if you prevail, it would simplify . . . things."

"Like?" Grace was intrigued.

"Well. If you're a tenured professor—that means there'll be less opportunity for conflict of interest concerns."

"You mean because you're my new boss?"

"Technically, I'm *not* your boss. I'm your boss's boss."

"Isn't that the same thing?"

Abbie shook her head. "Not really."

Grace twirled her glass around. "This is a mess."

"I know."

She met Abbie's incredible gray eyes. "I keep thinking about what Oscar Wilde said."

"What's that?"

Grace sighed. "That there are only two tragedies in life. One is not getting what you want, and the other is getting it."

"Which one is this?" Abbie asked.

"You tell me."

"I'm not sure I know yet."

They sat in silence for a few moments. Grace could hear rain pelting the kitchen window.

"I thought about trying to find you," Abbie said in a quiet voice. "More than once."

Grace put her glass down. She didn't really need anything else to drink. "Why didn't you?"

Abbie looked down at the tabletop. "I was a mess. I was confused. I didn't know what I wanted."

"And now?"

"Now? I'm still a mess—and I'm still confused." She raised her eyes. "But I think I know what I want."

Grace could feel her heart starting to pound. "You do?"

Abbie nodded. "But it's complicated."

Grace laughed out loud. "You think?"

Abbie smiled. "Did you ever think about trying to find me?"

"You're kidding, right?"

Abbie shook her head.

"Of course I did." She hesitated. "I nearly called Rizzo a dozen times. You know, I've never done anything like that before. It was . . . amazing."

"Yes. It was."

Grace waved a hand in frustration. "But you never *said* anything. You never asked me for my phone number—or even for my last name." She gave up and took a drink of the cognac. It went down her throat like liquid fire. She knew she'd pay for it tomorrow.

"I didn't think I could," Abbie said. "I felt too . . . vulnerable. Too exposed and inexperienced."

"I'm sorry about that."

"No." Abbie laid a hand atop hers. Grace noticed she was not wearing the gold ring. "Don't be. It was wonderful. *You* were wonderful."

Grace felt excitement and trepidation in equal parts.

But this was impossible. There was no way for them to go forward from here.

She turned her hand over beneath Abbie's. "Did you know I worked here?"

"No." Abbie squeezed her fingers. "I had no idea. I was as shocked to see you as I'm certain you were to see me."

"How did you find me?"

Abbie shrugged. "After dinner with the trustees, I had a few minutes alone so I could peruse the English department website. Once I found the profile for Grace Warner, I asked my assistant to get me your home address. I told her that we had friends in common, and that I had promised to look you up."

"Plausible."

"That's what I thought."

"But," Grace added, "knowing Lucretia Fletcher, I am sure your new 'assistant' is busy compiling a dossier about your real motivation in seeking me out."

"Why would you think that?"

Grace shrugged. "Let's just say her fame precedes her."

They lapsed into silence again, but they continued to sit there, holding hands. The coffeemaker beeped to signify that it had finished brewing, but they both ignored it. Abbie's fingers felt strong and solid. Grace was reminded of the time when she was ten, and had been horsing around on a neighbor's farm with her brother. They had been playing on top of a nearly empty grain silo, and Grace had slipped and fallen into it. When Dean managed to climb down the bin ladder and reach out to haul her up, she remembered the flood of relief she felt when she grabbed onto his hand. Right now, Abbie's hand felt like that—safe and sure. There was only one problem: now they were both stuck inside the same dark silo of professional quicksand.

She squeezed Abbie's hand. "What do you want?"

"Isn't it obvious?" Abbie replied.

Grace shook her head.

"I took this job, this particular job at St. Albans, because this appeared to be an open community—one that allows and encourages people to be who they are."

"That's mostly true," Grace said. St. Albans had a laudable history. It had been the site of the northern-most Confederate army attack during the Civil War. And before the abolition of slavery, the college had been a way station on the Underground Railroad. It had also been one of the first colleges in the country to admit students of color. Grace had been an out lesbian the whole time she'd taught here—and it had never been an issue—at least not overtly. She'd always regarded that as one of the perks of living in a blue state.

"So, you came here because you thought it would be a safe place to experiment with an alternative lifestyle?"

"No, Grace," Abbie said. "I came here because I wanted—finally—to have the latitude to be who I really am."

"And who is that?"

Abbie sighed. "You of all people should know the answer to that question."

"Abbie. I spent the better part of a day, and most of one incredible night with you, but I'd hardly say that qualifies me to know who you are."

Abbie slowly nodded her head. She started to withdraw her hand, but Grace held on to it.

"Not so fast," she said. "That doesn't mean I'm not interested in finding out."

Abbie's expression lost some of its sadness. "Really?"

Grace nodded.

They smiled somewhat shyly at each other.

"So," Grace asked, "how do we do this?"

Abbie shook her dark head. "Beats the hell outta me. I was hoping you'd have some ideas."

"Oh," Grace looked her up and down, "I have a few ideas all right."

Abbie smiled. "Not *those* kinds of ideas. Although," she tugged Grace forward until their noses were nearly touching, "those certainly have some relevance to our . . . deliberations."

"You think so?"

"I know so." Abbie kissed her. It was just a quick, light kiss, but Grace could feel her toes curling up inside her socks.

"It's still raining," she said when she could find her voice.

"It is."

"And we have this whole pot of coffee."

"We do, indeed," Abbie agreed.

They kissed again. This time, it wasn't remotely light and it showed no signs of stopping any time soon. Grace was losing focus. She forced herself to pull away while she still could.

It took her a few seconds to catch her breath.

"We're two . . . uncommonly . . . smart women. Aren't we?" she asked.

Abbie appeared to be taking deep breaths, too. "I'd say so. Between the two of us, we probably have about eight million years of postgraduate education."

"And in my case, twice that amount in unpaid student loans."

Abbie drew back and looked at her with a raised eyebrow. "I may need to rethink this idea."

"Nuh uh." Grace pulled her closer again. "Drop/Add day already came and went, sister. You're stuck in this little seminar until the bitter end."

"Oh really?" Abbie didn't sound too distressed by this revelation. "How will I know when we're finished?"

"Oh, that's easy." Grace laughed. "Just listen for the Nine O'Clock Dog."

"The nine o'clock dog?"

"Don't worry. It'll make sense soon enough."

Abbie smiled at her. "As much as I want to—and *believe* me, I want to—you know I can't stay the night."

"I know." Grace gave her a wry smile. "Lucretia would be leading a hue and cry to find you." She considered her remark. "With wolves," she added. "*Salivating* wolves."

Abbie squeezed her hand. "I'll be here a little bit longer."

"When are you back for good?" The words sounded strange to Grace, even as she spoke them. Abbie soon would be living there. *Permanently.*

"Ten days."

Ten days? Grace's head was spinning—and not just because of Abbie's proximity.

"We have a lot to figure out," she said, morosely.

"I know," Abbie agreed. "I don't mean to oversimplify how complicated this is."

"I don't think you could."

"No," Abbie released her hand. "Probably not."

"Well." Grace pushed back her chair and got to her feet. "If we're both gonna lie awake all night we might as well do it in style." She walked to the counter. "How do you take your coffee?"

"Black. Like my prospects."

"Don't you mean *bleak*?" Grace asked.

"That, too." Abbie smiled. "I was going for a bad movie pun."

"Oh, I get it. *Airplane!*" Grace shook her head. "Wrong week for me to give up a life of celibacy."

"Not from where I'm sitting . . ."

Grace filled two mugs and carried them back to the table. "If we're gonna quote old movies, we should go with the real classics."

"Such as?"

Grace sat down again. "Of all the gin joints in all the world . . ."

"I had to walk into yours," Abbie finished for her.

"Something like that."

"Do you want me to leave?"

"Leave?" Grace was confused. "Leave here?" She tapped the tabletop.

"No. *Here*," Abbie clarified. "*Uber* here. As in, St. Albans."

Grace blinked. "Are you kidding?"

Abbie shook her head.

"You'd do that?"

"If it meant having a chance at a relationship with you, I would."

Grace was incredulous. "That's nuts."

"Is it?"

"Well. Yeah. I could never ask something like that of you."

"Why not?" Abbie shrugged. "I would, if the tables were turned."

"But the tables aren't turned."

"No." Abbie sighed. "I can't change that."

"So." Grace leaned back in her chair. "What are we going to do?"

Abbie shrugged. "Figure it out as we go along?"

"That's hardly scientific."

"No, it's more . . . experimental," Abbie said.

"Which means?" Grace asked.

"Which means we take it one day at a time."

"Oh, I get it." Grace rolled her eyes. "Like some lame-ass kind of lotus-eating, twelve-step mumbo jumbo?"

"Yes." Abbie nodded. "Exactly like that."

Grace shook her head. "Well," She raised her coffee mug. "however the hell this turns out . . ."

Abbie finished for her. "We'll always have Paris?"

They clinked mugs.

"Here's looking at you, kid." Grace gave her a sad smile. "I sure as hell hope *this* drama doesn't end up with one of us saying goodbye at the damn Burlington *International* Airport."

"Me either," Abbie agreed. "I look terrible in hats."

Chapter Three

Grace was shocked when she woke up at the crack of 9:30 on Friday morning and realized she'd slept late. It was apparent that Grendel was falling down on the job. An even bigger surprise greeted her when she took her coffee out to her back porch and realized that her neighbors had decamped sometime during the night. Joe Simmons, who owned the house and half a dozen other rental properties in Franklin County, was striding around the soggy back yard like an angry crow, barking orders as a couple of beefy students wearing Nova Wrestling T-shirts hauled boxes—which seemed mostly to be filled with empty PBR cans—out of the house and deposited them onto the only patch of grass that passed for a lawn.

"Hey, Joe?" Grace called out to him. "What's up?"

Joe nudged one of the boxes of discarded beer cans. "Slimy bastards skipped out. Owed me four months' back rent and pretty much trashed the place. I came by this morning to kick their asses out." He snorted. "Too late for that."

Grace wasn't too surprised. Her now former neighbors hadn't been much for what you'd call housekeeping.

"Bummer," she commiserated. "Guess they took the dog, too?"

"*Dog?*" Joe sounded like he was chewing on a mouthful of glass. "*What* dog?"

"Um." Grace pointed down at his shit-covered boot.

Joe's eyes followed her gaze. "God fucking damn it!" He gave the box a swift kick and PBR cans dispersed across the lawn like a flock of shiny metal birds.

"Lemme guess," Grace offered. "You didn't know about the dog?"

"No. I didn't know about the fucking dog. I wonder what other damn surprises they have in store for me."

He didn't have to wait long to find out. His two helpers were fighting their way down the back steps wrangling what looked like the remains of a curiously stained and supremely ill-used mattress.

"Where do you want us to put this, Joe?" the taller of the pair asked. He looked familiar. Grace thought she recalled him not exactly enjoying a brief tenure in a section of her English Lit class . . . Tyler something. From Swanton. Or "Swa-in," as the locals called it.

"What the fuck is that?" Joe was trying to clean the dog shit off his boot.

"It was on the bedroom floor." The guy who was or wasn't Tyler jerked his head toward a gaping black hole that encompassed most of one side. "I think it got burned. There was a pizza box full of cigarette butts beside it."

Joe was nearly apoplectic. "They torched a goddamn mattress? Why didn't the fucking smoke alarm go off?"

"Oh." The other student set his end of the mattress down on the warped top step. He held up a round, plastic-looking disc cinched to his belt loop by a skinny black wire. "Here's the smoke alarm. It was in the pizza box, too."

Joe sucked in a deep breath and blew it out. He remained rooted in place while stray raindrops began to soak his thinning hair and anger swirled like a fog around his face. Eventually, he glared at Grace. "I hope to hell they *did* take their damn dog— 'cause if I find it, I'm gonna use it for target practice."

Grace knew better than to comment. She wasn't sure which fate would be worse for Grendel—having Joe take potshots at her with the .22 he was always packing, or having to face more of her life tethered to the loose whims of the people who'd just fled during the night.

She felt a pang of sorrow for the paranoid little dog. No wonder Grendel was so suspicious. It was apparent she didn't have much to feel secure about.

She raised her coffee mug in a mock salute. "I wish you better luck, Joe. Sorry you have to deal with this."

He shook his head and trudged across a minefield of dung and debris to join his helpers on the steps. Grace took advantage of the chance to beat a hasty retreat and stole back inside her house.

Her telephone rang while she was fixing herself a second cup of coffee. She glanced at the caller ID and smiled when she read the name.

"Hey, Grady. We still on for the weekend at the cabin?"

Grady and his wife, Karen, owned a sweet little weekend cottage out on Butler Island—a six-hundred-acre slice of heaven rising out of the middle of Lake Champlain. Life on Butler Island was simple. No phones. No electricity. No potable water. And—Grace's favorite part—a complete dearth of assholes. It was her idea of nirvana. She loved it out there and she jumped at any chance to spend time on the island during the season—which in Vermont, meant June through October. The place had been in Karen's family since the '60s, and was little more than a fishing shack when she inherited it from her bachelor uncle. But Grady had great plans for it and Grace was his willing accomplice. Together they had replaced windows, installed a new roof, added a screened porch, and were making good progress on the interior. The cabin now sported a propane-fueled stove and refrigerator. A couple of solar panels connected to a bank of 12-volt batteries generated enough power to run lights, an FM radio, and a ceiling fan.

It was bliss.

"Bad news, Grace." Grady sounded downright somber. "Karen's sister went into labor this morning. The whole friggin' family is heading for Manchester—including us."

"Oh, man," Grace's heart sank. "Can't you get out of it?"

"You know I would if I could." Grady's voice was near a whisper.

"I'd rather stick a branding iron in my eye than have to spend an entire weekend with Gladys."

Gladys was Karen's castrating mother. Grady said she had the charm of a stump grinder—and a voice that matched one in decibels.

"I'm sorry, dude," she said.

"Not as sorry as I am, believe me. But, hey," Grady continued. "Why don't you go on out by yourself? Take the pontoon."

"Are you sure?"

"Totally. It's not like we'll be using it. You know where the keys are."

Grace was elated. "Thanks, man. I could really use the solitude."

"Yeah. At some point, you'll have to fill me in on that. We have a lot of catching up to do. And I want to hear your thoughts about the superwoman who just became our new head honcho."

"It's nothing new, believe me."

"Grace? Don't kid a kidder. I know when you're lying. Besides, I ran into CK at the library yesterday. She told me your face had a textbook Catholic guilt streak about a mile wide—and that meant you were up to your ass in alligators about something."

CK? *Christ.* She'd be done for once CK got wind of this . . .

"Did she elaborate?"

"Nope. But she said she was gonna hammer you until you fessed up."

Fabulous. Now she really was in deep shit.

"Okay." Grace sighed. Grady and CK were her best friends in Vermont. She knew she could trust them—and she needed solid advice and a safe harbor where she could talk about the mess with Abbie. "I promise I'll come clean when you get back."

"Okay. And we also need to compare notes on the new prez. I never did get to hear your reaction."

"It's a deal." *That one was gonna be fun . . .*

"Hang on." Grady lowered the phone. Grace could hear Karen's voice in the background, telling him to hurry the fuck up. "I gotta go," Grady said. "You have a good time this weekend—and don't do any work out there. Just take it easy."

She knew better than to argue. "Okay. I promise."

"Cool," Grady said. "I'll catch up with you next week." He hung up.

She stood in the middle of her kitchen, tapping the phone against her thigh.

"I am so totally fucked . . ."

The persistent rain that had been hanging around since Wednesday was supposed to move out by early afternoon so Grace planned to head for the island after lunch. In the meantime, she resolved to take the bull by the horns and save CK a lot of sweat equity—and herself the pain of an inquisition—by asking her best friend to meet her for lunch. CK didn't hesitate. She accepted Grace's invitation immediately—an indication that Grace's come-to-Jesus moment was at hand.

CK wasn't known for her subtlety.

They had met two years ago when CK came to St. Allie's on a high-dollar, higher-prestige teaching fellowship. CK was the reigning rock star of the faculty—one of the youngest-ever recipients of a MacArthur Fellowship for her pioneering work in the "quantum physics of free will." And *that* fact, if you knew anything about CK, showed up in the dictionary as the best illustration of the word "paradox."

"CK" was short for "Clover Kale." Clover Kale Greene, BS, MS, M.Div., JD, Ph.D., LMNOP, XYZ, etc., etc. She had an academic pedigree that rivaled "floccinaucinihilipilification" in its number of letters. Knowing CK, she probably held advanced degrees in *that* field, too—especially since it referenced the estimation of things that were regarded as valueless.

Grace and CK were complete opposites. Grace was forty-six, CK was twenty-eight. Grace dressed in clothes she liked to think of as shabby-chic (her mother called them "early rummage sale"). CK looked like a higher-octane version of Cyndi Lauper. Despite her best efforts, Grace plodded through life dragging a guilt-ridden, Catholic world view behind her like a ship's anchor. CK had no time or patience for *any* of that. She believed Grace's "scruples" functioned entirely as bourgeois stumbling blocks that were nothing more than pathetic offshoots of Cartesian Dualism.

Grace wasn't exactly sure what all "Cartesian Dualism" entailed, but she assumed it was something like the philosophical equivalent of mixing plaids. Their energetic discussions of free will vs. determinism had kicked into high gear the day Grace came home from school early to discover CK and her brother, Dean, sprawled across the bed in her guest room, engaged in dualism of another kind.

Grace stood frozen in the doorway, uncertain about whether she most wanted to turn the garden hose on them—or claw out her eyes. They both were so engrossed they didn't realize she was there.

CK noticed her first.

"Um, Dean?" she muttered.

Her brother ignored her. He was too intent on the commission of his . . . errand.

"Dean!" CK smacked him on the back of his head.

"Whattsamatter?" he grunted. "Not hard enough?"

"No, you stupid asshole." CK smacked him again. "Your *sister* is here."

"Where?" he asked, dumbly.

CK pushed him off her. "In the goddamn doorway."

Grace had seen enough. "Take your time," she said. "I'm gonna go make coffee."

Five minutes later, CK joined her in the kitchen. Alone. Grace heard a door slam, followed by the grind and rumble of her brother's HEMI-Powered Dodge Ram.

"Dean took off," CK explained.

"I don't doubt it."

CK sat down and held up one of the three pottery mugs Grace had placed on the small table.

"Are you pissed?" she asked.

"That depends." Grace uncorked a bottle of Bar Hill and poured her a couple of ounces.

CK raised a red eyebrow. "I thought you were gonna make coffee?"

"I was." Grace filled her own mug. "But seeing my brother's hairy ass made me realize I needed something stronger."

CK laughed. "I won't disagree with that."

"What the hell were you doing?"

CK shrugged. "Wasn't it obvious?"

"Not *that* part," Grace clarified.

"Well." CK tossed back her gin in one gulp. "Do you really want me to explain it to you?"

Grace held up a hand. "No thanks. I nearly lost my eyesight."

CK reached for the Bar Hill and poured herself another healthy portion. "I really hate gin that's this heavy on the botanicals." She took another lusty swallow. "It's like drinking aftershave."

"All evidence to the contrary."

CK gave her the finger.

Grace sipped from her own mug. "Seriously . . . you and Dean?"

CK shrugged. "He's great in the sack."

"Yeah," Grace pointed toward the front of the house, "not *my* sack."

"Oh, don't get your panties in a wad. Any port in a storm."

"He's a total cretin." Grace waved a hand in frustration. "He chews fucking Red Man. He flunked out of Penn State—*twice*. He watches NASCAR . . . with the volume *on*. He has 'Trump Train' stickers all over the back of his pathetic, over-chromed pickup. He always leaves my TV tuned to the Fox News Channel." She shook her head. "You two have *nothing* in common."

"Not true." CK held up an index finger and wagged it back and forth. "We're exploring physics theory."

"What theory?"

"Relativity."

Grace blinked.

"Absolutely," CK explained. "How long he takes to shed his pants is relative to how fast he can get me off and still leave time for takeout."

Grace closed her eyes. "I so do not need to know this."

"That's the beauty of science. Once you establish a working principle, it's infinitely repeatable."

"CK? You have *no* scruples."

"Of course, I do. Unlike you, I simply do not allow them to get in the way of a great fuck."

"Give me a break."

CK smiled at her. "I might—once you get your shaggy head out of your ass and rejoin the land of the living."

Grace had no response to make, and they finished their too-florid gin in silence.

That had been more than a month ago. *Today?*

Today, Grace was meeting CK for lunch—and her shaggy head was no longer anywhere *near* her ass.

They agreed to meet at Twiggs, a popular gastropub on North Main Street. Grace could see CK, holding court at a table near the bar, as soon as she entered the place. She groaned when she saw, too, that Brittney McDaniel was working today. *Great. The hits keep right on coming.*

CK waved her over.

Grace dropped her messenger bag on a spare chair and sat down.

CK looked her over. "What the hell is the matter with you? You look like shit."

"Thanks."

"No." CK waved at a server. Mercifully, it wasn't Brittney. "Let's get you something to drink."

"Nothing alcoholic, okay?"

Too late. CK held up her glass and pointed at Grace. The server nodded and headed toward the bar.

"One beer won't kill you." CK narrowed her eyes. "Grady said you weren't right. What's up? Are you sick?"

"No." Grace shook her head. "Not sick . . . exactly."

Grace decided to cut to the chase. There was no reason not to. CK would drag it out of her eventually. "So, remember a few weeks ago when I told you about Rizzo's party?"

"Of *course*, I remember. How often do you hook up with

anybody—much less a total stranger? I added it to my finite roster of verified religious miracles."

"Yeah. Well." Grace fiddled with her menu. "Turns out she's no longer a total stranger."

"What the hell is that supposed to mean?"

Grace rolled her eyes. "I saw her again the other day."

CK's eyes widened. "No shit? Where?"

Before Grace could answer, their server appeared and deposited two fresh pints of dark brown beer. Grace eyed them with suspicion. "What is this?"

"Something you'll hate." CK handed her empty to the young waitress. "Thanks, Tif. Keep 'em coming."

"You got it, CK." Tiffany winked at her and sashayed off.

Grace shook her head. "Why do you let them call you by your first name?"

"Why not?" CK shrugged.

"I find it breeds too much familiarity and interferes with my ability to deliver constructive criticism."

"You would." CK snorted. "I don't give a flying fuck what they call me as long as they turn their work in on time and don't bug my ass after ten at night."

Grace knew it was pointless to argue. She held the pint glass up to her nose. "This smells like ass."

"Yeah, but it tastes like ambrosia."

"Whatever." Grace set the glass down. "What are we eating?"

"Nachos. Extra beer cheese. I already ordered."

"Veggie?" Grace asked, hopefully.

"Nope." CK shook her red head. "Beef—the way god intended them."

"You're really trying to kill me, aren't you?"

"No. But I might consider it if you don't soon get to the point."

"What was I saying?"

CK rolled her eyes. "You were about to tell me where you saw the ephemeral Madam X."

"Yeah. Okay." Grace decided to try a cautious sip of the beer.

CK was right—it didn't quite taste like ass. It tasted more like . . . a damp basement. "It was here," she said.

"Here? Like *here*, here?" She waved a hand to encompass their surroundings.

"No. *Here* as in St. Albans. On campus."

CK was incredulous. "Where?"

"Well. It was the other day. In the auditorium. During the announcement." She paused before continuing. "On the stage."

"On the . . ." CK repeated. Her eyes were like saucers. "*No fucking way.*"

Grace sighed. "Way."

"*Williams?*"

Grace nodded.

CK dropped back against her chair. "Boy, when you finally decide to fuck around, you don't fuck around."

"It *wasn't* intentional."

"No." CK shook her head. "I don't imagine it was."

"So." Grace knew she'd probably regret asking, but she took the plunge anyway. "What do I do now?"

CK snickered. "You're asking *me* this question?"

"Apparently." Grace nodded. "You should correctly understand this request as an indication of my level of desperation."

CK laughed. "In retrospect, you could've done a lot worse. She's pretty hot."

"Thanks a lot. That doesn't really help."

CK leaned toward her. "Say more about that."

"Nice try. You're not my shrink."

"Do you *have* a shrink?"

"No," Grace took another cautious sip of her beer. "But I might need one by the end of this lunch."

Tif arrived and plopped a massive platter of cheese-covered nachos onto their table with a thunk. "Enjoy," she said, before sailing off.

"That looks revolting," Grace observed.

"I know, right?" CK picked up her fork. "Dig in while it's hot."

"That's pretty much your advice for everything, isn't it?"

"See?" CK shoved a chip loaded with chili and gooey cheese into her mouth. "I knew you were trainable."

"CK? I'm not kidding. I'm in one hell of a mess."

"I know you are. You're faced with a big damn choice."

Grace watched her friend lift another chip that sagged beneath the weight of its toppings. "Just for the sake of discussion," she asked, "what, in your view, are my so-called choices?"

"I can't really answer that without understanding some of the variables." CK wiped her fingers on a napkin.

"Such as?" Grace asked.

"Well, for starters, what does 'Abbie' want?" CK raised an eyebrow. "I'm going to go out on a limb here and postulate that the two of you have met to discuss this unhappy dilemma?"

Grace nodded.

"And?"

Grace shrugged. "She came by my house the night after the announcement."

"Aaaaand . . ." CK made an entreating gesture.

"And . . . nothing."

"*Nothing?*"

"Yeah. 'Nothing' pretty much covers it." Grace shrugged again. "We didn't reach any resolution."

"A wasted opportunity." CK shook her head. "Did you at least bump uglies?"

"Hey," Grace hissed before shooting panicked looks around the restaurant. "Would you mind lowering your damn voice? There are students all over this place."

"Oh, give me a break. None of them would ever suspect *you* of having a sex life."

Grace rolled her eyes and loaded a few of the nachos onto her plate. "I still need to keep this on the DL. I don't want to lose my damn job."

"Why the fuck would you lose your job?"

Grace was incredulous. "Does your spinal cord touch your brain? I'm up for tenure this year . . . remember?"

CK waved a hand dismissively. "Those assholes wouldn't dare use something like this to disqualify you."

"With all due respect, not all of us enjoy the perks that come with an academic pedigree like yours. Finding someone else to teach four sections of freshman English is pretty much a cake-walk."

CK ignored her argument. "Ah, but you've *also* made a name for yourself by editing one of the country's most prestigious literary journals."

That much was true. Grace had been at the helm of *Borealis*, the college's highly esteemed quarterly, for two years now. During her tenure, the journal had continued its lauded tradition of publishing short fiction and poetry by luminaries in contemporary literature.

"Yeah, well." Grace replied. "Don't think Bryce Oliver-James wouldn't happily step into the void."

"Oh, good god. A pencil-dick with three first names and no chin? I don't think so."

Grace glared at her. "*Seriously?* Would you stow the commentary? He could be *in* here."

"I highly doubt it. Blowjob wouldn't darken the door of *any* establishment that boasted beer cheese as its leading refinement."

"*Blowjob?*"

"Hey." CK waved a hand dismissively. "If the acronym fits, claim the title."

Grace shook her head. "Nevertheless. He's up for tenure in the department, too—and there's only *one* slot available."

"They'd never choose that waste of skin over you."

"They might—if they found out I was sleeping with the boss."

For once, CK didn't have a ready response. They ate in silence for a bit.

CK changed the subject. "So, you're heading out to the island for the weekend?"

Grace nodded.

"Gonna work on that book?"

"Maybe. Grady made me promise not to do any work on the cabin."

"I so do not understand you." CK sat back and folded her arms. When her sleeve rode up, Grace noticed that she'd added yet another tattoo.

"Why the hell do you keep getting those things?" Grace pointed at the angry-looking patch of skin. "You're starting to look like a headliner for Strates Shows."

CK rolled her eyes. "If I knew what that meant, I'd deliver a crushing reply."

"It's a *carnival*," Grace explained. "I keep forgetting that you're, like, eighty years younger than me."

"Yeah. Well. Get over it." CK drained her glass. "Do you want another beer?"

"Nope. I gotta get going. I want to get out there before the rain decides to circle back around."

CK looked over her shoulder toward the big front windows that faced the street. "You think it's going to?"

"Probably. It's Vermont. It might even snow before dark."

"True." CK waved at Tif, who was passing their table, carrying a stack of fat menus. "Could we get our check?" Tif flashed her an okay sign. "As I was saying," CK resumed. "You need to get your thumb out of your ass and submit that book to some publishers."

"We've had this conversation before. It doesn't work that way."

"Says who?"

"Says every set of submission guidelines I've ever read," Grace explained.

"Okay. So, screw publishers. What about literary agents?"

Grace shrugged.

"What does that mean?"

"It's . . ." Grace didn't finish her explanation.

"Yes? It's . . . what?" CK leaned toward her. "I'm waiting."

"It's not ready for that."

"Not ready? When the fuck will it *be* ready? When it's nine times the length of *Ulysses?*"

"Give me a break, CK."

"Nope. Don't think I will."

Grace decided it was her turn to change the subject. "What are you doing this weekend?"

"You don't want to know."

Macabre images of CK, tangled up with Dean, flashed through Grace's mind like a profane slide show. "Yeah," she agreed. "You're probably right."

CK smiled. "You head on out and get a jump on that weather. Lunch is on me."

"Really? That's awfully generous."

"Yeah, well. Consider it my contribution to great literature."

Grace shook her head. "You're nuts."

"We'll see."

Grace extended her hand and CK gave it a warm squeeze.

"See you on the flip side, pal."

"That you will, my friend." Grace smiled at her. She didn't bother adding that CK would likely be seeing a *lot* more of her—as a potential roommate, once she got rejected for tenure and lost her job.

Grace had spent enough time on the island to have a good routine down for getting ready. She didn't need to take much besides whatever food she wanted to eat, drinking water, and a change of clothing. Everything else was already there. She always found it odd that Karen didn't often accompany Grady on his weekend work trips. It seemed her friend's wife found the cabin's spartan conditions and relative isolation more off-putting than charming. More than once, Grace asked him why they kept the place when it was so abundantly clear that his wife did not enjoy spending time with him there.

"Karen's too much of a mall rat," Grady had explained during their last trip. "If there are no available stores to hit, she's definitely not spending twenty-four hours without access to Amazon Prime."

"I don't get you two sometimes."

"Join the club." He laughed. "I don't get us *any* of the time."

Grace had often fantasized about buying the place, but it would have taken a minor financial miracle. And even then, she knew there was no chance Karen could let it go while her mother was still alive.

"Gladys would have a shit fit," Grady once told Grace when she asked if Karen would ever consider selling the place.

"Why?"

"Because the place is a monument to Karen's big ole, queer uncle, Martin." Grady shook his head. "Gladys still believes her brother used the cabin for fishing expeditions. She's determined to cling to her delusions." He laughed. "Ole Martin was 'fishing,' all right—but not for anything that swam in the lake."

Grace thought about it. "That certainly would explain some of the eclectic reading material we found piled up inside the outhouse."

"You think? Although I have to say—that's not a place I'd ever be inclined to tarry long enough to read anything."

"Grady?" Grace asked. "I don't think anybody stockpiles those publications so they can linger over the prose."

He blinked.

Grace laid a hand on his shoulder. "I have so much to teach you, young Skywalker."

Grady sighed. "I really don't understand your people."

"*My* people?" Grace withdrew her hand. "I beg your pardon. *My* people read prolix monographs, not porn."

Grady waved a hand dismissively. "You know what I meant."

"Not so fast, bucko. You don't get a pass for making a stupid and ill-informed observation just because you're black."

"What the hell does that have to do with anything?"

"Nothing. That's my point."

He squinted at her. "Am I supposed to know what that means?"

"It means the ability to make bigoted and ignorant generalizations about an entire population has about as much relevance to race as my sexual orientation has to some pathetic wanker, holed up on an island ogling guy-on-guy porn."

He sighed. "You're spending too much time with CK."

"I see we understand each other." Grace smiled at him.

She didn't mean to be so hard on Grady. But, sometimes, despite her best efforts to retain *nothing* from her forced attendance at all those CYO summer camps growing up, a random aphorism would rouse its sleepy head and invade her consciousness. "Sweep your corners, girls," Sister Merry Larry would lecture her captive crew of fledgling campers, as they sat huddled together around a campfire that smoldered beneath the weight of wet kindling. "That's the best way to make positive change in the world—one small bit at a time."

Grace wondered what advice Sister Merry Larry would have for her today . . .

Slap the unholy passion that smoldered inside her until it was safely extinguished?

Turn her back on her own happiness—and probably, Abbie's—to save her career and shave a few hundred millennia off her sojourn in purgatory?

Tuck her tail and run like hell in the opposite direction?

No. That last bit was more like her mother's one-size-fits-all brand of advice.

Shit. There was no wisdom that could save her or provide a ready exit from this mess.

The only way out is through. Merry Larry's voice again. Grace often wondered if the upstart nun had spent her free time penning proverbs for fortune cookies.

Grady and Karen kept their pontoon in a slip at St. Albans harbor. Grace topped off the fuel tanks and stowed her bags in the dry storage wells beneath the front bench seats. The lake was only mildly choppy after several days of steady rain. The winds were blowing in from the south—an ominous sign that the weather system might decide to loop back around and wage a dorsal assault . . . usually the worst kind.

She was not an experienced boater, but she could manage the

straight shot from the harbor to Butler Island—just. And if she took care to head in slowly and toss out all the bumpers on the docking side, she could usually moor the damn thing without too much hassle—or collateral damage. Grady and Karen shared a dock with two other Butler Island property owners.

One of the neighboring camps belonged to a pair of elusive octogenarians who, if they ever left their house at all, did so under cover of darkness. Grace had never caught a glimpse of, much less met, the antisocial pair. Grady said the man, Ed Simpson, was a retired investment banker from Manhattan, and that he and his wife arrived on June the first every year, and departed on Halloween—without exception. Grace would sometimes see smoke belching from their stone chimney—or hear the bang and clatter of their gasoline-powered generator on cold nights. But she never *saw* either of them—not even during the island's monthly, communal binge-drinking and trash-burning rituals.

Grace called the reclusive couple, "Edward and Mrs. Simpson."

The other resident who shared Grady's dock was an avid "freecycler" named Roscoe. Nobody really knew what Roscoe's last name was—or whether he even *had* a last name . . . or a first name, for that matter. He was just "Roscoe." Every week, Butler Island's self-styled Mr. Haney would show up with his gargantuan Mandalay pontoon heaped to the gills with . . . junk. Roscoe spent his free time cruising neighborhoods on the mainland, looking for any promising castoffs. Old furniture. Discarded hunks of wood. Doors. Bits of old scrap metal. Broken tools. Buckets. Mismatched tires. Any kind of waste that might be headed for a landfill or a burn pile was fair game for Roscoe. He snapped up all of it. And he was always quick to make sure the other island inhabitants found ways to put his eclectic gleanings to use.

Roscoe's high-dollar salvage barge was tied up at the dock when Grace arrived. He waved enthusiastically when he recognized her.

"Hey, Doc?" he called out. "You gotta come take a gander at what I brung today. Got some real finds in here. Things you'n Grady will want to use for that new deck railing."

Grace secured her boat and tossed her bags onto the dock. "Whattaya got, Roscoe?"

Roscoe threw back an old, stained canvas tarp and shifted some of his haul to the side. He pointed at a bundle of twisted iron rods. There had to be at least three or four dozen of them, strapped together with frayed bungee cords.

Grace knelt to examine them more closely. "Oh, wow. What are these? They look like parts of an old fence."

"Exactly." Roscoe beamed. "They're from the Greenwood cemetery in St. Albans—back in the oldest section where all them Revolutionary War soldiers is buried. These were all part of a fence they had way back before they started building all them houses up in that area. I figure these iron spikes was all hand-wrought. Look close and you can see the hammer marks and how the patterns is irregular from one to the next."

Grace ran her fingers over the rough texture of the narrow iron pickets. It was incredible to think that these hunks of metal had been heated, pounded and twisted into such intricate ribbon-like shapes by hand.

"They just let you have these?" she asked Roscoe.

"Waaall." He rubbed a calloused hand across his jaw. "Didn't nobody try to stop me from takin' them. They was all piled up behind an old mausoleum—and mostly buried beneath a couple years' worth of grass clippin's, so I figured nobody'd kick up a fuss if I dug 'em out and hauled 'em off."

Grace shook her head. "How'd you even find out they were there?"

He winked at her. "I got my sources."

"I just bet you do, Roscoe."

He smiled at her. "Grady not comin' this weekend?"

"Nope. I'm doing a solo."

"Waaall." Roscoe plucked at his chin. "You give a holler if you need help with anything."

Grace fetched her bags from the dock. "Thanks, Roscoe. But I think I'm gonna have a quiet couple of days—just grading papers and working on my book."

He scoffed. "I wouldn't be countin' on that."

"What do you mean?"

He waved a hand at the landscape behind them. "Some ass-wipe ditched a stray dog out here . . . again. Damn thing barked up a storm last night—and again this mornin'."

"Oh, man. What kind of person can do something like that?"

"Beats the hell outta me. But I'll tell you one thing—if ole Bud Wyatt gets sight of it, he'll pump its hind-end full of lead."

Grace was horrified. "Well that's not any better than ditching the poor thing in the first place."

Roscoe shrugged. "Maybe not. Might be better'n starvin' to death out here in the middle of the lake."

"Unless it can swim?" Grace suggested.

"You never know."

Grace shook her head. "Why would somebody go to the trouble to bring a dog out here by boat and abandon it?"

"Hell if I know. But I seen a lot a stranger things in my time. Couple years back, some doofus tied off in the cove and dumped out a crate of ferrets. Did you know them little rats can swim? And they breed like rabbits. They was all over this dang island." He clucked his tongue. "But that first winter out here did for them. Maybe the same thing'll happen with this dog."

Grace didn't want to think about that. She didn't want to think about anything freezing to death, all alone in a Vermont winter. She gave him a salute and headed for the path that led up a steep incline to Grady and Karen's cabin. "See you later, Roscoe."

"You tell Grady about these here spikes."

"I will," Grace called over her shoulder. "Thanks."

She reached the clearing at the top of the rise. The view of the lake from here always took her breath away. It made everything else seem smaller. More fleeting. Less important. Even her angst about the situation with Abbie got up from its anxious perch in the front row and retreated to the cheap seats at the back of the hall.

She never got tired of it. Winter. Spring. Summer. Fall. This view of Lake Champlain woke something up inside her. The cranky, old sleeping dog that inhabited the better part of her psyche would stir and lift its head, nosing at the air like it caught a whiff of something tantalizing on a stray breeze. Hope? A second shot at happiness? *Brisket?*

She turned her head away from the view and inhaled.

Yep. *Brisket.* The scent was unmistakable. Somebody was grilling. *Probably the Simpsons.*

Her stomach growled. The sooner she got her stuff stowed inside, the sooner she could get everything hooked up and humming. The propane-powered fridge took a couple of hours to cool down.

She hefted the backpack higher onto her shoulder and walked the remaining distance to the cabin. The place looked great. She'd talked Karen into letting them paint the clapboard exterior a rich mustard color. Now the brightly colored little cabin seemed to vibrate at the center of its cleared patch of ground. It was a simple saltbox—four side walls and a stand-up loft. It had a kitchen, a small bedroom, and a big living area topped by the loft that was only accessible, for now, by a wooden ladder. The cabin had an outhouse, too, located a short but respectful distance away.

Grady kept a spare key stashed beneath some empty clay pots that were artfully stacked beside the porch. Once she was inside, it only took her a few minutes to stow her few grocery items and open all the windows. Flipping a switch on the inverter allowed access to solar power stored in a bank of batteries. A quick trip outside to open the valve on the propane tank completed her chores.

The rest? The rest was easy. The "rest" for this weekend meant dragging one of the big distressed Adirondack chairs into a scrap of shade and sitting down with her stack of four dozen English Lit papers. The topics ranged from "Epic Themes and Conventions in *Beowulf* and How They Mirror Contemporary Culture" to "Social and Political Contexts of the Heroic Code." The writing and quality of research in the papers seesawed wildly between woefully arcane and wholly incomprehensible.

If this was a movie, Beowulf *would be a coming of age story. Grendel has been dealt a crappy hand his whole life. Nothing has ever been fair. His mom was a nasty old hag that never talked to him, except when she warned him about smelly fish. He spent most of his time wandering around stabbing animals because he was so full of anger. He's mad that humans all refuse to care about his pain at being such an outcast. His archenemy Hrothgar is a really ugly dude that still manages to marry a great-looking queen while Grendel is cursed and being mocked all the time by climbing goats. His life is full of injustices.*

Grace dropped her red pen in disgust and stared out at the water.

I just had to do this—consign myself to an endless purgatory where I'm forced to read drivel vomited out by bored and completely disinterested twenty-somethings—instead of going into . . . I don't know . . . dentistry.

Her brother, Dean, didn't have to deal with crap like this. *His* social contract was a lot simpler. When a subordinate of his did a shitty, subpar job, Dean fired him. End of story.

She glanced down at the paper again. *At least this one isn't as bad as Brittney McDaniel's.* Brittney had managed to crank out an entire theme paper composed of sound bites that each contained no more than 140 characters. It took Grace a while to catch on and, at first, her interest was piqued by the unusual, albeit dubious, approach. After the first five pages, she picked up the clue phone and realized that Brittney wasn't intending to be clever. Brittney genuinely believed that a flimsily connected string of *tweets* was a legitimate form of written communication. Small wonder. Cultural mores like that tended to trickle down from the top—unlike most economic schemes.

"Yeah." She collected the stack of papers and stuffed them back inside a bulging accordion folder. "Maybe later—after I'm good and *drunk*."

She indulged herself by watching the water for a few minutes. There was a fair amount of boat activity today. She figured that most people would be eager to get an hour or two of recreation in before the weather went south. She could see a bank of dark clouds building on the horizon. It was an ominous sign. She guessed they all would be in for some fireworks later on.

That was okay, though, because if your solar panels racked up about five good hours of sunlight, your power stores would be just fine for the evening. The only bad part about rotten weather was having to trudge outside to use the privy. Grady had grand plans in place to install a proper bathroom inside the cabin—one with running water pumped up from the lake, and a composting toilet. But for now, the outhouse was the only recourse—at least for females. They'd done a lot, though, to make the tiny space a bit more hospitable. It was scrupulously clean—at least, as clean as it could be without any kind of climate control. And they'd installed a pergola linking it to the main cabin. That had been an attractive addition, but it didn't make trips outside during inclement weather any less onerous. Grace had insisted on insulating the outhouse walls and painting them a brighter, more inviting color—the same mustard yellow that adorned the exterior walls of the cabin. She'd even installed a magazine rack and filled it with back issues of *Borealis*—although Grady argued that people visiting the island privy wouldn't be any more inclined to plow through *those* tomes than any of the articles contained in his gay uncle-in-law's back issues of *Unzipped*.

A warm breeze blowing in from the lake and the soft, insistent purr of boat motors lured her into closing her eyes. She didn't realize she'd fallen asleep until the first few drops of rain hit her face and jolted her awake. She blinked at the lake. *Damn.* The sun was well along its collision course with the horizon. She glanced at her watch in shock. She'd dozed off for nearly ninety minutes.

That part was really no surprise. She hadn't gotten much sleep since Abbie turned up. She collected her folder of papers and headed for the cabin. The rainfall was gaining steam. Just as she reached the cabin steps, she heard a distant rumble of thunder. It was going to be an early night.

Once inside, she turned on the receiver and tuned into Vermont Public Radio. She got lucky. Instead of one of their ubiquitous no-one-ever-listens-to-this-so-we're-going-to-play-it programs, the live Chicago Symphony broadcast was starting in just a few minutes—and Anne-Sophie Mutter would be wrangling her way through the twisted machinations of Mozart's *Turkish Concerto*.

Grace hadn't planned on making much for dinner—her beer cheese- and ground meat-laden lunch with CK had just about killed her appetite, she thought forever. But the aftermath of her nap outside in all that fresh air must've jump-started her metabolism. It was either that or her memory of how great that damn brisket smelled. She wandered into the small kitchen and considered her various food options. She'd brought along a big container of the black bean soup she'd made for Dean last week. That might work. She could trick it out with some plain yogurt, a chopped scallion, and a grate or two of cheese. Or she could fire up the gas grill—which, handily, was under cover—and toss some chicken and fresh veggies on it. She'd also brought along a few late-season, fat heirloom tomatoes she'd picked up at the local farmer's market on her way to the marina. They were gorgeous—more like works of art than produce with their brilliant yellow, orange, and deep purple skins. They vibrated from their perch on the windowsill like background *objets* in a Matisse painting.

Why not?

She set about mixing up some marinade for the chicken from the cache of oils and dried spices she kept on hand in a cabinet. The upcoming fireworks of the Mozart concerto encouraged Grace to add greater flourish to her meal. So, she decided to cobble together a modified curry baste with onion, garlic, paprika, honey, some grainy mustard and a dash of cinnamon. *That* combination was sure to liven up any stormy night.

There was another, more sonorous roll of thunder. The rain was becoming more insistent now. Grace could hear its staccato tapping against the metal roof of the cabin. For a moment, she thought she heard something like hail, until it persisted and she realized the sound wasn't coming from the roof—it was the door. Someone was knocking—softly but persistently—on the cabin door.

Roscoe? That seemed unlikely. But who else on Butler Island would be out wandering around in weather like this?

Grace wiped her hands on a towel and crossed the living area to open the door. The sight that greeted her stopped her cold.

It wasn't Roscoe. It was a *woman*—dripping wet, and with a countenance that was a perfect blend of hope and uncertainty.

It was Abbie.

Chapter Four

Grace stood frozen in place for so long that Abbie finally sighed and broke the silence.

"If you're not going to invite me in, then I've definitely overplayed my hand."

Grace blinked at her in disbelief. "How'd you get here?" she asked—before quickly regretting her response. "I'm sorry," she corrected. "Of course." She stepped back and swung the door open wider. "Come inside. You're getting soaked."

"Thanks." Abbie did her best to shake off as much of the water clinging to her—*everything*—as possible before stepping over the threshold. And even dripping wet, the sum total of that "everything" presented the most bona fide, USDA-certified, prime and perfectly aged hunk of pure perfection that Grace had ever seen. "I'm sorry," Abbie said. "I don't mean to make such a mess." She smiled at the obvious irony of her comment. "I mean—any more of a mess than I've already created for you."

"It's okay." Grace closed the door behind her. "It livens things up in a dull Vermont town."

Abbie gave her a dubious look. "I somehow doubt that's what you really think."

Grace shrugged. "You're well advised to doubt it. I honestly don't know what I think."

Abbie nodded but didn't say anything.

Grace fought hard not to stare at everything that was amplified by Abbie's wet clothing. She cleared her throat. "Is that why you're here?" she asked. "To find out what I really think?"

"That, and other reasons."

"What other reasons?"

Abbie shivered.

"God." Grace felt like an oaf. "Let's get you outta that t-shirt."

Abbie raised an eyebrow.

"I mean . . ." Grace was mortified. "I *didn't* mean it like that. I meant you're so wet . . . I mean . . . so *damp* . . . from . . . from the rain." She hung her head. "I don't know what the fuck I meant."

"It's okay." Abbie laid a hand on Grace's arm. "I know what you meant. And, yes. I'd love something dry to put on."

"Okay," Grace said meekly. "Follow me to the bedroom."

Abbie smiled at her again.

Grace rolled her eyes. "You're *not* helping, you know . . ."

"I know. I apologize." She waved a hand. "Lead on. After I've changed, I'll explain the whole sordid business to you." She held out a hand. "Here—I brought this along as a kind of peace offering."

Grace had been so determined not to stare, she failed to notice that Abbie was carrying a bottle of wine. She took it from her and read the label. It was an Oregon pinot noir—a good one from the Willamette Valley.

"'Whole cluster,'" she quoted. "Nice choice."

Abbie smiled. "It seemed to be in sync with our situation."

Grace had to laugh at that. "Follow me." She led Abbie to the bedroom.

"Something smells wonderful," Abbie commented as they passed through the kitchen.

"It's my curry baste."

"You like to cook?"

"I do. I don't know how good I am at it, but I enjoy it just the same." Grace stood back so Abbie could precede her into the bedroom. "Let me grab you some shorts and a clean t-shirt. I keep extra stuff here."

Grace retrieved the items and set them on the bed. "I'll wait out there while you change." She pointed at the living room.

"Thanks." Abbie gave her a shy smile.

Grace left her alone and tried not to swoon as she crossed the kitchen.

What the hell is Abbie doing here? How did she know where to find me? And how in the hell did she get out here?

There was another rumble of thunder. One thing was for sure, Abbie was stuck there for now. Nobody would be leaving the island any time soon.

Grace didn't know if that thought filled her more with jubilation or dread.

"Grace?"

Abbie's voice—coming from the bedroom.

"Yeah?" Grace replied.

"I think I may need something a bit—larger."

Larger? That seemed unlikely. Abbie was taller than Grace, but not really *bigger*.

"Are you sure?" Grace called out.

"I'm sure." Abbie's voice came from just behind her.

Grace jumped, and turned around to face her.

"Oh. Um . . ." The words died in her throat. The t-shirt fit all right—well enough for Abbie to moonlight as a server at Hooters. "Yeah. I see what you . . . um . . . mean."

Abbie glanced down at her chest. "I fear this one is a bit too snug."

Are you kidding? Grace wanted to scream. *I'd offer my retirement savings to bribe you never to take it off.* "Yeah." She cleared her throat. "Let's get you something of Grady's."

"Thanks." Abbie gave her another one of her thousand-watt smiles. "I'd appreciate it."

"His things are in that tall chest by the closet. Top drawer."

"Great. Be right back." Abbie turned around and headed back to the bedroom.

Grace watched her go. There was definitely *no* problem with the sweat shorts. They were just the right fit to show off all nine miles of her perfect legs.

She sank down into a chair. *I'll never fucking survive this.*

The symphony broadcast was just beginning. Riccardo Muti was giving program notes for the evening performance. Grace tried to pay attention, but it was a losing battle.

"This is much better." Abbie rejoined her. She held out her arms. "See?"

Abbie was wearing one of Grady's ratty, Nova hockey t-shirts—with long sleeves.

It should've been illegal . . .

"Aren't you too hot in that?" Grace asked. What the hell was she saying? *Abbie could never be too hot in anything.* Even if she'd appeared trussed-up in a biohazard suit, she'd still trip every meter on every dial.

"No." Abbie raised her arms, and the impossibly long sleeves drooped from her hands. "I'll just roll these up and I'll be right as rain—no pun intended."

Grace looked at her bare feet. "Want some dry shoes?"

"That would be great."

"I have some spare Crocs."

"Very stylish."

Grace got up and retrieved the pair of battered, lime green shoes and handed them to her. "Beggars can't be choosers."

Abbie put the shoes on. Miraculously, they fit. But with Crocs, it was kind of a moving target. "Is that what I am?" she asked. "A beggar?"

Grace shrugged. "You tell me."

Abbie perched on the arm of the sofa because its cushions were strewn with pages from Grace's manuscript. "Maybe I should start by explaining why I'm here?"

"That's a thought. I'd also like to know how the hell you got here."

Abbie laughed. "That part is easy. Captain Polly."

Captain Polly? Captain Polly ran a small-scale island charter service out of Burton Island. She knew these waterways better than anyone—even better than the coterie of crusty old bass fishermen who hauled in the biggest catches year after year in all the high-dollar tournaments the lake was famous for.

"How'd you find out about Captain Polly?" Grace asked. "I thought you'd already left for North Carolina."

"I got a later start than I'd planned because I had a couple of things crop up that I needed to take care of. And when I finally got on the road, I saw her sign on my way out of town—near the turnoff for the marina—and changed my mind."

Grace sat back down in a chair facing her. "Why'd you change your mind?"

"That part is a bit more complicated."

Grace waved a hand at the big front windows that faced the lake. It was pouring now. "Doesn't look like either of us is going anyplace for a while."

"No," Abbie agreed. "It appears we're stuck with each other." She met Grace's eyes. "For now," she added, softly.

How about fucking forever? Grace cursed herself for her own weakness.

Time for a reset. She forced her eyes away from Abbie's. *Beyond this point, there be dragons.*

"That still doesn't explain how you knew I was out here."

Abbie sighed. "CK told me."

What the hell? CK?

"When the hell did you meet CK?" Grace shook her head. "I mean . . . I only just saw her about . . ." Grace looked at her watch, "five hours ago. I swear, that woman spreads news faster than a 5G network."

Abbie laughed. "It was less dramatic than that. I ran into her at the bookshop on Main Street. We both were trying to avoid that energetic Québécois who appears to hang out in there. We ended up hiding behind the same bookcase."

"You mean Pierre Paul? And nice French, by the way."

"Yes. That would be he. And thank you—I grew up in Québec."

"I didn't know that." Grace was fascinated. "Your interest in St. Albans begins to make more sense now. Remind me to grill you about that after you explain meeting CK?"

"Okay," Abbie agreed.

"So," Grace continued, "you two introduced yourselves to each other?"

"Kind of," Abbie explained. "I recognized her right away."

"She is hard to mistake," Grace agreed. "She has more ink on her body than the combined total from every term paper written in the storied history of St. Allie's."

Abbie laughed. "That's *not* why I recognized her. She delivered the keynote address at last year's Q-Knot Conference in Banff."

"Do I want to know what the hell a 'Q-Knot' conference is?"

Abbie smiled. "Quantum Knot Invariants. This is a leading forum to explore research in the intersections of modular forms and quantum knots in invariants."

Grace blinked. "Which translated into English means?"

Abbie thought about it. "Imagine the *Klutz Book of Knots* with a greater emphasis on algorithms."

"Ah. Now I get why CK was there. But why on earth would you be attending something that dense?"

"It wasn't by choice—not to say that Alberta isn't rife with charm in the wintertime. The conference was partially funded by a grant from our foundation."

"So, it was a working gig?"

"Precisely."

"Tell the truth." Grace narrowed her eyes. "How much of the content did you really understand?"

Abbie seemed to consider her answer. "Not. A. Single. Word."

"Well, thank god."

Abbie laughed.

"But that's where you met CK?" Grace clarified.

"No. I didn't *meet* her there. But I was impressed by her speech. So, when I saw her in the bookstore, I introduced myself."

"I'd have loved to have overheard *that* conversation."

"She's very devoted to you."

"Really?" Grace raised an eyebrow. "And my name happened to come up *because*?"

Abbie shrugged.

"Oh, come on. You don't get off *that* easily, Williams. Dish."

Abbie looked down at the carpet. "After we made our introductions, I told her that I'd heard her speak before. She seemed surprised by that, but went on to say she knew a bit about me, too."

Grace closed her eyes. "God . . . I'm sorry Abbie. CK is my best friend. I didn't tell her about us to boast. She could see I was miserable and she knows me well enough to . . . to . . ."

"Interpret the algorithms?" Abbie suggested.

Grace nodded morosely. "Something like that."

Abbie reached out to touch Grace on the knee. "It's okay. I'm not upset. I'm . . . glad."

"Glad? I doubt that."

"Don't. It's true. It makes me happy you have someone you trust to talk with about . . . things."

"Yeah. *Things*."

Abbie squeezed her knee. "I mean it. I wish I had someone like CK to confide in."

"You don't?"

Abbie shook her head.

Grace tentatively placed her hand on top of Abbie's. It felt every bit as warm and solid as it had the other night when they sat together at her kitchen table drinking cognac. It was raining like hell that night, too. Grace wondered if the weather's instability was an omen for their prospects.

"I'm sorry about that, Abbie."

"Me, too. But I have no one to blame but myself for living such an insular life."

"If it helps, I'll be happy to share CK with you."

"I'd like that. She seems pretty special."

"Special?" Grace laughed. "Yeah. She's definitely . . . *woke*."

"Woke?" Abbie quoted. "Is that the same thing as *lighted*?"

Grace narrowed her eyes. "Don't you mean *lit*?"

70

"I always get those colloquial expressions wrong. I'm such a nerd."

"You're adorable." The words were out before Grace could keep them back.

Abbie looked at her.

Time stood still. They stared at each other while the rain continued to thrum against the roof and the Chicago Symphony began to work its way through the first movement of Tchaikovsky's *Sleeping Beauty*. Grace didn't miss the irony. She felt like she was finally waking up from her own stupor of repressed longing. And its object wasn't the product of some manufactured fantasy—it was the Word become glorious flesh. And the whole human enchilada was seated right in front of her in all its quick and vibrant glory.

The question was what she was going to *do* with it. It was a colossal mess.

And it was tying her invariants up in quantum knots . . .

She smiled at her own musing.

Abbie noticed and gave her hand a tug. "What?"

"It's . . . nothing."

"It's not nothing."

"I was just thinking about the irony of both of us taking advice from CK."

"Would that be a bad thing?" Abbie asked.

"Bad?" Grace thought about it. "Not bad. But definitely messy."

Abbie seemed intrigued. "*Messy*? She seems a bit eccentric, I'll grant you. But otherwise pretty well put together."

"Not *that* kind of messy," Grace corrected. "I mean the kind of messy that requires a half-gallon of Resolve and a drop cloth."

Abbie blinked. "I have no idea what that means."

Grace let out a long, slow breath. "Tell you what—let's make some dinner and I'll explain it to you. Then we can listen to the symphony concert. Maybe things will be clearer with a small dose of curry and a big dose of Mozart."

"At least our sinuses will be clearer, even if our understanding lags behind."

"Such an optimist." Grace stood up, but retained her hold on Abbie's hand. "Come on. Let's go sling some hash."

Abbie got to her feet, too. Once again, Grace was struck by how much taller she was. She stared at Abbie with the open-mouthed awe of a tourist gawking up at all six feet, six inches of Mary in Michelangelo's Pietà.

Yep. Into the hand basket and straight on to hell . . .

She dared to allow herself a fleeting hope that her own prospects might be a tad brighter than the Blessed Virgin's.

Fat chance.

"Come on." Grace led the way to the kitchen. "You can open the wine."

Anne-Sophie Mutter was killing it.

Even with the herculean level of distraction that accompanied sharing her medley of curried chicken and vegetables with Abbie, some still-functioning part of her mind managed to be blown away by how great Mutter's performance was.

Abbie seemed to read her thoughts. "I love this concerto. I once heard Isaac Stern play it, and although I was very young, I recall being mesmerized by his musical gymnastics."

Grace was impressed. "You heard Isaac Stern?"

"My grandmother used to take me to performances by the Montréal Symphony." Abbie smiled. "I was only eight years old when I heard him, but I'll never forget the experience." She took a sip of her wine. "Mutter is playing this superbly."

"So, you grew up in Montréal?"

"Near there," Abbie explained. "In Québec City. I lived in Canada until I finished college at McGill."

"So, you grew up speaking French?"

"*And* English. My parents are both committed Francophiles, but I was determined to become proficient in both languages. And McGill is an English-speaking college." She smiled. "They weren't particularly happy with my choice."

Grace was intrigued. "Why not?"

"Before his retirement, my father was a professor of economics at Laval. He was determined for me to attend one of the province's French-speaking universities."

"But you didn't share his enthusiasm for that idea?"

"Not in the least. I found that level of cultural sophistry offensive. So, after grad school at Chicago and Princeton, I just never went back."

"Until now?"

"Well—my parents are a lot older, and I'm their only child." Abbie shrugged. "This seemed close, but not too close—if you know what I mean."

"I know exactly what you mean."

"Where is your family?"

"My mother is in Wilkes-Barre. My brother, Dean, lives in Plattsburgh—the headquarters of his home improvement stores."

"What about your father?" Abbie asked.

Grace refilled their wineglasses. "He died when I was a year old."

"Oh, dear god." Abbie's jaw dropped. "That's *terrible*. May I ask what happened?"

"The flood."

"The flood?" Abbie repeated.

"I'm sorry. The Susquehanna Flood of '72," Grace explained. "In three days, tropical storm Agnes dumped eighteen inches of rain on the Wyoming Valley in Pennsylvania. The river rose more than a foot per hour. When it finally crested at forty-one feet, the dikes just couldn't hold it back. It overran its banks and nineteen feet of water roared through all the little towns in the valley. My dad was one of the unlucky ones. He drove a delivery truck for the Sanitary Bakery in Nanticoke. He got caught in flood waters while trying to move the truck to higher ground."

"Oh, my god. How horrible."

"Yeah." Grace shook her head. "He died trying to save a load of spice cakes. Most of the other fatalities were people who drowned trapped in their cars, too. My mom managed to get my brother and me to our grandparents' house in Ashley—but, oddly, our house was one of only three on our street that wasn't destroyed. I don't remember anything about the experience, of course. But Dean says he remembers the smell of mud and oil—how it hung around the whole area and seemed to cling to everything for years. He's a big bubba, but to this day, he won't change the oil on his own truck. He says the odor makes him sick."

"I don't doubt it. What did your mom do after your father's death?"

"She stayed. It's what people did. They pushed the mud and debris out of what was left of their lives and they went on. Eventually, she got married again, but it didn't last long. He was a shift supervisor she worked with at the garment factory—but it turned out his real life's work was perfecting his role as a drunk and a womanizer—quite a change from our sainted father, whose worst excess was overindulging on his beloved Polish spice cakes. Mum later said that since her new husband chose to spend more time at the VFW hall than he did at home, it made sense to pack up his stuff and drop it off over there. I remember riding along with her in our old, beat-up Ford station wagon." Grace smiled at the recollection. "She was so calm. Like dumping all this guy's shit out on the sidewalk in front of a bar was the most natural thing in the world. Afterward, she took me to Howard Johnson's for ice cream."

"Just like that?"

"Just like that," Grace repeated. "When Agnes is done with something, she's *done*. No second thoughts. No apologies. No going back."

"Agnes?" Abbie asked.

"Oh, yeah," Grace explained. *Just like the storm.* She smiled. "It's no accident that Agnes shared the same name. That bit of irony regularly conspired to compound my escalating load of Catholic guilt."

"*That* parallel must've been interesting to grow up with."

"Was and *is*," Grace corrected. "It's no accident that I ended up with a job more than four hundred miles from home."

"You said your brother lives in Plattsburgh?"

Grace nodded.

"I suppose he feels the same way?"

"Hell no." Grace laughed. "Dean is her fair-haired boy. He can do no wrong. I'm the black sheep in the Warner family."

"You?" Abbie seemed surprised. "Why?"

Grace raised an eyebrow. "Seriously?"

"Surely not because you're gay?"

"No. Not because I'm gay." Grace leaned over her plate and dropped her voice to a whisper. "Because I'm something much worse than gay: I'm a *lesbian*."

"How on earth is *that* worse?"

"Hell if I know. If I had to guess, it's because the word 'lesbian' summons up all kinds of murky, seamy and vaguely foul-smelling unnatural acts. Gay men don't much threaten staunch Catholic women. I mean . . . think about it: most of our priests are closeted gay men. But homosexual women? *Nuh uh*. They're all up to something subliminal and corrupting. Why else would all those generations of nuns make little girls sleep with their hands *outside* the covers? *They knew things.* They didn't want us figuring that shit out."

Abbie seemed confused. "I'm trying very hard to follow your line of reasoning here—but I'm having difficulty connecting these dots."

"Okay." Grace sat back. "Let's go at this another way. I'm gonna go out on a limb here and assume you also were raised Catholic?"

"You might say that."

"So, do your parents know about your newfound . . . *curiosity* about sexual relationships with other women?"

Abbie sighed. "For starters, I wouldn't characterize my attraction to you as a function of 'curiosity.'"

"You wouldn't?"

"No."

"Then what is it?"

It was Abbie's turn to lean forward. "Why do you want to know?"

"I thought we'd established that."

"So, your question is part of some academic exercise?"

Grace thought Abbie sounded a little disappointed. "No. It's not."

"Then what is it?"

"Hey, wait a minute." Grace held up a hand. "Isn't that what I just asked *you?*"

Abbie tapped her fingers on the side of her wineglass. The gesture was in perfect syncopation with the *allegro aperto* of the Mozart concerto. "I forget," she said.

"You're lying." Grace called her bluff.

"Maybe I just want you to answer first?"

"Okay." Grace sighed. "I thought I was trying to make a point about why Catholics view lesbians as a greater threat than gay men. But now it appears that what I'm really asking you is why you're interested in me."

"*Interested* seems like a pretty benign term, Grace."

"It does?"

Abbie nodded.

Grace thought about what to say next. "Well, what term would you use, then?"

"I think I'd have to go for something a bit more—visceral. Certainly, something thoughtful that implies greater emotional intensity and . . ."

Grace wondered why Abbie was struggling to complete her statement. "And . . . what?"

Abbie met her eyes. "Investment."

"Oh." Grace didn't have a ready response.

"Is that okay?" Abbie asked. Her voice sounded uncertain.

Grace nodded.

"So," Abbie continued, "maybe now you can answer my question. Why do you want to know?"

Grace took her time. "Maybe because *I'm* emotionally invested in your answer."

"Are you?"

"I think so." Grace closed her eyes and shook her head. "Hell. I *know* so."

There was an ominous roll of thunder.

Abbie sighed and looked at her watch. "Why did we have to wait to have this part of the conversation when I need to be heading back to St. Albans?"

Grace looked out the front window of the cabin. The rain was coming down in sheets. It had been pouring like this an hour ago while she grilled their dinner. Abbie had stood there beside her on the tiny back porch and mused about when the system might blow itself out. Grace knew better than to say anything about her certainty that this storm wouldn't be letting up anytime soon. By now, she was ninety-nine percent sure Abbie would be marooned on the island with her for the rest of the night.

She waved a hand at the window. "You're kidding me, right?"

Abbie followed her gaze. "I wasn't . . ."

"Trust me. You aren't going anyplace by boat in this."

"No?"

Grace shook her head.

"But, Captain Polly . . ."

"Captain Polly would be the first person to tell you to stay off the water."

"Should I text her?"

Grace shrugged. "You could try. Sometimes, if you hold your mouth just right and manage to stand in precisely the right spot on the island during a solar flare, you can grab a stray signal."

"Great." Abbie met her eyes. "So, I guess that means I don't need to be out on the dock in twenty-five minutes to wait for her to fetch me?"

"I'm thinking not."

"Are you . . . will you be okay with that?"

"I dunno." Grace pretended to mull it over. "Lemme think . . ."

Abbie tossed part of a dinner roll at her.

"Hey!" Grace caught it in midair. "Don't start something you can't finish."

Abbie's chin went up. "You think you can take me?"

Grace was no longer sure what they were talking about—which she quickly realized wasn't much of a change from their normal conversations. "You mean in a food fight?"

"I mean in *any* kind of fight."

"Why do I suddenly feel like we're playing three-dimensional chess . . . again?"

Abbie took her time before answering. "Maybe because we are."

"I don't want to play games," Grace declared.

"I don't either. I want to bask in how much I'm enjoying this meal—and this company."

Abbie was right about one thing: the food had turned out better than Grace had planned when she cobbled together the makeshift marinade. But although it had come together nicely, she still regretted that the first and only meal she'd probably ever get to cook for Abbie would be so—forgettable.

Oh, well. At least it didn't totally suck. And the wine was great . . .

Abbie raised another forkful of the curried vegetables to her mouth and made happy, moaning sounds—which made it hard for Grace to concentrate on anything but her memories of the *other* happy sounds she remembered hearing her make once.

She made a valiant effort to distract herself. "It's so amazing to me that we can listen to this virtuosic performance and recall that Mutter once cut off part of her finger while chopping carrots." Grace wagged her pinkie. "I never trusted taproots, and after hearing that story, I knew my suspicions were well-founded."

Abbie laughed. "Right story. Wrong musician. That happened to Salerno-Sonnenberg, not Mutter."

"My bad. I *always* get them confused." Grace shook her head. "It's those damn hyphens. They invariably portend the certain onset of something ominous."

"Really?" Abbie raised an eyebrow. "As in the case of Bryce Oliver-James?"

Grace was surprised. "You know about him?"

Abbie nodded. "Of course."

Grace narrowed her eyes. "Why, I wonder?"

"I don't know." Abbie speared a slice of grilled chicken. "Maybe I did my homework and researched the faculty."

"Uh huh. Or maybe a little sprig of Clover got stuck in your ear while you were hiding from Pierre Paul?"

"It's been known to happen."

"Abbie. You know you cannot get involved in this."

"I'm already involved in it."

Grace felt a surge of panic. "Not *yet* you aren't. And after today, you won't ever have reason to become involved."

"Meaning?"

Grace sighed. "You don't really need me to spell this out for you again, do you?"

Abbie avoided her gaze.

"Abbie?" Grace tried again. "You know it's impossible. You know we can't."

Now Abbie did look at her. "It's *not* impossible. But it pains me to confront the reality that you believe it is."

Even though her somber and futile view of their prospects was vindicated by Abbie's grudging acceptance, Grace still managed to feel a contradictory pang of sadness. It was like living with the suspicion that you were afflicted with an incurable disease, and finally getting a diagnosis that confirmed your fears. That sliver of hope you thought lay buried in the sub-basement of your consciousness managed to reappear and writhe in silent agony as it died a miserable death.

Abbie must've noticed Grace's morose expression. She reached across the table and took hold of Grace's hand. "We still have right now," she said softly.

"What makes right now different from any other day?" Grace asked.

Abbie squeezed her hand. "Because, according to your definition—I'm not the president of the college yet."

"Isn't that splitting hairs?"

"Maybe. But today, it's a hair that *can* be split—and that's the only part that matters to me."

"I'm not sure many people would agree with that logic, Abbie."

"Ask me how much I care about what other people think."

"Maybe I have to care for you."

Abbie released her hand and sat back against her chair.

"Or not . . ." Grace added. She pushed back her chair and stood up. "How about a compromise? How about we confine ourselves to one dimension for a change?"

"Okay." Abbie belatedly got up, too. "What'd you have in mind?"

"Grab our wineglasses." Grace walked to a cabinet beside the bank of batteries and extracted another bottle. "I keep a few of these out here for emergencies." She held it up so Abbie could read the label.

"You must have pretty high-toned emergencies."

"I find it's best to be prepared. CK bought me six bottles of this last year for my birthday."

"Impressive. How many do you have left?"

"After this one? Five."

"I guess you don't have many emergencies."

Grace retrieved the corkscrew from the kitchen. "None of this caliber."

Abbie laughed. "Until now?"

"You might say that." She gestured toward the sofa. "Have a seat. Just push that stuff to the side."

Abbie put down their wineglasses and began collecting the pages from Grace's manuscript. Something on one of the pages must've caught her eye. She paused to read it more closely.

Grace closed her eyes. *Oh, shit . . .*

Abbie held up the stack of papers. "What is this?"

"It's nothing."

"It's not nothing." Abbie continued to peruse the pages. "It's captivating."

Grace reflexively began to apologize. "It's not anything—just some drivel I hammer away on whenever I'm . . ."

Wait a minute . . . did she just say it was captivating?

80

Grace walked toward her with the wine. "Did you just say *captivating?*"

"Yes."

"Well, I'll be damned. This from the woman who reads Boccaccio for fun?"

Abbie rolled her eyes. "I was *only* reading that to improve my Latin."

"Of *course* you were. Because you needed to sharpen those skills for your upcoming debut as the newest president of an indifferent, northeastern liberal arts college."

"Don't be an ass." Abbie frowned at her. "And don't try to change the subject because you're uncomfortable."

Grace didn't reply. She plopped down on the end of the sofa and deposited the bottle of wine and the opener alongside their two glasses on the coffee table.

"And don't pout, either," Abbie added. She sat down next to her and their arms brushed together.

Grace knew right away this wasn't going to end well. All of her internal alert sirens were blaring. Her head remained caught up in the same unending swivel it acquired the moment Abbie had stepped out onto that stage less than a week ago. And right now, Abbie's sudden, physical proximity was pushing her agitation into hyperdrive.

"I'm sorry. I don't mean to be an ass. I'm just—self-conscious about my book."

"That's what this is?" Abbie asked. "You're writing a novel?"

Grace nodded.

"What's it about?"

"I dunno." Grace shrugged. "Life. Loss. The differences between reality and illusion. You know . . . the usual."

"The usual," Abbie repeated. "Right." She shifted on the sofa. "How long have you been working on it?"

"What year is this?" Grace asked. Abbie laughed. It was a silvery sound that Grace wished she could bottle up and carry with her through all the dark years that surely lay ahead—a soft, sad, and secret reminder of what might have been. "I started it years ago," she explained. "It was an idea I got in grad school. It's now what I have in lieu of a social life."

"How near finished is it?"

Grace shrugged. "I dunno. Sometimes I think it's finished and I leave it alone for a few months. Then I have the misfortune to reread it and realize it's still a total mess. So, I tear it up and start over." She paused. "You'll soon learn that this exercise mirrors my general approach to life."

"Hmmmm." Abbie looked at her watch again.

"What's wrong?"

"Nothing." Abbie smiled at her. "I'm just wondering if I could *swim* back to Burton Island before dark."

"Hey." Grace bumped her shoulder. "No fair. I was trying to be self-revealing."

"Self-revealing?" Abbie quoted. "That's not self-revealing."

"It isn't?"

Abbie shook her head. "Nope."

"Well what is?"

"I've always found that actions speak louder than words."

"Which means?" Grace asked.

Abbie leaned forward and kissed her lightly.

Grace didn't wait to find out if this was intended as a test to see how she would respond—not unlike that first tentative kiss by the bay in San Francisco. She didn't wait for anything. She reached out and pulled Abbie closer.

She could feel the pages of her manuscript crumpling between them like a harbinger of destruction, but she didn't care. Right then, she didn't care about anything. Not the impropriety of intimate contact. Not her job. Not her prospects. Not the colossal chaos all of this certainly portended for Abbie. Not the fact that Anne-Sophie Mutter was working up to a thunderous expression of wild and unleashed adventure in the *rondo finale* of the concerto. Not the storm that continued to roll and rage outside around them. Not the fact that they were isolated on a damn island in more ways than just one. Not any of those things. For once, she allowed herself to live *in* the moment—instead of second-guessing what might occur in the next moment, after reason and sanity prevailed.

She could tell that Abbie was surprised by the initial way her body stiffened. But that didn't last long. Within moments, they had sunk down onto the sofa cushions, strewing pages from Grace's GAN all around them. A frail voice of better sense fought valiantly to bleat out a warning—but it quickly faded beneath the roar of shared passion that surged over them. Better sense didn't have a prayer. *Not now.* It was clear that right now, in this perfect moment, neither of them cared about being sensible.

Together, they were too strong for it.

Abbie's warm body moved beneath her. It felt both solid and fluid. Heady scents of bergamot orange and late-summer rain filled up Grace's world and clouded her judgment. Abbie's tongue tasted spicy and sweet—with fleeting hints of paprika, cinnamon and honey. It was an intoxicating medley of flavors that should never work together—yet they did. Perfectly. Wonderfully. Mysteriously.

Exotic—and a certain recipe for disaster . . .

Abbie managed to find her voice first.

"We shouldn't." She was breathing heavily.

Grace nuzzled the smooth fragrant skin on Abbie's neck. "I know."

"We should stop." Abbie's hands were roaming beneath Grace's shirt.

"I know that, too."

Abbie kissed along the side of Grace's face. "Do you want to stop?" Her voice was a husky whisper.

Grace decided to give her a definitive, nonverbal reply.

Abbie gasped. "I take it that's a no?"

Grace chuckled and began to tug on Abbie's shorts. "That would be a *big* no, Dr. Williams."

"Wait." Abbie stopped her hands.

Grace looked down at her with alarm. "I'm sorry . . ." She immediately withdrew her hand. "I thought you wanted to . . ."

"No," Abbie stopped her with a kiss. "I *do* want to." She pushed Grace up into a sitting position, then shifted herself around to straddle her lap. She wound her arms around Grace's shoulders and pulled her closer. "This time," she said in a voice that was soft and low, "*I* want to drive."

They dissolved into each other. *This was right*, Grace's tired mind told her. Right in ways she'd never experienced before. Her head was reeling. She could feel the cold, hard terrain of reason slipping away beneath her feet. The world was upside down. It was getting harder to breathe. Grace could feel the floodwaters rising inside her. Soon they would overspread their banks and carry them both away. For the first time, she understood what drove her poor, misguided father to risk everything in a passionate display of devotion to his cake of many spices.

Abbie proceeded to make good on her pledge to take the lead. Grace was only too happy to surrender control—although she hardly remained passive. The roar in her head grew louder and succeeded in drowning out all other sounds. Even the music on the radio faded into oblivion. She was surprised when she slowly became aware of a dim and persistent sound that was more like a wail than a moan.

She lifted her head. "Was that you?" she asked Abbie.

Abbie looked back at her with a dazed expression. Her lips were moist and slightly puffy. "Was *what* me?" she replied. "This?"

Grace jumped at the intimate contact. "No," she gasped. "Not *that*. The noise."

"What noise?"

The wail sounded again, closer this time.

"*That* noise," Grace asked. "Outside."

Abbie cocked her head to listen. "What *is* that?"

"It sounds like some kind of animal." Grace's eyes widened. "Oh my *god.*"

"What's wrong?" Abbie shifted back on Grace's lap. She laid a hand against the side of her face. "You look like you've seen a ghost."

"Close. I think it's Grendel."

"Grendel?"

"The Nine O'Clock Dog . . . remember?"

Abbie blinked. "Your neighbor's dog?"

Grace nodded. "Former neighbors. They skipped out during the night."

"And came out here?"

"Not all of them."

Abbie looked surprised. "You mean they abandoned their dog out here on an island? That's contemptible."

The low-pitched wail sounded again—closer this time.

"We need to go find it." Abbie climbed off Grace's lap. "The poor thing is probably starving."

Grace was surprised. "Are you serious?"

"Of course." Abbie was busy straightening her clothing. "Don't you think we should?"

"Well, yeah. I just didn't think you'd . . ." Grace didn't finish her sentence.

"Care?" Abbie asked her.

"No." Grace laid a hand on Abbie's leg. "That's not what I meant. I didn't think you'd want to go trolling around outside in the rain again."

"Oh. *That*." Abbie gave her a coquettish smile. "Why not? I mean . . . if I end up getting soaked—*again*—it will simply provide you with another flimsy excuse to get my clothes off."

The rain was still coming down in sheets, and that made seeing in the dark—which on the island was difficult under the best conditions—next to impossible. Grace kept a tight hold on Abbie's hand to try and prevent her from tripping as they navigated the rugged path that led to the highest point on the island.

She'd lent Abbie one of Grady's rain slickers, and the thing was impossibly large on her. With its cavernous hood pulled low over her face, she looked like a shadowy caricature of the Grim Reaper. Grace noted the irony of that, and recalled how Abbie had looked the first time she showed up at her house—in the rain and wearing a long, black cloak.

It didn't take them long to find Grendel. The frightened creature was huddled beneath some cast-off sheets of plywood that were leaning against a tree near the community burn pile. The beam from Grace's flashlight reflected off a pair of owlish eyes.

"There she is," Grace said, waving the beam around in a tight circle. "Beneath that wood."

"What do we do now?" Abbie asked.

"Hand me that bag with the bits of chicken in it."

Abbie retrieved the Ziploc bag from the pocket of Grady's raincoat. "Do you think she'll take it?"

"Only one way to find out." Grace took the bag and handed Abbie her flashlight. "Here goes."

Grace extended a piece of the chicken and approached Grendel cautiously.

"Here, girl." She tried her best to sound nonthreatening. "I know you're hungry."

The closer Grace inched toward the dog, the more it ducked its head and growled. She finally gave up trying to coax it forward and tossed it the bite of chicken. The dog lunged forward and snagged it, then retreated to its spot beneath the plywood.

Grace turned to face Abbie. "She's not going to come to me."

"I have an idea," Abbie said. "Come hold the flashlight."

Grace complied. "What are you gonna do?"

"Give me the bag of chicken."

Grace handed it over.

"Wish me luck. I'm going in." Abbie turned and slowly approached the cowering dog. She stopped about six feet away and calmly sat down on the ground. She opened the bag of chicken and poured a handful of bites into her hand. She didn't say anything, she just sat there in the rain with her hand extended. Grace couldn't believe her eyes when Grendel slowly got to her feet and took a few tentative steps toward Abbie.

"It's okay," Abbie cooed. "I won't hurt you, baby. Come on."

Grendel walked to within a few feet of where Abbie sat and

slowly stretched out her neck to take the chicken from her palm. She did not retreat to her hiding place, however. She sat down on the ground and stared up at Abbie with saucer-like eyes.

Abbie patted her hand against her leg. "Come on. I won't hurt you."

Grendel shimmied closer—close enough to rest her head on Abbie's thigh.

"Good baby." Abbie cautiously began to pet the soggy dog. "Have some more to eat." She emptied the rest of the bag into her hand and Grendel ate it without hesitation. "You want to come with us?" Abbie slowly got to her feet. She patted the side of her leg. "Come on. Come on." Grendel got up, too. Grace fully expected the dog to retreat to her hiding place. But she didn't. Grendel cautiously followed Abbie back to where Grace stood, holding the flashlight.

"Let's go," Abbie said. "Before she gets spooked and changes her mind."

Grace didn't bother to argue with Abbie. She simply turned around and began lighting their way along the slow hike back down to the cabin. She resisted the impulse to look back to see if Grendel was still following them.

Abbie must've read her mind. "She's following us," she whispered. "Don't stop—just keep going."

When they reached the cabin, Grace didn't bother to stop and shake the water from her raincoat. She opened the door and stepped inside. Abbie followed suit—and so did Grendel, who immediately ducked behind the sofa to claim a spot on the floor near the corner. Before lying down, she gave her small body a vigorous shake and sent water flying everyplace.

"Do you have any old towels?" Abbie asked. "Something we can give her to lie on?"

"Yeah." Grace took off her soggy jacket and held out a hand. "Give me your coat. I'll hang these out on the back porch."

Abbie complied. "She looks pretty comfortable—like she's used to being inside."

"I think they let her in at night."

"We need to feed her something else."

Grace nodded. "Wanna take a look in the fridge while I hang these up and get her some towels?"

Abbie nodded.

Grace headed for the back porch with their dripping coats.

Who ever saw this *one coming?*

If she'd stopped to think about it, she probably could've come up with a hundred ways their . . . *assignation* . . . could've been disrupted. A flash flood of epic proportions? The International Space Station crashing through Earth's atmosphere and landing smack-dab on top of Grady's cabin? An invasion by marauding Canadians determined to reclaim their island chain? Or maybe Lucretia Fletcher with a searchlight and a salivating pack of bloodhounds?

Any of those would've made more sense.

But Grendel? Out here on Butler Island?

Not in a million years.

When Grace came back inside after hanging up their rain gear, Abbie was pulling containers out of the fridge.

"There's more rice," she said. "And we could scramble her some eggs."

Grace peered over her shoulder. "Sounds delicious."

Abbie leaned back against her. Neither of them said anything for a moment. Grace felt like she could stand there forever. She leaned her head against Abbie's shoulder.

"Why does it have to be this way?"

Abbie didn't seem to have any trouble understanding the non sequitur. "I don't know. It should be so simple. Yet it isn't."

Grace wrapped her arms around her. "I want it to be."

"I do, too. But it's not, and we both have to face that."

"I know."

"Do you also know that we can't see each other this way again?"

"Yeah," Grace replied. "I kind of figured."

"At least not until we can figure something out."

Abbie took hold of Grace's hands. Grace was surprised at how warm her touch still felt—even after their seek-and-rescue mission in the rain. "You think we can figure something out?"

"I'm counting on it, Grace."

"I wish I shared your optimism."

"It's not really optimism. It's more like—determinism."

Grace laughed. "Now you sound like CK. 'Dam the torpedoes' has always been her mantra."

"I knew that coming out here was wrong of me—that it was totally selfish." Abbie squeezed her hands. "But I couldn't stop myself."

"I'm glad you didn't."

From her corner in the living room, Grendel began to whimper. The sound was soft and sad, and it perfectly matched how Grace felt in that moment.

"I guess we'd better feed her," Abbie suggested.

"Probably." Grace kissed Abbie's neck before releasing her. "Then what?" she was brave enough to ask.

Abbie turned around to face her. "Then you take me to bed, and we make this night last a thousand years."

Grace was not inclined to argue with her.

Chapter Five

The storm blew itself out sometime during the night. Grace wasn't sure exactly when because she was too preoccupied with trying to memorize every detail of her waning hours with Abbie.

They didn't sleep much.

In the end, Grendel wound up making a nest out of a couple of old quilts they'd piled up on the floor in the corner of the bedroom. Once the tired dog had eaten and taken another trip outside for a bathroom break, she trotted over to her makeshift bed, curled up in a ball, and never made another sound. Grace was incredulous. To be fair, she had never really paid attention to where Grendel spent her nights—but it seemed apparent that she was used to being inside.

It also seemed apparent that the jittery little dog was more than slightly attached to Abbie.

"You may end up having to adopt her," Grace pointed out, after the pair returned from their respective trips to the outhouse before bed.

"Oh, I don't know about that." Abbie bent down and scrubbed the top of Grendel's head. "I think she'd be a lot happier living with you."

"*Me?* Why me?"

"Because you have a fenced yard and a perfect back porch. And I have a life and a ridiculously overwrought new home—both filled with contradictions and uncertainty."

Grace narrowed her eyes. "Almost thou persuadest me."

Abbie smiled a bit rakishly. "Spoken like a woman accustomed to running around in a toga."

"I only did that once."

"I know. As I recall, it made undressing you a whole lot easier."

Grace rolled her eyes. "I would've packed it for this weekend if I'd known I'd have occasion *not* to wear it."

"About that." Abbie stood up to face her. "Got anything I can borrow to sleep in?"

"Sorry." Grace did her best to sound sincere. "I appear to be fresh out of sleepwear."

Abbie raised an eyebrow. "Why do I think you're lying?"

Grace took a step closer to her. "Beats me."

"Well. When in Rome . . ." With one smooth gesture, Abbie shed Grady's oversized hockey shirt.

She wasn't wearing anything beneath it.

Grace's spring-loaded inner Catholic reared up to remind her that a God-fearing, decent person should look away. But she wasn't feeling particularly decent right then, and, although she certainly did fear God, she didn't have the emotional bandwidth to aspire to anything approximating behavior sanctioned by the Church. All she wanted was to collapse into a heap and stare stupidly at the beatified vision before her.

But that wasn't going to happen, either. Abbie had other ideas. Before she could concoct something pithy to say, Grace was flat on her back with Abbie's face hovering above her.

"I think I remember this part."

"Do you?" Abbie asked. "Then maybe you'll remember this, too." Abbie kissed her.

As they dissolved into each other, Grace understood with a hazy kind of clarity that her doleful memories of this amazing night would always be wrapped in the sounds of Grendel's soft snores and the gentle patter of a waning storm.

When she woke up in the morning, Grace was immediately aware of two things—Abbie and Grendel were nowhere to be seen, and the air was rife with the intoxicating aroma of coffee.

She threw on her discarded clothes and headed out to the kitchen. Sure enough, there was a pot of coffee. It was about half full, so Grace surmised that Abbie had been up for a while. She poured herself a generous cup and headed outside in search of her companions. She found them sitting together in the same spot where she'd fallen asleep yesterday. Abbie didn't hear her approach, but Grendel, who was dozing in the scrap of shade beneath Abbie's chair, lifted her head like a prairie dog and stared as Grace drew closer.

Abbie was wearing her own clothes. Grace figured they must've dried out overnight. Her hair was loosely knotted on top of her head. One hand held a coffee mug; the other held a stack of papers. She looked fabulous. But Grace was learning that Abbie tended to look fabulous in anything—or nothing.

Seeing her sitting there against the backdrop of the lake and the distant, smoky-blue contours of the Green Mountains seemed . . . right. It was like she completed the landscape—a final flourish at the end of a near-perfect composition.

Grace could have stood there all day.

Abbie seemed particularly engrossed in whatever she was reading. As she drew closer, Grace felt a jolt of panic when she realized that the stack of loose-leaf papers balanced on Abbie's lap were pages from her manuscript.

Oh, holy fucking shit . . .

She cleared her throat.

Abbie looked up at her. "Good morning." She smiled. "I see you found the coffee."

"Oh, yeah." Grace took a healthy sip. "It's good, too. You've managed to capitalize on another weakness of mine."

"Another?" Abbie's face relaxed into a long, slow smile that made Grace go weak at the knees. "Do tell. What was the first?"

"It was . . . um . . . you know . . ."

Abbie raised an eyebrow. She lifted the pages from her lap. "Richly crafted descriptions like that would seen to cast doubt on the authorship of this stunning prose work."

Stunning prose work?

"Um . . ." Grace waved a hand at the pages. "So, you're reading something . . . *interesting?*"

"Oh, yes. I've been reading for more than two hours now. It's one of the best novels I've picked up in a very long time."

Grace did her best to feign calm. "Do tell. Where'd you find it?"

"On your sofa." She smiled again. "Mostly."

"Mostly?"

"In our haste, we did knock a few pages onto the floor. It took me a while to get them back into their correct order."

Grace pulled another battered Adirondack chair over so she could sit beside Abbie. "Scrambling up the page order could only improve the narrative."

"I disagree. This narrative flows superbly."

Grace extended a hand toward Grendel, who inched forward on the grass to sniff at her palm. "I guess I should be grateful that at least one narrative in my life is flowing superbly."

"Meaning?" Abbie asked.

Grace shrugged.

"Grace?" Abbie leaned forward and rested a hand on Grace's knee. "Not talking about it won't help either of us."

Grace met her eyes. Today, they looked as blue as the lake, shimmering beneath the morning sun.

"I don't want to talk about it. I want to pretend that right now is our new normal."

Abbie sighed. "I do, too. But we can't, and it isn't."

"I know."

"I'm sorry." Abbie squeezed her knee. "I didn't mean for this to happen."

"Define *this*."

"Coming out here the way I did. It was a reckless impulse. I should never have given in to it. I just couldn't . . ." She didn't finish her sentence.

"Couldn't what?" Grace prodded.

Abbie sighed. "Couldn't stop myself. I had to see you again. Just once more—as *me*—not as the new president of St. Albans."

"Is there a difference?" Grace wondered if she sounded as morose as she was beginning to feel.

"You know there is."

"Yeah," Grace said with resignation. "I do know." She rested her hand on top of Abbie's. "I'm sorry, too."

Abbie bent forward and kissed her on the temple. The gesture was soft and slow—and its sweet simplicity was the most deeply romantic thing Grace had ever experienced.

"So," Abbie said, after sitting back against her chair, "how about I ask you some questions about this book of yours while we enjoy what's left of the morning?"

Grace gazed out across the water. A couple of small fishing boats were visible—both idly drifting along over the usual favored spots. She watched the dark silhouettes of the standing fishermen as they cast their lines and slowly wound them back in. Over and over they repeated the practiced maneuver—as if they had all the time in the world to wait for the sleepy fish to rouse and decide to take their bait.

She looked back at Abbie. *What did* they *have? Another hour? Maybe two?* Then she'd take Abbie back to Burton Island, so she could catch the ferry to retrieve her car. And that would be that—an ellipsis at the end of their unfinished sentence.

No. Not an ellipsis. *A period.*

"Sure." Grace took another sip of her coffee. *Why not answer questions about another thing in her life that was going no place?* "Fire away."

Grendel accompanied them on the boat ride across the lake. Grace didn't question it when the odd little dog trotted along behind them as they descended the path to the dock. She was surprised, however, when Grendel leapt from the dock onto the pontoon, where she quickly took up residence on a padded seat in front of the helm. Grace wasn't sure if the dog was used to boats, or whether she simply feared being ditched . . . again.

Abbie followed along more sedately, and soon they'd pushed off and were underway.

Abbie sat just behind Grace and inconspicuously held her hand as they made their way across the lake. The winds were calm today so they didn't get bounced around too much. As they drew closer to land, increasing numbers of recreational boaters slowed their progress.

They didn't talk much. That didn't really surprise Grace. What, after all, remained unsaid?

Not much.

It was all pretty straightforward. Once Abbie returned from North Carolina, she'd be inaugurated as president. That, as they say, would be that.

End of story.

At least, it would be the end of *their* pathetic little story.

Burton Island was hopping when she slowed the pontoon to search for a place to dock. The harbor was choked with boats. People crawled all over the waterfront and clogged the paths that led to campsites and the public restrooms. Grace began to think that coming here wasn't the brightest idea. She'd thought most people would be heading out of town for the long holiday weekend. She didn't count on the legions who would opt to stay around at the public parks.

She rummaged in a compartment beside her seat.

"Here." She handed Abbie a pair of oversized sunglasses and a ball cap emblazoned with a Bass Pro Shops logo. "Put these on."

Abbie took the items from her. "Why? Are we gonna knock off that hotdog stand?"

"Yes. That's precisely what I had in mind. And after that, we can dance topless on the boat and try to draw even more attention to ourselves."

Abbie laughed. "Feeling a little paranoid?"

"Aren't you?"

Abbie adjusted her cap. "Not particularly. I don't think I'm especially recognizable around here."

Grace thought about telling Abbie she was nuts—that she'd be a standout even if she tried to hide behind a gang of mummers, sashaying down Two Street in Philadelphia. But she didn't. Besides, maybe Abbie was right, and Grace was just being paranoid.

It wouldn't be the first time.

"I guess you're right," she apologized. "I didn't want you to have to endure the fallout if anyone saw us together."

"Fallout? Is your reputation that toxic?" Abbie donned the enormous sunglasses—a castoff pair of Karen's. They were absurdly large and made her look ridiculous. "To whom did these horrible things belong?" she asked. "Jackie O.?"

Grace was on the verge of delivering a snappy reply when she saw someone she recognized.

Fuck. Fuckity, fuck, fuck, fuck.

It was Brittney—her fucking, starry-eyed stalker. *Of course*. She was standing near the water's edge with another girl Grace didn't recognize. They both were eating ice cream cones.

"Sit down," she barked at Abbie. "*Now*."

Grace couldn't read Abbie's expression because of the plate-sized lenses that covered most of her face, but she complied immediately. "I assume you'll tell me why you look like you've seen a ghost?"

"In a minute," Grace replied. She navigated the pontoon around an enormous motorboat that had stopped to off-load a couple of jet skis. "We're getting out of here."

"Okaayyy . . ." Abbie sat back against the side of the boat and refrained from comment while Grace steered them out of the harbor. Once they had safely returned to open water, she got to her feet and took off the sunglasses. "Care to tell me what that was all about?"

"I'm really sorry." Grace looked at her sheepishly. "I saw someone I knew . . . a student of mine." She rolled her eyes. "An overly-*attentive* student of mine."

"Young love?"

"You might say that. She drives me crazy."

"She?" Abbie raised an eyebrow.

"Yeah." Grace held up a hand. "Don't worry—it's not what you think."

"Really? How do you know what I think?"

"I can imagine."

Abbie squinted her eyes. "I'm not sure you can, actually."

"Forget about Brittney. We're gonna have to drop you off back at Kamp Kill Kare."

Abbie looked confused. "Won't that increase the likelihood that we'll run into *other* people you know?"

"Probably," Grace agreed. "At this point, it doesn't much matter. If Brittney saw us, the news will beat us back to the mainland."

"Grace?" Abbie took hold of her elbow. "I'm sorry about this. And I'm even sorrier that all I can manage to do is keep repeating the same pitiful phrase."

"It's okay. No pain, no gain—right?"

"If you say so."

"Besides, I need to hit a store in town to get some food for this damn dog."

Grendel's head whipped around as soon as Grace uttered the words, "damn dog." Grace had a sudden, uncanny sense that Grendel possessed highly developed language skills. Either that, or she was used to hearing the phrase "damn dog" a lot. Knowing her former neighbors, she opted for the latter explanation.

"Where did you leave your car?" Grace asked.

"In the main lot near the park entrance." Abbie hesitated. "Thanks for the curb service."

Grace gave her a rueful smile. "I'd say 'my pleasure,' but I'd be lying."

Abbie smiled, too. "I'm glad."

They approached the boat landing at Kamp Kill Kare in silence. This time, Grace didn't have any trouble docking—although there were a lot of families scattered about, and hordes of free-range kids splashing in the shallow water and racing across the sandy beaches. This was the last big weekend of the tourist season—and the final one in which camp visitors could hike, picnic, swim or paddle about in the Kamp peninsula's clear, blue water. Grace loved this place, which had been an elegant and sought-after tourist retreat in the late 1800s before its decades-long tenure as a summer boys' camp. The park's stately, three-story Rocky Point House now stood as a monument to the elegance of traditional lakeside architecture. Grace thought it was the best of Vermont—and when she couldn't get out to Butler Island, her favorite pastime was to pack up a book and spend an afternoon or early summer evening out here—sprawled across a blanket in the long shadows cast by the former hotel.

"I love this place."

Grace looked at Abbie with surprise. "You must've read my mind."

"I seem to be making a habit of that."

"Yeah. Go figure."

Abbie sighed. "No use putting it off. If I leave now, I can try to make it as far as Harrisburg before stopping for the night." She walked toward the bow to give Grendel a few pats and quick kiss on the head. "You be a good girl and don't run off."

Grace thought she heard a faint keening sound from the dog when Abbie turned away. She didn't blame her one bit.

Abbie was certainly agile enough to not require any help getting off the pontoon, but Grace hopped onto the dock and reached down a hand to her, just the same. She knew the phony act of courtesy was nothing more than a flimsy excuse to touch her again before they said goodbye. If Abbie guessed her real motivation, she didn't seem to mind it. She took hold of Grace's extended hand and climbed up to stand beside her. She didn't let go right away and the two of them stood together, stupidly holding hands for what felt to Grace like both the longest—and the painfully shortest—moments of her life.

"I'll miss you," Grace whispered.

Abbie squeezed her hand before releasing it. "Not as much as I'll miss you."

Grace closed her eyes. When she opened them, Abbie had turned away and started walking toward the parking lot where she'd left her car. With each step she took, Grace felt another leaf of hope wither and die on the vine inside her.

When she was nearly out of sight, Abbie stopped abruptly and turned around. She raised a hand to her head.

"The cap," she called out. "I forgot to give it back."

Grace smiled at the imposing picture she made: Élisabeth Abbot Williams—the esteemed fifteenth president of St. Albans College. A complex and accomplished scholar with an impeccable academic pedigree—provocative enough in appearance to command the cover of any fashion magazine—cast against a tumbled backdrop of recreational excess and faded elegance. The absurd cap with its garish, Day-Glo jumping fish logo was spot-on as a burlesque icon of her many contradictions.

"Keep it." Grace smiled sadly and gave Abbie a mock salute. "It's you."

Grace was able to snag a bag of dry dog food and a box of Milk-Bone biscuits for Grendel at a mini-mart within walking distance of the harbor. She didn't worry too much about Grendel disappearing if she left her alone on the pontoon. The little dog had already had numerous opportunities to bolt and had shown no inclination at all to flee. When she returned to the boat with her purchases, Grendel was exactly where Grace had left her: curled up on her bench seat at the bow of the pontoon.

Grace opened the box of dog biscuits and fished out a couple. She walked over to Grendel and held one out to her.

"Want this?" she asked, waving the tiny bone-shaped treat back and forth. "Want a cookie?"

Grendel ducked her head and scooted forward on the seat, wagging her tail. Grace gave her the cookie and sat down beside her.

"Looks like we're stuck with each other, kiddo."

Grendel looked up at her with sad brown eyes.

"Yeah." Grace stroked the dog's head. "We're both a couple of castoffs, aren't we?" She gave Grendel the other biscuit. "It's okay. Tonight, we can howl at the moon together."

Grendel sat beside her on the short ride back to Butler Island. Grace noticed that another rig was tied up at the dock Grady shared with Roscoe, and when she got closer, she recognized the souped-up deck boat belonging to her brother, Dean.

Why the hell is Dean out here on a holiday?

She didn't have to wait long to find out. She saw him coming down the path from the cabin while she was mooring the pontoon.

"Yo," he called out. "I thought you'd taken off already."

"No. I had to run over to St. Albans to pick up some stuff. What are you doing here?"

"I came out to drop off some salvage wood I got yesterday in Hinesburg. Nice stuff. Wormy chestnut. Not enough of it to do anything with at your place so I thought maybe Grady could use it out here. Where you been? And what's with the mutt?"

Grace and Grendel climbed up onto the aluminum dock. She had no idea why Roscoe had the damn thing set so high. He was either too lazy to adjust it, or he suspected the lake level would mysteriously rise up another two feet when no one was looking.

"She's a stray. Somebody dumped her out here yesterday. Don't you recognize her?"

"Recognize her?" Dean looked at Grendel more closely. "Why the fuck would I recognize her?"

"She belonged to the people who lived in the house next door to me."

"No shit? Those assholes who took off during the night and skipped out on all that back rent they owed Joe?"

Grace nodded. "They would be the ones."

"Fuckwads. I hate people like that. They're what's wrong with this country."

"In this case, I won't disagree with you."

Dean reached out to take the bag of dog food from her. "Seems like they went to a lot of trouble to ditch their dog out here. Why not just dump its ass out along the road someplace?"

"Beats me. Maybe they actually cared about her and thought she'd have a better shot at getting taken care of on an island."

Dean laughed. "Well they figured that one right, didn't they?"

Grace shrugged.

"You always had a damn soft spot for things nobody wanted. How many bimbos who were kicked out or knocked-up did you drag home while we were in school?"

"I dunno, Dean. Didn't you keep track of how many of them you fucked?"

"Can't say I did." He chuckled. "Besides, I only hit the good-lookin' ones who were already preggers."

"You're really a pig, you know that?"

"Hey? It's not like *they* didn't want it. Nobody had anything to lose."

"Yeah." Grace led the way back up to the cabin. Grendel raced on ahead of her like she'd made the trip a hundred times. "Great economy in that, I guess."

"No shit." He huffed along behind her. Grace could tell by his breathing that he was smoking again.

"Speaking of women who should have better sense—where is CK?"

Dean didn't bother to pretend he had no idea. That ship had sailed. "She's working on some grant thingamajig. She's gonna be in the library all day. We're hooking up later."

"Yeah." Grace waved a hand. "TMI, dude."

"Oh, get over it. We weren't hurting anything. I don't know why you had to get so bent out of shape about it."

"Maybe because I had to boil the damn sheets." Grace unlocked the cabin door so they could go inside. She began to wonder if the salvage wood was just an excuse for him to come out here and finally face the music about CK. She hadn't spoken with him since the day she caught them together in her guest room.

"CK is my friend, Dean. I don't want her to get hurt."

He set the bag of dog food down on the floor beside the sofa. "Why the hell would she get hurt?"

"Forgetting something?"

He looked at her with a blank expression. "What?"

"Let's see ... Dina, Donna, Debbie, Darlene." She ticked them off. "*Four* wives, Dean. Oh. Wait ... I forgot about Dolly."

"Hey, I never married *her*."

"Only because you found out on your way to Vegas that she was *already* married to two other men—*at the same time*."

"*That* one was not my fault. She was from Utah."

Grace held up her hands. "Which means?"

"Hell if I know. It's *Utah*. They're into weird-ass crap out there." He scratched the back of his head. "They all wear that magic underwear shit, too."

Grace rolled her eyes. "They're called 'temple garments,' Dean. And they're supposed to be an aid in resisting temptation—something you, in particular, would derive great benefit from."

"Whatever." He sniffed. "I don't see how any man can walk around in that getup—it'd be like having your junk in a straightjacket."

The mention of "junk" was like a Skinner bell—causing Dean to hike and resettle his baggy jeans.

Grace shook her head. "Therein would be the point."

Dean sniffed again.

Grace stared at her brother and tried again to solve the riddle of how he and CK could be . . . whatever the hell they were.

Fuck buddies?

What a stupid phrase to describe an even stupider concept. Besides, Dean only dated—or married—women who fit within his alliterative approach to relationships.

"I guess I don't need to worry too much about you and CK," she said. "Her name doesn't begin with *D*."

Her brother gave her a crooked smile. "Maybe I'm making an exception."

"Branching out to a new frontier of the alphabet?"

"It could happen."

"I doubt it." Grace folded her arms. "You're too damned cheap to replace all those monogrammed towels Mum gave you when you married Dina."

"So? They're nice towels . . . eighty-zillion thread count or something. I'm not gonna trash 'em."

"Dean? I'd venture a guess that four divorces have cost you more than a set of Egyptian cotton towels."

"Yeah, well." Dean picked up the bag of dog food. "Where do you want this? I gotta hit the head and get back to town before noon."

"I've got a plastic bin in the kitchen." Grace led the way. "Where'd you leave the wood?"

"Under a tarp on the back porch. It'll be fine out there until you and Grady can figure out what you wanna do with it. If you think it'll be longer than another month or two, you'll wanna bring it inside before he closes this place up for the season. I think it would make a great accent wall—maybe in this dining area."

Dean's ability to shape-shift from knuckle-dragging bubba to feng shui master never ceased to amaze Grace. He was simply a genius at interior design and space utilization.

"I like that idea. Why can't we do this at my place?"

Dean shook his head. "You don't need this at your place because we don't have to cover anything up. All we need to do is rip shit out to show off what's already there."

Grace opened the Rubbermaid bin, and Dean stashed the big bag of dog food inside.

"Why don't you apply these searing insights to your personal relationships?"

Dean looked at her. "Why should I? Last time I checked, your scruples didn't seem to be doing you any good."

"Touché."

Dean seemed to think better of his comment. He laid a hand on Grace's shoulder. "Hey. I'm sorry. That wasn't fair. I know you're still having a rough time of it since that bitch took off."

Grace patted her brother's hand. "It's okay. You're right. I need to get my head out of my ass."

"Yeah. CK said you might be starting to come back to life."

Grace felt a tinge of panic. She had a momentary, irrational fear that CK would say something to Dean about Abbie. *But she'd never do that . . . would she?*

"She did?" Grace tried to make her voice as casual as possible. "What prompted that conversation?"

He shrugged. "It wasn't really what I'd call a conversation. I was telling her about Agnes coming for Thanksgiving—and how you'd probably throw a rod."

"Wait a minute. Mum is coming for Thanksgiving?"

He nodded.

"When the hell was that decided? I thought we were going to Wilkes-Barre?"

"Nope."

"Dean. What the fuck? I'm not ready to have company—especially not Mum's brand of company."

"First off—it's not 'company.' It's Agnes. Second, she's only staying a week."

A week? Grace would never survive a week under the same roof with her mother.

"She's not staying with me."

"Oh, come on, Grace."

"I'm not kidding, Dean. She's staying with you."

"In Plattsburgh?"

"Why not? Don't they have turkeys in New York State?"

Dean rolled his eyes. "What's your problem? She's a nice old lady who doesn't want to be alone for the holidays."

"She's an overbearing virago who defines me as a lesbian with bad shoes."

"So? You *are* a lesbian," Dean dropped his eyes to look at Grace's feet, "with bad shoes."

"Fuck you."

Dean laughed and kissed her on the cheek. "Fuck you, too. See you on Tuesday."

"Okay."

Grace held the back door open for him. He left the cabin and made a beeline for the outhouse. She knew he'd be disappointed to discover that none of his favorite reading materials were left out there.

"Hey, Dean?" she called out. "Be careful with CK. And quit having sex in my guestroom."

"What-ever." He waved a hand over his head without looking back. "You and that mangy mutt stay safe out here."

He disappeared inside the privy.

Grace was determined to spend the rest of the day and evening working on her GAN.

She tried to convince herself that she was motivated more by a surge of creative enthusiasm than by the lavish praise Abbie had heaped on the story that morning.

She set up a makeshift desk on the north side of the cabin, in some shade cast by a cluster of cottonwood trees. She hadn't bothered to bring her laptop along, so she was writing longhand.

This introduced a new set of variables to the exercise.

Grace found this style of writing led her to work more thoughtfully. The prose she generated wasn't actually *better*—it was just more *careful*. There was something about the exercise of mechanically crafting the letters with a pen and ink that led her to be more precise about the words she chose to use. Handwritten sentences took on greater meaning—probably because anything she typed on a mechanical device seemed, by definition, to be less permanent . . . immediately tagged as a candidate for change or revision. Strings of words that were backlit on a computer screen existed more like placeholders than actual prose.

She sometimes mused about the possible benefits her students might derive if she insisted that they write their theme papers out in longhand first, before typing them up for submission. For one thing, it might provoke them to actually notice things like missing punctuation, dangling participles, or sentences without verbs.

Not very likely . . .

She had been making halting progress. It was a battle to stay focused on the words and not let her attention wander to the boat traffic on the lake. The weather was glorious today—a nearly cloudless sky and soft winds from the north. There was next to no chop on the water—which meant jet skis were out in droves, furiously racing behind motorboats to zigzag back and forth across their wakes. It was a textbook, late-summer Vermont day.

She was now writing a scene where Ochre had taken up reluctant residence on the back wall of a booth choked with indifferent antiques housed inside a barn-sized "super flea" complex that sagged inelegantly near an off-ramp on Interstate 80 in South Bend. The proprietor of the booth had acquired her—along with twenty-two other works of "art"—from a back room full of "everything's five bucks" *objets* at an estate auction in suburban Muncie.

Ochre knew the drill. She'd hang here, unadorned, overlooked and unrecognized, until the day some poor loser took a liking to her unique color palette or her '50s-era gestalt. Although any would-be buyer would never be able to articulate what it was about Ochre that made her so alluring. More often than not, some untutored lummox would eventually notice her bare breasts and decide that her family of warm mustard tones was a perfect match for his natty harvest-gold recliner.

Then her unending American Gothic nightmare would commence its next chapter . . .

But for now, Ochre was content to rest quietly in obscurity, nestled among the mishmash of Hoosier cabinets, distressed Coca-Cola crates, castoff Lodge skillets and motor oil cans that doubled as coin banks. Sometimes, like today, a weary individual would stop and stare at her—long enough for Ochre to wonder if, at last, her true provenance was about to be divined.

Why do you look so familiar? the pensive one would ask.
Because, like you, I do not belong here, she would answer.

I don't know what you mean, the stranger would say.

Then sit down here beside me, Ochre would reply, *and I will explain it to you.*

And so their dialogue would begin.

I am not what you perceive—yet am the culmination of all you seek.

I don't understand.

You will gain understanding when you stop seeking it.

Why must you speak in riddles?

A riddle is a mirror that reveals a hidden path to meaning.

Another riddle.

Another path.

I have another question.

What was your first question?

Why you look familiar?

I abide in the temple of all familiars.

Yet you are here—naked and unashamed.

I am enlightened. That is true.

What else is true?

It is true that you fear my power over you.

I fear only what I do not understand.

That is your curse.

Why is it a curse to be cautious?

Because you have allowed your fear to become your pearl of great price.

Are you saying I'm wrong to avoid risking my happiness on an unknown?

I am saying the known and the unknown are two sides of the same coin.

So there are no wrong answers?

There are only wrong questions.

How do I learn the right questions?

If you have to ask, you will never know the answer.

I am afraid.

To face your fear is to embrace your humanity. To flee it is to embrace a life of misery.

I no longer wish to be miserable.

Then it behooves you to change your perspective.

How do I do that?

What do you seek?

Happiness.

The known and the unknown are two halves of a whole.

Which means?

To embrace one is to possess the other.

Which one are you?

I am the known that remains unknown.

And what am I?

You are a mirror without a path . . .

Grace abruptly closed her notebook.

Where the hell did that come from?

She held her pen up to the light and examined it. No telltale glimmers of diode-emitting ink. No residue of perspicacious pixie dust. No magic. No *nothing*. Just a plain old 41¢ Bic Cristal ballpoint.

That meant all the sophomoric, Kierkegaardian mumbo-jumbo came from *her*.

She stood up and heaved the pen over the cliff into the lake.

She blamed Dean. Damn him and his fucking inferences about her pathetic sex life.

Damn him for being right. She was a coward who was a prisoner of her scruples.

Something needed to change. Something needed to give.

And soon . . .

Chapter Six

Grace fought hard not to yawn. It wasn't easy.

It was only her third day back after the long weekend, but already, it felt like a month. She was trying hard not to pay attention to the calendar, but it was impossible not to count off the days until Abbie returned to St. Albans—for good.

This was the fourth student appointment she'd had since ten o'clock. Most of the thirty-minute meetings were with students from her Freshman Lit 101 surveys. Papers that comprised one-quarter of their total grades were due and, based on the sneak previews she'd had, several of them were skating perilously close to ruination.

Fortunately for her, Brittney hadn't bothered to show up for her nine-thirty appointment. Grace wasn't sure what to make of that, but she was confident it meant something. She knew Brittney had recognized her on Burton Island—it was unclear if she knew who Abbie was. That part was a crapshoot.

She wondered for the millionth time if Abbie had made it back to North Carolina safely. She had halfway thought Abbie might try to call her on Saturday night—she even stayed up late under the guise of watching a meteor shower, just so she'd be outside, camped out at one of the island's best locations to catch a random cell signal. She ended up seeing a lot of meteors, but got no calls. She'd actually fallen asleep on her blanket and probably would've stayed there all night if Grendel hadn't started barking her head off at the crack of nine. Grace bolted up like someone had fired a gun next to her head. She did her best to try and shush Grendel—she certainly didn't want Bud Wyatt filling either of their derrieres with lead. But it was useless. Grendel was going to bark until she was finished—which Grace supposed would only happen once the moment of unseen threat had subsided.

So she sat quietly next to the dog and stroked her back while she howled. Once Grendel finished her sacred ritual, she simply rotated in place three quick times and collapsed into a happy heap, resting her head on Grace's thigh.

"What a pair we are, Grendel girl. We both fear things we cannot see, and rail at imaginary foes."

Grace felt like a fool for spending the better part of three hours staring up at a blazing night sky, hoping that each flash of a meteor racing across the horizon might be carrying a message from Abbie. She was sore from lying on the ground and entirely dejected when she finally gave up and went back to the cabin to cash it in for the night. It was only when she got back to St. Albans on Monday morning that her cell phone roared to life and her message alerts went off in a frenzy of minuets.

Abbie had called her. *Four times.*

Bless Babel. Maybe she wasn't such a loser after all.

"So, I still think that contrasting Hrothulf's evil tendencies and blatant treachery with Queen Modthryth's scheming dishonesty makes a good parallel for our last presidential election. Don't you, Dr. Warner?"

Grace looked across the desk at Hannah Sweeney, a very determined honors student from New Hampshire. Hannah had desperately wanted to enter the journalism program at Emerson, but got wait-listed and ended up settling for St. Allie's on the rebound. She still had hopes to transfer out after her freshman year. Grace had the sense that every text the aspiring investigative reporter studied presented a new opportunity for a show-stopping admission essay.

"I dunno, Hannah. That seems like a bit of a stretch to me. I find it's better initially to focus on what's unique in the construction of the text, before we strain to cobble together narrative fragments that lie buried in subtext."

Hannah looked crestfallen. "But isn't searching for contemporary cultural relevance in these iconic works of literature something we should do?"

"It's absolutely something we should do, Hannah. But before you go too far down the rabbit hole of past is prologue, it's my job to help you appreciate how important it is to understand the ways this epic poem functions *as a poem*—and teach you to explore its skillful introduction of literary methods and conventions that have made it survive as high art. That's the primary focus of these introductory survey classes—and it's why they're a part of a liberal arts curriculum. You are right that part of why *Beowulf* endures is precisely because it grapples with so many epic themes. But I'd be failing as your guide if I didn't encourage you first to read and appreciate the text before you seek to reframe it with present-day modifiers. Does that make sense?"

Hannah sighed and stared down at the draft of her theme paper. The subtle droop to her shoulders made Grace feel like she'd just lopped off the girl's arm with Unferth's rusty sword.

What possible good came from pushing this kid to suspend her enthusiasm for viewing this damn text with *anything* besides boredom and disdain? Most of her students thought *Beowulf's* only possible relevance was providing inspiration for a slash-and-burn video game.

Grace relented.

I'm such a damn weenie . . .

"Tell you what, Hannah. Why don't we find a path that allows you to do both things?"

"Can we do that?" Hannah practically chirped out the words.

"I don't see why not. How about you divide your exposition into two distinct parts: first discuss your thesis; then describe how the poem's literary conventions—alliterative verse variations, dramatic reversals, litotes—all serve to advance the themes you describe. What do you think about that?"

Hannah was already collecting her papers and stuffing them into her backpack.

Grace smiled. "I take it we have an agreement?"

"Do we ever." Hannah got up from her chair. "Thanks, Dr. Warner. I really appreciate this—and I won't let you down."

Grace stood up, too. She held out a hand to Hannah, who shook it with great enthusiasm.

Dear god . . . why are they all so waifish? Her little bones are like papier-mâché.

"See you in class." Hannah waved and hurried from the office.

Grace suspected she was headed straight for her study carrel in the library. She could hear the staccato tapping of Hannah's shoes as she descended the old wooden steps that led to the first floor lobby of Ames Hall.

Another day. Another dollar.

CK was already seated when Grace arrived at Twiggs to meet her for lunch. Grace noticed two things right away—CK was already halfway through her glass of iced tea, and she wasn't alone.

Oh, great. Please don't tell me that's her . . . again.

It was.

Grace fought an impulse to turn around and flee, but instead, she approached their table and dropped her messenger bag onto a chair that already contained two others.

"Sorry I'm late," she explained. "It's nice to see you again, Lorrie." Laurel "Lorrie" Weisz was this semester's Fournier Artist in Residence. She'd won the PEN/Voelcker prize back in 2011 for *Listing to Port: At Sea with Madness*. Grace admired a few of the darkly sinister poems in the collection, but thought that most of them, regrettably, paid full obeisance to the critically lauded subgenre of navel-gazing favored by wealthy white alumnae of the Sister Colleges.

Weisz hadn't published much since winning the PEN prize, but who could blame her? If Grace had laurels equal to Lorrie's, she'd certainly be resting on them, too.

Lorrie was teaching two sections of creative writing, and another part of her tenure at St. Allie's involved "helping" Grace and Bryce Oliver-James with the fall issue of *Borealis*. They were having their first editorial meeting later today, so Grace was surprised to see Lorrie at lunch.

But then, CK had a knack for attracting the best and brightest—her friendship with Grace notwithstanding. So it probably was no surprise that Lorrie would latch on to the winner of a MacArthur genius grant. She figured that Lorrie's ambition probably roared to life within her when she first met CK—just like the unborn prophet, John the Baptist, leapt inside his mother's womb when she first drew near to the Holy Mother of Jesus.

Why not? Shit like that happened every day at St. Allie's . . . it was a Catholic thing.

"I know we're getting together later today, but when CK mentioned you were meeting for lunch, I leapt at the chance to see you again."

Leapt?

Grace blushed. Had she spoken her words aloud?

"Yeah. Well. It's nice to see you, too. As always," she added, belatedly.

Grace forced herself not to look at CK, who she knew was trying hard not to laugh.

Lorrie pushed out a chair. "Sit down, Grace. What would you like to drink?"

Strychnine?

"Um, maybe just some water. I'm already jittery from eight cups of coffee."

"A woman of excess—just like me." Lorrie delivered a perfect stage laugh.

Grace had an impulse to kick CK beneath the table, but her legs were too jammed up against Lorrie's to pull it off.

What the fuck is with this woman? She's not even gay . . .

But then, meaningless lesbian dalliances were indexed in the Sister College canon, too.

Grace glowered at CK while Lorrie tried to flag a server. "I'm going to fucking kill you for this," her gaze said.

CK did laugh then. It was lusty and hearty, like she was the damn Franklin from *The Canterbury Tales*, presiding over the prelude to a full-fledged debauch.

"Lorrie, why don't you fill Grace in on your ideas about livening up the social scene at St. Allie's?" CK looked at Grace. "I think you, in particular, will find her proposals . . . stimulating."

Lorrie flipped her mane of perfect blond hair so it would resettle behind a bony shoulder. It must've been a maneuver she practiced a lot. It was like watching a discus thrower move through his windup. Her watery blue eyes locked on Grace. She resembled a younger, wispier version of Laura Dern.

"We should discuss it—but privately. I think some of my thoughts might be too . . . mature for a general audience."

"What are we talking about, exactly?" Grace asked. "Nameless Tupperware orgies?"

"I'd pay good money to see your scantily clad ass in a lettuce spinner," CK snorted with mirth.

"So would I." Lorrie laid a hand on top of Grace's arm.

Grace resisted the impulse to yank her arm away. Lorrie's hand felt hot and clammy at the same time.

CK cleared her throat. "So, Lorrie . . . who all should we invite to this eclectic group exercise?"

"I've been giving that some thought." Lorrie removed her hand and picked up her frosty glass of . . . something thick and green. Grace was certain that whatever it was, it clearly contained micro greens and kale as primary ingredients. "No men, of course—unless they're special."

CK leaned forward. "Define 'special.'"

"You know . . . *special*."

CK squinted her eyes. "If you mean men who like boys, we're talking half the population of the diocese."

"Not *that* kind of special," Lorrie clarified. "I mean men who aren't cretinous louts."

"Oh," CK sat back against her chair. "I think the last few we had just died out. It was a hard winter."

Grace tried to change the subject. "So, Lorrie—do you know yet what piece you're contributing to *Borealis*?"

"I have some thoughts. I want to wait to get a sense of the overall theme of the issue before I commit."

Of course you do, love chunks . . .

"I can see that." Grace nodded. "We should have a pretty good sense by October first—that's when all the submissions are due."

"October first?" Lorrie asked. Grace thought she saw a glimmer of panic blaze in her pale eyes. "That's awfully early, isn't it? I mean . . . most journals don't go to bed until late December."

CK chuckled—probably at Lorrie's use of "go to bed."

"Well, you're right," Grace clarified. "We do go to . . . *press* . . . at the end of the term. But it takes a full three months in advance of that to edit, proof, and typeset the book. So even an early October deadline for final copy is pushing it by most standards."

Lorrie's already ghostly pallor seemed to grow even paler.

"Excuse me." She pushed her chair back and got to her feet. "I need to use the restroom. Back in a flash."

Grace and CK watched her make her way through the crowd of students choking the bar area of the restaurant.

"And she's off." CK finished off her remaining iced tea. "Wanna bet she's back there yacking up her frosty colon-blow?"

"What the hell is the matter with you?" Grace hissed. "You know I have not the slightest desire to . . . socialize . . . with that woman."

"Oh, get your head outta your vise-like ass. It wouldn't hurt you to play the field a little bit."

"With St. Allie's resident Anaïs Nin?" Grace jerked a thumb toward the restrooms. "I don't think so."

CK chuckled. "Before she gets back, fill me in on how your weekend assignation went."

"What assignation?"

"Nice try, Laura Ingalls. I happen to know Her Eminence joined you out there for a little tête-à-tête."

"What could possibly make you think that happened?"

CK leaned toward her. "Because I ran into Captain Polly in what passes for the wine aisle at Price Chopper. It was horrifying."

Grace was surprised at CK's reaction to Abbie's visit to the island. "I'll grant you it was a surprise—but I wouldn't exactly call it horrifying."

"Not you and the Prez," CK clarified. "The *wine* Polly was buying. It was in a big fucking *box* with shiny silver diamonds all over it." CK shivered. "It gave me the willies."

"CK? Please tell me you didn't mention anything about this to Dean."

"Dean? Why the fuck would I tell Dean?"

"He came out there on Sunday." Grace shrugged. "It was such a random visit . . . I just wondered. That's all."

"No. Stuff all your little paranoid delusions back into their holding cells. I didn't say anything to Dean." CK twisted her head to look past Grace. "Fuck. Here she comes. You'll have to fill me in later."

"I'm still going to kill you for this."

"Relax. You could never have sex with Lorrie. If you accidentally rolled over on her, she'd snap like a twig."

"Thanks a lot."

CK gave her a withering look. "You know what I meant." She held up a menu. "Hey, Lorrie? Grace here was just saying we should share a double order of the junkyard nachos. You in?"

Grace understood with sick certainty that she had just been cast as the lead in a macabre reprise of *The Ploughman's Lunch.*

Bryce Oliver-James was dressed to the nines for their editorial board meeting—just as he always was. Normally, Grace would feel a bit sheepish about her own casual attire—which she was certain he intended—but today, she didn't really give a shit.

"Hey, Bryce," she said after claiming a seat across from him at the small round table in the office *Borealis* shared with the campus newspaper, *The Ledger*. "Nice tie. Going to a funeral later—or do you have a job interview?"

Bryce blinked at her, but didn't reply. Grace knew he hated her guts. They both were vying for the same, single tenure position in the English department, and Bryce was determined to out-maneuver, outsmart and outclass Grace at every interval. Most days, she didn't worry too much about it. Bryce was an officious blowhard with an indifferent resume and a shitty reputation among students. His only claim to fame was his legacy connection to the college's former board chair, Holman James. Grace figured the tenure decision was binary: either she'd get it, or Bryce would—and that would be that. Until Abbie had appeared on the scene, Grace was actually growing pretty confident that she'd persevere in her seven-year audition to join the musty ranks of the aging St. Allie's faculty.

Today? Today she was anything but sure. And, frankly—she no longer knew if she even *wanted* to fight to hang on. Not if succeeding meant seeing Abbie day after grueling day, and knowing they could never even have a shot at finding out if they could make it as a couple.

A couple. *Hell.* She sounded like one of her lovesick freshmen.

"I took the liberty of typing up an itinerary for our meeting." Bryce handed Grace several sheets of crème-colored St. Allie's stationery, presenting a somewhat lengthy but perfectly formatted roster of discussion topics.

"Thanks, Bryce. You're a regular Della Street."

Bryce looked confused, which was not an uncommon reaction for him—especially around Grace.

"Della Street?" Grace explained. "Perry Mason's gal Friday?"

"I don't watch television," he replied drily.

"Nor do I," Grace responded. "I was referring to the novels by Erle Stanley Gardner. If you haven't read them, you're missing out on eighty of the greatest hallmarks of Western literature."

"I find that hard to believe."

"To each his own," Grace quipped. "I'm thinking about adding *The Case of the Velvet Claws* to my syllabus for next semester's 'Intro to the American Novel' seminar."

"Are you serious?"

Grace thought she detected a hint of giddy optimism in Bryce's question.

"Why not?" She co-opted a handy rationale from Hannah Sweeney. "As faculty, we have a responsibility to encourage our students to find contemporary cultural relevance in iconic works of literature."

"That's certainly a departure from established curricula."

"Isn't it?" Grace agreed. "I often lie awake at night, exploring avenues to shake up the status quo. Don't you?"

Bryce cleared his scrawny throat. "I rarely lie awake at night."

I just bet you don't, you limp-dick fainting goat . . .

"I know *I* do," a singsong voice from behind them chimed in.

Grace swiveled around on her chair. It was Lorrie . . . *of course*.

Lorrie winked at Grace. "I sometimes have the sweetest fantasies in the wee hours before dawn."

Just like I have night terrors in the gloaming . . .

Bryce bolted to his feet and pulled out a chair. "Miss Weisz, do, please, sit down and join us."

"Why thank you, Dr. Oliver."

"Oliver-James," he corrected.

"Pardon me?" Lorrie asked.

"My name," he explained. "It's Oliver-James."

"Oh," Lorrie gushed. "I thought your first name was Blake."

"*Bryce.*"

"Bryce James?" Lorrie tittered. "Bryce like *Rice*—as in a James *Rice* cooker? How very Iron Chef! Were your parents cooking aficionados?"

Grace sat back and crossed her arms. This kept getting better and better. For the first time, she thought maybe there was more to Lorrie than her glittering Phi Beta Kappa key.

"It's not *Bryce James*," Bryce said with exaggerated patience. "It's Bryce *Oliver*-James. The last name is hyphenated."

"Do tell? I went to Radcliffe with a hyphen—Hester fforbes-Morgan. That's 'fforbes' with two small *f*'s. An extremely mousy girl, as I recall—with an oddly Welsh name." Lorrie beamed at Bryce. "Did you know her?"

"Why, no." Bryce seemed surprised by the suggestion. "But then, I don't share kinship with any fforbeses."

"Or hyphens, I daresay." Lorrie reeled off another one of her practiced stage laughs.

Bryce cleared his throat again.

Lorrie ignored the chair that Bryce had drawn out for her and plopped down on one beside Grace.

"This is all very exciting," she gushed. "I've never been in an actual editorial meeting before. What do we do first?"

"Um. Well." Grace handed Lorrie her copy of Bryce's agenda. "We make a valiant effort to hack our way through this terribly aspirational agenda."

"Oh, my." Lorrie flipped through the pages. "We may be here all night." She bumped shoulders with Grace. "Wouldn't that be a lark?"

Yeah, Grace thought. *We could brush each other's hair and take turns huffing cans of chocolate Reddi-wip . . .*

"I hope it won't come to that," she said instead. "We'll do our best to have you on your way by three o'clock."

"Party-pooper." Lorrie pouted. "I was actually looking forward to trying some takeout from Thai House. I heard the curries are to die for—especially if you like things . . . hot."

"Why don't we get started?" Grace suggested. "Is Brittney joining us, Bryce?" She looked at Lorrie. "Brittney McDaniel is our student intern."

"I don't think she will be joining us," Bryce replied. "She called before you arrived and said she was under the weather."

Grace was beginning to grow concerned. This would be the second appointment Brittney had missed today. It wasn't like her. She thought about checking in on her after the meeting, just to be sure she was really okay.

"All right. Well, I suppose we should just soldier on. Bryce, do you want to review the new submissions we've received since we met last week?"

"Of course." Bryce opened an accordion file folder that had colorful labels attached to each of its tabs. He withdrew several stapled sets of pages. "The first is an essay on global terrorism by Don DeLillo. We also received a new short story by Dorothy Allison, and two poems by Isobel Van Dyk."

Lorrie perked up. "Izzy Van Dyk submitted something?"

"Two somethings, to be precise." He passed the pages across the table. "Her note said *The New Yorker* rejected these, so she sent them on to us."

Lorrie rolled her eyes. "That sounds like her." She proceeded to read the poems.

Grace's interest was piqued. "What do you think of them, Bryce?"

"I like them. They're gutsy. Raw. Very cutting edge."

Lorrie snorted and thrust the sheets of paper at Grace. "They're *crap*. She's a has-been who drinks her own Kool-Aid."

Bryce blinked. "I disagree."

"Oh, give me a break, *Blake*. She writes like Annie Dillard on a testosterone patch."

Grace laughed. *Maybe ole Lorrie hasn't lost her mojo after all . . .*

"Very well." Bryce chose to ignore Lorrie's faux pas. "How about we set these submissions aside for now, and take another look later on?"

"Fine," Grace agreed. "What's next?"

"It's been suggested that we ask our new president to write an introduction to the fall issue. Not only is it a courtesy, she's a scholar of some repute in her own right, and I think having her name on the masthead as a contributor would be a good boost for the academic cred of the journal."

"I wouldn't disagree with that." Lorrie looked at Grace. "It wouldn't hurt circulation to run her photo, either. I met her last week at one of those insufferable common hour coffees." Lorrie fanned herself. "She's a hot commodity in more than one way."

"I, um. Well . . ." Grace fidgeted with her pencil.

"Would you approach Dr. Williams about writing the intro, Grace?"

Grace stared at Bryce. "I'm sure she's very busy. I don't think I could get an appointment with her between now and the inauguration."

"Sure you can." Lorrie dug into her bag and withdrew a thick embossed card. "We'll both be attending a dinner with her next Thursday. You can ask her about it then."

Dinner? With Abbie?

Grace took the card from Lorrie. "What dinner?"

"It's a pre-inauguration soirée. We're both invited to represent the English department. I know because I asked Lucretia Fletcher to show me the entire guest list." She looked at Bryce. "I wanted to see it before I committed . . . you know how incredibly dull these things can be."

"I wouldn't know," he said coldly.

Grace's heart was pounding. *Dinner with Abbie? Next week? At her fucking mansion—with half the damn faculty and trustees in attendance? Who the hell thought this was a good idea?*

Kill me now . . .

She wondered if Abbie knew about the guest list yet?

Lorrie was staring at her with a mixture of curiosity and concern. "What's wrong?" she asked. "You look unwell."

"I think it's lunch. Something in those nachos . . ." She got to her feet. "I'm sorry Bryce. I think I need to go lie down. We'll have to reschedule."

Bryce was squinting at her with suspicion. She figured he probably knew she was lying—but he didn't say anything. He just nodded curtly and began collecting his papers.

Grace grabbed her messenger bag and headed for the door.

"Take care of yourself, Grace," Lorrie called after her. "I'll check in on you later on."

Grace didn't bother replying. She just waved a hand and headed for the nearest exit.

The first thing Grace discovered when she got home was that she was totally out of wine.

The second thing was that Grendel, who'd spent the day in her fenced back yard, had decided to amuse herself by digging holes . . . a *lot* of them. In fact, Grace's yard looked exactly like photos she'd seen from some of the joint excavation sites in Milton, undertaken by anthropology students from St. Allie's and UVM.

"Oh, good god," she yelled from her back porch. "What the hell?"

Even though she was pissed at the destruction, she couldn't help but be impressed by the dog's industry. Grendel's efforts were remarkable. And empirical evidence suggested that her dig had yielded more findings than all of the student digs at the Civil War-era Stannard House site, combined.

"What the fuck are these?" Grace walked outside and randomly kicked at one of about six barrel-shaped, hard plastic bins.

It didn't budge.

Grendel had done a credible job unearthing the things, which were spread out across the lawn in a figure eight pattern—almost like there had been some method to how they'd been buried.

She began to get a sinking feeling. Something about the containers looked familiar. Something she recalled seeing once in a Cabela's catalog.

At Dean's.

It had to be.

She knelt beside one of the bins. *Dear god, don't let this be what I think it is. Let it just be pick hits from his porn collection . . .*

She forced the mini-barrel free from the ground and used both of her hands to twist off its thick, black lid. Inside the drum was another, smaller container. That one opened more easily.

Yep. There it was. *Ammo.* Enough of it to start a small range war—or fend off the feds when they finally came to take your guns.

That asshole . . .

She had no doubt that the other bins contained similar caches of ammunition.

Grendel sat nearby and stared over at her like she was waiting to be flogged.

Grace sighed and got to her feet. She patted her thigh.

"Come on, girl. Let's go find something alcoholic. Then we'll sit on the ground and tell sad stories of the death of kings."

Grendel happily followed Grace inside.

"Too bad I don't have any more of that pear vodka."

Grace rummaged in a cupboard until she found what was left of the bottle of Rémy she'd shared with Abbie. It was only about a third full—but she was pretty sure it would get the job done.

She carried it and a glass to her study—one of the only rooms in her house that wasn't completely torn up or under tarp—and dropped into an old leather chair that sat beside an oak table loaded with ungraded papers. Grendel curled up on a faded rug at her feet with a new rawhide bone from a pack Grace had purchased on Tuesday.

She concentrated on getting at least one full drink down before she picked up the phone to call Dean.

He answered on the second ring.

"Warner Restoration," he barked. It sounded like he was driving someplace.

"Yeah," she began. "I'm calling about some defective shrubs I bought at your Plattsburgh store. I planted them in my back yard and now the fucking things are covered with 9mm spores. Any advice?"

The line hissed for a moment.

"Grace?" Dean finally asked. "Is that you?"

"Of course it's *me*, you big jerk. What the fuck did you think you were doing, burying all those damn ammo caches in *my* back yard?"

He chuckled. "Lemme guess. Your new dog found 'em?"

"Bingo, asshole. Why'd you stash it all over here?"

"Because you're such a big lib, nobody would ever look for it at your place."

"Nice try, Dean. If you don't come get this shit outta here by tomorrow—*and* bring along a crew of your minions to fix my damn yard—I'm gonna turn it all over to the state police. I *mean* it."

"Oh, come on, Grace. Don't get your panties in a wad. It's not that big a deal."

"Seriously?" Grace poured herself another shot of cognac. "If it's not a big deal, then why didn't you bury this crap in your own damn yard?"

"Hey—I have an underground sprinkler system."

"Yeah. I can see that maintaining proper lawn irrigation trumps your need to defend your Second Amendment rights. I always wondered what that pecking order was."

"All right, already. I'll come get the shit tomorrow."

"And you'll fix my lawn, too. I'm not kidding, Dean."

"Okay, okay. Jesus. What climbed up your ass?"

She sighed. "It's just been a bad day." She paused. "One of many."

"Anything you wanna talk about?"

He sounded so sincere that Grace nearly relented and spilled the beans—about Abbie, about Lorrie, about Bryce and Brittney—about *everything*. But she didn't. Not yet. She wasn't drunk or desperate enough.

"No," she said. "I'll be okay. Thanks for asking, bro."

"You know you can call me any time, right?"

Grace smiled. "Yeah. I know. Ditto. And, Dean?"

"Yeah?"

"I'm still not putting Mum up for a week."

She hung up.

Fuckwad. Even though he drove her crazy, he really was a good guy. And it wasn't like she was faring any better in the relationship derby. She just didn't marry them all like Dean did. And she had a healthier respect for other letters in the alphabet.

She laughed bitterly. "This evening of domestic bliss is brought to you by the letter *A* . . ."

She drained her glass.

Dean really was a good guy. *It's too bad he voted for that asshole, Trump.*

She shook her head in an attempt to clear it.

"Here's to genetics. Somewhere, somebody is getting their rocks off on this mixed-up mess." She raised her tumbler toward heaven—then noticed that it was empty. Again.

"At this rate, I'll be drunk by five-thirty."

She thought about heading to her kitchen to cobble something together to eat, but she wasn't really very hungry. At her feet, Grendel stopped chewing on her rawhide and looked up at Grace with a worried expression.

Grace bent down and scratched her head. "Don't worry. I'll make you some dinner even if I don't partake."

But, apparently, it wasn't food Grendel was concerned about. A second later, she cocked her head, then scrambled to her feet and took off for the back door.

"Oh, great." Grace got up to follow her. "What now? Vermont militia in search of their missing ordinance?"

But Grendel wasn't barking, so Grace surmised that the implied threat must not be a major one. She was only beginning to get a handle on Grendel's hierarchy of DEFCON codes.

What she discovered when she reached the open interior door that led to her porch made her rethink her conclusion. A tall woman, who looked a helluva lot like Abbie, was standing outside the door, cooing and waving at the happily dancing dog. Her visitor was wearing faded jeans and a distressed-looking red polo shirt that bore a McGill shield with a pair of crossed lacrosse sticks.

Grace blinked her eyes a few times and tried to clear her head. She hadn't had *that* much to drink. Not yet, anyway. She took a closer look—and this time, the woman who was or wasn't Abbie saw her standing in the doorway, and gave her a tentative little smile.

Holy shit. It *was* Abbie.

What is she doing back so soon? And why the hell is she here?

Grace walked over and opened the screened door.

"Surprise," Abbie said. It sounded more like a question than a statement.

"I'll say." Grace stepped back so Abbie could step inside.

Grendel was beside herself with excitement. Her tail was spinning like a helicopter rotor. Grace half expected the little dog to lift off from the down draft.

Abbie stood there patting Grendel and shooting glances at Grace without saying anything. Grace finally broke their stalemate.

"So, I guess you came back early?"

Abbie nodded. "I did. It was absurd. I was wandering around the house like a zombie, unable to concentrate on anything. After two days, I realized how ridiculous it was. So I gave up and hired packers." She shrugged. "Most of my personal stuff is going into storage, anyway. I just pulled together the clothes I'd need for the next few weeks, and left North Carolina yesterday." She smiled. "The folks at the City House in Harrisburg were surprised to see me again so soon."

"So you're here for the duration, now?"

"Guess so."

Grace didn't know why she was continuing to stand there like a totem pole when all she wanted to do was wrap Abbie up in a giant bear hug.

What the hell . . .

She crossed the room and pulled Abbie into her arms. Abbie reciprocated immediately.

"I know it was crazy to come over here," she muttered into Grace's shoulder, "but I really needed to see you."

"It's certifiable," Grace said. "Thank god."

"I missed you."

"I missed you, too." Grace closed her eyes. She could feel Grendel struggling to insinuate herself between them. She loosened her death grip on Abbie and stepped back. "She also missed you."

Abbie smiled. "You know, I think she did." She stroked the happy mutt's head. "I'm glad." She met Grace's eyes. "And I'm especially glad that you missed me, too."

"Wanna come inside and let me count the ways?"

"I was hoping you'd ask."

"Hey? In for a penny, in for a pound."

Abbie laughed. "The only reason I managed to pull this off is because Lucretia doesn't know I'm back. I basically dropped my bags at the house and headed straight over here. I guess I figured I'd be safe. I don't think I'm recognizable around here quite yet—especially dressed like this."

In your dreams, sister.

Abbie was apparently clueless how *entirely* recognizable she was in this small community. "Yeah, well, I wouldn't count on that," Grace said. Your photos have pretty much been plastered on every available surface around here since the big reveal. I'd say your gorgeous mug is just about the *most* recognizable thing at St. Allie's right now—except for maybe the faces of the four knuckle-dragging SAE brothers who just got bounced for hazing."

Abbie rolled her eyes. "That's one horse race I'm happy to lose."

Grace led the way to her kitchen. "Well, as I recall, our agreement was to make sure you lost the *I got axed in the St. Allie's derby*."

"Is that what we agreed? I forget."

"You seem determined to forget a lot of sensible things."

"I know." Abbie leaned against the kitchen counter. She shook her head. "I'm going to suck at this, Grace. It's delusional to pretend I won't. And before you think I'm incapable of traveling a straight line, I need to assure you that this level of . . . *suckage* . . . is not common for me."

"Suckage?" Grace asked.

Abbie shrugged. "Got a better word for it?"

Grace thought about it. "No. I think 'suckage' pretty much covers it—for both of us."

Abbie sighed. "Well that's a relief. I thought maybe I was the only one slouching toward misery."

"Nope. I'm pretty much a write-off, too. This week has gone from ridiculous to impossible at, like, warp six."

"Is warp six fast?"

"I'd say so. It's when manned space ships travel six times the speed of light."

Abbie looked dubious. "Is that actually possible?"

"Well," Grace clarified. "It is in all the *Star Trek* movies."

"Of course, it is. How silly of me. I've never been much of a fan of sci-fi epics."

"You might want to rethink that—especially since you're now living in one."

Abbie laughed.

"I'd offer you a drink," Grace began, "but all I've got on hand are trace elements of cognac and half a bottle of red wine vinegar."

"Mixed together?"

"Not yet. But the night is young."

"I think I'll pass. How about some hot tea?"

Grace smiled. "That, I'm sure I can manage." She opened a cabinet. "Chinese Gunpowder, Lemon Zinger or Earl Grey?"

"Surprise me."

"Given your totally uncharacteristic ensemble, I think we'll throw caution to the wind and go with Lemon Zinger. In fact, I think I'll join you."

Abbie glanced down at her clothes. "What makes you think this outfit is uncharacteristic for me?" She sounded amused.

Grace filled a kettle with water and set it to boil on the gas range.

"Well. You said you were in disguise—or words to that effect."

"No, I didn't. I said I didn't think I'd be recognizable dressed this way."

"Is there a difference?" Grace asked.

"Absolutely. No one at St. Albans has seen enough of me to know what 'typical' is. Since I've only ever appeared here dressed like a Kelly Girl, I felt my casual attire would conceal my true identity."

Grace was intrigued. "Which is?"

"Someone who eschews convention."

"As your presence here would indicate?"

Abbie smiled. "Precisely."

The kettle began to rumble and hiss.

"That was fast," Abbie observed.

"Yeah." Grace took two mugs down from a shelf and dropped a tea bag into each one. "One of my recent improvements. Dean talked me into it. This thing boils water in about twelve seconds. And, because it's gas, it still works when the power goes out—which you'll learn happens a lot up here in the tundra."

"Oh, I remember. Growing up in Québec, I had to learn how to do all kinds of things in the dark."

"Well, that explains a lot."

Abbie laughed. "I guess it does."

"And here I thought you were just a fast learner."

"You do tend to inspire me."

Grace didn't have a snappy response for that one—at least, not one she could make without blushing. So she feinted and held up Abbie's mug of tea. "Cream? Sugar?"

Abbie shook her head. "Just plain."

"Wanna go sit down in my study? It's the only room in the house that's not covered in tarps or sawdust."

"I'd love to."

Abbie followed her down the hall, with Grendel trotting close behind her. Grace fought hard not to veer off and make an immediate detour into the downstairs bedroom. The only thing that stopped her was a lingering vision of Dean and CK.

I really need to burn some smudge sticks of white sage in there . . .

"Have a seat." She waited for Abbie to get settled before handing her the mug of tea.

Abbie glanced at the open bottle of Rémy and empty tumbler. "I take it you were in here when I arrived?"

Grace nodded. "As I said, it was a shitty day. It didn't help when I got home and took a look at the back yard."

"I was going to ask you about that."

"Yeah. Ole Grendel here could work for Sunbelt."

"You mean *she* dug all those holes?"

"Yep. In *one* day." Grace sipped her tea. "The best part was when I discovered what she dug up."

"That sounds ominous."

"Only if your last name isn't Bundy."

Abbie's eyes widened in understanding.

"Yep," Grace nodded her head. "It's ammo. A lot of it. In just about every caliber."

"Where in the world did *that* come from?"

"Oh. Cabela's. Walmart. Bass Pro Shops. The bed of my brother's pickup. You know," she waved a hand, "the usual places."

"Wait. You're saying your *brother* buried ammunition in your back yard?"

"Ten-four, Kemosabe."

Abbie's jaw dropped. "Dear god."

"Don't worry. I expressed the magnitude of my displeasure. He's coming over tomorrow to collect his contraband—and to repair the lawn."

"So what else happened this week?"

"Apart from the detestable monotony of grading about ten thousand badly written theme papers, it appears I've been invited to a fancy dinner party."

Abbie raised an eyebrow. "Really? Where?"

Grace smiled at her. "Your place."

"My place?" Abbie asked with confusion.

"Yep. Next Thursday. You. Me. A soupçon of trustees. And about thirty other members of the St. Albans community. I gather it's some kind of pre-inaugural soirée. I got tagged to represent the English department," she rolled her eyes, "much to the chagrin of my nemesis, Bryce Oliver-James—or, as CK calls him, 'Blowjob.'"

Abbie nearly spewed Lemon Zinger across the room.

"Sorry," Grace apologized. "I guess that was TMI."

"I don't get it," Abbie mused. "How is it you know about this and I don't?"

"Beats me. Apparently, the invites went out yesterday. I guess they kind of figured you were a captive audience."

"I guess."

"So. Any thoughts about how we navigate this one?"

"Oh, god." Abbie shook her head. "I have no idea."

"Maybe I can come down with something," Grace suggested. "Something exotic and highly contagious." She gave the idea some thought. "Anthrax? Norwegian scabies?"

Abbie knitted her brows. "What on earth are Norwegian scabies?"

"Not something you wanna fuck around with, believe me."

"And you know about them, because?"

"I watch a lot of Nat Geo on sleepless nights."

Abbie shook her head. "I have so much to learn."

"Well you'd better take a couple of crash courses on playing it cool, because I'm gonna be a damn basket case."

Abbie ran a hand across her forehead. "When did you say this is taking place?"

"Next Thursday night."

"*Merde.* My parents will be here. They're arriving early for the big event on Monday."

"Oh? *Great.*" Grace wished she had more cognac. Right now, even a red wine vinegar cocktail was sounding pretty good. "That'll be cozy."

"Believe me when I tell you it will be anything but."

"Do you want me to get out of it? I could ask Bryce to take my place . . . he'd probably soil himself with excitement."

Abbie looked at her. "Absolutely not. I refuse to have you take a back seat to anyone because of me."

Grace exhaled dramatically. "Even though it goes against my nature to say this, we should try to be optimistic. I mean . . . I'm pretty much plankton when it comes to the taxonomy of St. Allie's. Therefore, it's *entirely* likely that the event-planning gods will stash my place card at the darkest, remotest table reserved for lower life forms."

"Not if I have anything to say about it."

"Abbie . . ."

"Grace? If I had my way, you'd be seated in a place that doesn't require a place card—or a chair."

Grace blushed. The more she tried to minimize it, the worse it got. "You're not helping," she said.

"I'd say I'm sorry . . ."

Grace finished for her. "But it would be a lie?"

"Yep."

"Great. So what do we do?"

"We manage it. Just like we'll learn to manage a thousand other things."

"I dunno, Abbie. I think we're gonna get busted." She didn't tell Abbie that she was pretty sure Brittney had already busted them. And there was no way to know how many people she'd already poured her heart out to. It was only a matter of time before the whole thing imploded on them.

"Grace." Abbie leaned forward in her chair. "We aren't doing anything wrong. We're both consenting adults. We have the right to explore our feelings for each other."

"I don't know, Abbie. If it were a year from now, I'd probably agree with you. But there is no way a person like Bryce won't view this as anything but a profound conflict of interest. And he won't be alone in that—he'll have a significant pocket of support in the faculty. And probably among many of the older board members—especially the ones with historic ties to the church."

Abbie took a deep breath, but didn't say anything.

"That's not all." Grace leaned forward, too. "You have to decide if you're ready to permanently tar your professional reputation with the discovery that you're romantically involved with another woman."

Abbie nodded slowly.

Grace wasn't sure what the simple gesture signified agreement with. "You just expressed frustration that your parents would be present on Thursday night. Is that because you don't want them there, period—or because you don't want them to find out about . . ." Grace didn't complete her sentence.

"You?" Abbie asked.

"Well. Yeah."

"Is it fair so say both?"

Grace gave her a sad smile. "Maybe not fair. But honest."

Abbie took hold of Grace's hand. "My reasons for not wanting my parents to know about us isn't because of you or your sex. Please believe me about that. They've never approved of anything I've done in my life—*nothing*. Having them here, piously sitting on the sidelines and weighing in on *any* aspect of this experience—the reputation of the college, the appropriateness of the position, the intentional changes in direction I've chosen to make with my work *and* my life—will only serve to undermine my peace of mind—and my resolve." She squeezed Grace's fingers. "This is a referendum on my need to be free from their unceasing censure—not a plan to conceal the depth of my honest attraction to you."

Abbie's speech was a lot for Grace to take in. And she felt it would take more than the moment at hand to process the depth of it. Grace wasn't sure how much to read into any of what Abbie had said about the two of them—or what it meant about how she should conduct herself on Thursday night.

She wasn't really sure about anything.

But right now, she cared less about pushing for clarity, and more about offering Abbie some show of acceptance and support.

She turned her hand over beneath Abbie's and tugged her forward.

This time, it wasn't really a kiss—although anyone else who'd happened to be on hand to witness it would have disputed that claim. For Grace, it was a more a direct acknowledgment of the sad and sweet gratitude she felt for all that Abbie had just expressed. And the act of making that connection came cascading down around them, wrapped in faint, dull flashes of what Grace now recognized as the same hopeless longing that always lurked on the perimeter of their deepest interactions.

Abbie raised a hand to Grace's face. The gesture was simple and calming. Grace leaned into her warm touch and wished the contact could infuse her with a tenth of the certainty Abbie seemed to feel.

But the road to getting something worth having was *never* simple—at least, not if the Sisters at Bishop Hoban High School were to be believed. And they, like the sanctified sideshow barkers they were, had hammered into Grace—and generations of other pockmarked adolescents—the rote belief that enduring a path of hardship and strife would lead to glorious rewards for the exercise of faith and perseverance.

That was the story, anyway.

But right now, sharing such close and intimate space with Abbie, she wanted to raise her hand and declare her fealty to this holy quest—and any other impossible idea.

Abbie began to rain soft kisses along the side of her face.

What about believing six impossible things before breakfast?

Abbie kissed her throat.

I can do that.

Abbie kissed her again—on her collarbone this time.

Dear god . . . you can make it an even dozen . . .

Any betting person would've set the odds at better than evens that this evening would end with Grace and Abbie making the short trip upstairs.

It had to be *her* bedroom, however, because there was no way Grace would be able to exorcise the graphic images of Dean atop CK that were burned into her gray matter like a profane daguerreotype. That meant the handy downstairs bedroom was off limits. So Grace led Abbie, in halting and deliciously productive fits and starts, up the kitchen stairs to her dormer room.

"I thought we weren't going to do this again," Grace muttered against Abbie's lips.

"What are we doing?"

Grace had her pinned against the wall on the second landing. They were actively engaged in an energetic exploration of anything but reason.

"I think it's called willful commission of acts constituting conflict of interest?"

"Really?" Abbie was beginning to breathe heavily. "I'm not feeling the least bit conflicted." She demonstrated the veracity of her declaration by means that made Grace's head spin. "Are you?"

Grace couldn't reply because she was too busy trying to remember how that thing called standing up was supposed to work.

Abbie was right. She *was* feeling a lot of things at that moment—but conflicted was no longer among them.

Once more unto the breach, dear friends . . .

In her happy haze of uncharacteristic optimism, Grace failed to notice that Grendel hadn't followed them on their halting journey upstairs—not until she heard her barking somewhere at the back of the house.

It wasn't nine o'clock already, was it?

Then she heard the knocking, followed by a voice calling out—a decidedly *female* voice. It was an irritatingly waifish and gratingly thin female voice that still managed to communicate an air of insistent privilege.

Lorrie. Oh, shit.

Grace dropped her head to Abbie's shoulder. *What a time for another fucking test of faith and perseverance.*

"Grace? Are you home?" It was the voice again. Followed by louder and more determined knocking. "I'm here as promised." Another series of knocks. "Grace? Please come rescue me from this salivating beast."

"Who is that?" Abbie whispered.

"It's Lorrie."

"Who's Lorrie?"

More knocking on the back door.

"Laurel Weisz." Grace sighed and began to straighten her clothes. "The poet who's our visiting artist this year."

"You had a *date?*" Abbie sounded . . . Grace wasn't sure how she sounded.

Grendel was really getting wound up now. It sounded like she was about to go through the screened door.

"*No.* Look. Lemme get down there and get rid of her before Grendel buries her in one of those ammo caches." Grace squeezed Abbie's arm with what she hoped was reassurance. "I'll be *right* back."

She took off down the steps and headed for the back porch.

"There you are," Lorrie exclaimed when Grace appeared in the open doorway to the house. "I began to wonder if you were hiding from me."

No flies on you . . .

Grace called Grendel off and motioned for Lorrie to come inside. She was carrying a large paper bag with a grease-stained receipt stapled to its folded top.

"I brought dinner," Lorrie exclaimed. "From the Thai place. I got both red *and* green curry, not knowing which degree of spice you'd prefer."

Tell me this is not happening.

"Where should I set it down?" Lorrie asked. "The kitchen?" She pushed past Grace and entered the house. "How quaint this is. Are you renovating?"

I'm in a nightmare. Grace closed her eyes. *This is my nightmare. Things like this don't happen to real people. They only happen to Lucy and Ethel.*

Grace herded Grendel outside so she wouldn't be tempted to go fetch Abbie from the stairwell and drag her downstairs by her pant leg. Then she went in pursuit of Lorrie so she could nip this visit in the bud before it went any further.

Lorrie was already busy unpacking her paper satchel.

"You won't believe who I saw on my way over here. Abbie Williams. She was cutting across Bank Street when I drove past. I almost didn't recognize her because of how sloppily she was dressed—she looked like a *student.* I didn't think she was coming back this early, did you? Maybe it won't be as hard as you thought to get an appointment with her to ask about the magazine intro." Lorrie was now opening and closing cabinet doors. "Where are your plates, Grace? I'm starving."

Food was the last thing on Grace's mind. She felt like she might pass out.

"Look, Lorrie . . . it's awfully sweet of you to come by like this—and to bring dinner, but . . ."

"Oh, nonsense. I told you I was coming by to check on you, silly. Don't you remember? So I thought we should make an evening of it. You looked so sad and out of sorts at our meeting today. I wanted to do something special to cheer you up."

"I do appreciate that." Grace made another valiant effort to let Lorrie down without coming across like an insensitive ass. "But I'm not really feeling up to company this evening."

"Oh." Lorrie crossed the kitchen and took hold of Grace's face. Her hands felt like damp dishrags. "You poor baby. You *do* feel kind of warm. Are you running a fever?"

I was before you showed up.

"No." Grace took hold of Lorrie's hands and lowered them from her face. "I'm just a little overwhelmed right now by . . . things."

Lorrie sighed. "I get it. It's the tenure business, isn't it? That Blake is an officious ass. I've known plenty of sniveling academics like him before—they're all alike. You're right not to trust him. He'd use anything to gain an advantage over you."

Grace stared at her in amazement. *Did somebody give her a fucking script?*

Not to mention—Abbie was about twenty feet away, hearing all of this.

"No, Lorrie. That's not it. I really think I'm coming down with something." She tried to disengage her hands from Lorrie's, but it wasn't happening. Lorrie had latched on to her like a beggar tick.

"Oh, no," she cooed. "Well, let's get you into bed, then, and I'll make you some hot tea."

Bed? There was no fucking way she was getting anywhere *near* a bed with this Lilith in tow.

137

"Do you have any green tea?" Lorrie hauled Grace across the kitchen to commence scavenging inside her cupboards. "It keeps me right as rain."

I just bet it does. Along with all the other diuretics you ingest.

"I don't need any tea, Lorrie, honest." Grace finally wrested her hand free. "I just need to . . . rest." There was no way Grace was saying the word *bed* again.

"Well then, let me come with you and get you safely tucked in."

"I think that's a good idea." The icy voice came from the doorway behind them. "You do seem a bit under the weather."

Lorrie started and whirled toward the stairs. "*My god.*" She backed into Grace. Her expression exuded shock and confusion. "I didn't realize you had *company*, Grace."

"Oh, I was just leaving," Abbie explained. "I only stopped by to drop off Dr. Warner's invitation to dinner on Thursday night. Lucretia told me that some of them had managed to go awry." She smiled thinly at Lorrie. "You're Laurel Weisz, aren't you? I look forward to seeing you there, too." She extended her hand to Lorrie.

Lorrie shook Abbie's hand. "Oh, believe me—the pleasure is *all* mine." She looked Abbie up and down. "Since we're all here together, why don't we share the food I brought?" She gave Abbie a brittle smile. "It'll give us a chance to get better acquainted."

Grace ran a hand over her face before stealing a glance at Abbie, who stood there like a somber hunk of stone. She cleared her throat.

"I'm sure Dr. Williams has other things to do this evening, Lorrie."

"That is true," Abbie agreed. "Thank you for the kind invitation, Laurel, but I just drove in from North Carolina, and I'm very tired."

"Odd then, that you chose this evening to make your hand deliveries," Lorrie observed in her singsong voice. She beamed at Abbie. "What dedication. And please, call me Lorrie. All of my intimate friends do."

Grace rolled her eyes. "Let me walk you to the door, Dr. Williams."

Abbie held up a hand. "That won't be necessary. I've navigated my way out of bigger mazes than this one." She shook hands with Lorrie again. "Good night, Laurel. I hope to see you again, soon."

Abbie turned on her heel and left the kitchen. Grace's heart sank when she heard the back door open and close.

"Well *that* was certainly a surprise." Lorrie regarded Grace with narrowed eyes. "She's really much more striking up close, isn't she?"

"I hadn't noticed."

"Really?" Lorrie resumed unpacking her bag of food. "You may need to have your eyes checked."

Grace crossed the room and dropped onto a chair. "My eyesight is fine."

It's my head that needs to be examined.

After Lorrie left—which wasn't until ten—Grace called Abbie . . . six times. Each time, her calls rolled immediately to voice mail, meaning Abbie was either on the phone with someone else, which Grace doubted, or she'd turned the damn thing off.

Grace was furious with Lorrie for just showing up unannounced and posturing that they were—anything other than what they were. There was no way Abbie could believe she had any interest in Lorrie—or that she'd had a prior commitment with her that night.

Was there?

The whole thing was ridiculous—and surreal. What were the fucking odds?

And she knew better than to underestimate all that lurked behind Lorrie's *Little Miss Sunshine* routine. The woman's motivations were about as benign as a good dose of mustard gas.

How did I get into this mess? It's like being caught inside a snowball, rolling ass-over-teakettle down a double black diamond run at Stowe.

Grace quit pacing and grabbed the phone again.

"Come on, Abbie. Pick up."

No dice. Her voicemail message began. Even in her distress, Grace stood there like a heartsick schoolgirl and listened to the entire thing. Abbie's voice was so goddamn sexy . . .

Fuck it. She wanted to throw her damn phone across the room.

Abbie *had* to talk with her. *Tonight.* This was absurd. There was no possible way she could think Grace would two-time her with Lorrie. Hell. Grace was barely capable of one-timing with *Abbie.*

She sat down and tapped her cell phone against her leg.

It would be delusional to think Lorrie wouldn't blab about this. It was too juicy a tidbit not to share. And Lorrie was someone who would use this information like currency.

But to what end? Her better self took up the argument. *Lorrie had no stake in anything at St. Allie's. When the semester ended, she'd be gone.*

Not so fast, her darker self argued. *If she innocently blabbed about it to, say, Bryce—it would be "game on."*

But Lorrie knew Bryce was a conniving shit who would only use the salacious tidbit to hamstring Grace's chances at beating his ass out for tenure. She'd *never* do something that stupid. *Would she?*

Grace snagged the near-empty bottle of cognac from the table beside her chair. She was lifting it to her mouth when her cell phone rang. The sudden noise scared the shit out of her and the bottle slipped from her hand, spilling its precious, final few ounces all over her pants.

Great. Just great.

She answered her phone and wiped furiously at her leg.

"Hello?" she said expectantly, hopeful it was Abbie calling back.

"What the fuck is the matter with you?" a voice barked. "I put you into the path of one of the greatest, not to mention *available* and totally hot, women on the planet—and you manage to blow it to bum-fucking smithereens in two goddamn seconds."

Grace sighed. "Hello, Rizzo. Nice to hear from you."

"Spare me the social niceties." Rizzo took another bite out of the phone. "I just got off the horn with Abbie and she's pissed as hell."

"At me?"

"No. At the Emir of Qatar. Of course at *you*, you imbecile. What the fuck are you doing?"

"Hey, I'm not doing *anything*."

Rizzo snorted. "That sounds about right."

"Come on, Rizzo. It was a simple misunderstanding."

"Aren't they all?"

"Look, I don't know what Abbie told you, but what happened tonight was totally innocent."

"Sure, it was," Rizzo agreed. "Just like that time your sainted Denise fell into bed with that flight attendant."

"Hey, wait a minute . . ." Grace began.

"No. YOU wait a minute," Rizzo cut her off. "I don't know who the fuck this fluffy little stick-figure poet is, but you'd better get your thumb outta your ass, get your priorities straight, and get this shit sorted out. Abbie is about ready to bail."

Grace was horrified. "On me?"

"No. On the *job*. She's talking about stepping down and heading back to fucking Swaziland, or wherever in the hell that foundation was."

Grace began to panic. "That's crazy."

"We finally agree on something. This is a great opportunity for her, Warner. Don't ruin it."

"I'd never do that."

"Which we should be able to deduce from the implied context of these events, right?"

Grace slouched down in her chair. "I really care about her, Rizzo. Really, really care about her."

Rizzo sighed. "Against my better judgment, I do believe you. Besides, you aren't sharp enough to engineer something with this many moving parts."

"Thanks. I think . . ."

"Listen, Trixie Belden—you've got about ten seconds to make this shit right with her. That's if you mean what you say about your soft, gooey center and all those 'really' deep feelings you have for her."

"Of course I mean it." Grace sat up. "But I can't make things right if I can't get her to talk to me."

"Give me a break. St. Albans is a one-horse town. There can't be that many places for her to hide."

"Come on, Rizzo." Grace's frustration was starting to boil over. "What do you expect me to do? Sneak through her garden, climb a trellis, and break into her house?"

"Now you're finally using your head." Rizzo chuckled. "Be sure to wear something provocative."

She hung up.

Grace sat staring at her cell phone like it had just sprouted horns.

She can't be serious . . .

She slammed the phone down on the table beside her chair and sat watching the lake of cognac on her thigh dry to a brownish-colored stain. After a few catatonic minutes, she gave up.

"This is fucking ridiculous." She got to her feet.

Where'd I leave that flashlight?

Grace hadn't advanced very far into Abbie's back yard before she began to realize how ill advised this venture was. She'd already tripped over two loose pavers on the patio, and sent three clay pots full of geraniums on to their eternal rewards. The noise made a dog start barking.

It was probably Grendel, who was more like an omniscient prognosticator than a watchdog.

Why don't I just go ring her fucking doorbell?

Her Socratic dialogue continued.

Because if she won't take my calls, she sure as hell won't let me inside. And I absolutely don't wanna get dumped on her front steps, in full view of anyone who is out walking across the quad.

She made her way toward the four sets of double atrium doors that opened onto the patio. Locked. Of course. And all of them had big, blue and white ADT stickers on them.

That'd be just about right. Why not add breaking and entering to my list of crimes?

"It takes less time to do a job right," Sister Merry Larry had cautioned, "than to do it poorly and have to go back and do it over."

Fucking nuns. They were all show and no go.

She sighed and took a step back to look up at the second story of the house. There were lights on in rooms at the back. No doubt, they came from the private apartment that was the president's actual residence. The rest of the house was pretty much public space the college reserved for fancy dinners, schmoozing big-bucks donors, and hosting teas for blue-haired stalwarts of the church.

Grace took out her little flashlight and shone it against the brick wall beside the atrium doors.

Sure enough, there was a trellis. The things were ubiquitous at St. Allie's. This one was overspread with some kind of flowering vine. Roses? Jasmine? Wisteria? She really had no idea. She walked over and took hold of one of the trellis rungs. It felt pretty sturdy. She'd only have to climb about twelve feet to reach an open upstairs window.

She hesitated for a few seconds.

What was she going to do when she got up there? Climb inside and shout, "Heeeeeeere's Merv!"? Or simply creep around until she scared the bejesus out of an unsuspecting Abbie?

And maybe risk getting shot in the process?

Shit. It had never occurred to her that Abbie might have a *gun.* Her thoughts swung wildly back to their conversation about Dean and his ammo caches. Abbie seemed completely clueless about what they were. That had to be a good sign. *Right?* And Canadians had no legal right to possess firearms. She never actually asked Abbie if she'd maintained her Canadian citizenship.

Here's hoping.

She took a deep breath and stepped up onto the rung closest to the ground, and then gently bounced up and down on the ball of her foot to test it and see if it would bear her weight. It did. She raised her other foot and started to climb. The hardest part was finding places to get a handhold around all the damn vines. And they were *sharp*—studded with pointy little rows of piranha teeth.

Shit! She nearly lost her balance and had to grab wildly for a handhold. She felt about two dozen obliging spurs sink into the flat of her hand.

"Jeez Louise . . ." At this rate, she'd end up with more punctures than a soaker hose.

Why didn't she think to bring along a damn pair of gloves?

It was becoming clear she didn't have the chops to be a successful second-story man.

She gritted her teeth against the pain in her palms and kept climbing. She'd just gotten high enough to reach for the sill of an open window when she heard someone below gasp.

"What on earth are you doing up there?" It was a woman's voice—full of alarm and panic.

Grace was so startled and scared, she missed the sill entirely and found herself flailing desperately for something to grab hold of. The sudden, lurching shift in her weight was enough to overtax the trellis. She could feel it giving way beneath the soles of her shoes. First one rung cracked, then the other.

"Don't you *dare* move," the voice below her commanded. "I'm calling the police."

But Grace couldn't help moving. She started to fall, slowly and inelegantly, shouting profane epithets as she slid down the toothy vines.

"Jesus, Mary and chia seeds on a brisket!"

Suddenly, her downward momentum jerked to a halt when her jacket got snagged on one of the broken trellis rungs. She hung there, demoralized, battered and bleeding from a thousand tiny punctures, cursing her life and wondering how the headline in tomorrow's *Ledger* would read when it reported on how a former professor's ill-fated attempt to break into the new president's house got foiled by a thicket of avenging vines.

"Grace? Is that you?" The voice from below sounded a tiny bit calmer now. It also sounded more familiar.

Grace closed her eyes. *It couldn't be . . .*

"It *is* you. Grace? What on earth are you *doing* up there?"

Yep. It was Abbie, all right. *But what the hell was she doing outside?*

"It's a long story," Grace began. "But it involves Rizzo, so I'm hoping you'll cut me some slack."

"Rizzo?" Abbie asked. "Never mind that right now. Can you get down from there?"

"You mean without falling the last seven or eight feet?" Grace asked.

"That would be ideal, yes."

"Could you maybe, help me out?"

"How?" Abbie stepped closer to look up at Grace through the thicket of vines.

"Can you get a chair or something to stand on and help me get unhooked? My jacket is caught on one of these crosspieces."

"Okay. Stay put."

"Oh, I promise," Grace replied.

"You know, I've never heard anyone rail against chia seeds before," Abbie said while she grabbed a substantial-looking wrought iron chair and dragged it across the patio, near to where Grace hung suspended in space.

"Yeah. I guess that was kind of a give-away, wasn't it?"

"That and your shoes. Not many cat burglars wear red Chucks."

Abbie climbed up on the chair and took hold of Grace's hips. "If I support your butt, can you lift up and set yourself free?"

Grace actually laughed, even though her hands felt like they were on fire. "Is this a rhetorical question?"

"No. A pragmatic one. Can you do it?" To prove her intent, Abbie moved her hands to cup Grace's butt.

"You know, under other circumstances, this would really be pretty hot."

"Don't make me laugh. I'm still pissed at you."

Grace used all her might to lift her weight and try to shake herself free. Abbie did a more than credible job holding up her end of the bargain.

"Eureka!" Grace cried. "It's loose."

Her excitement was short-lived, however. The vine she was clinging to sagged, then snapped like a dry twig. Grace crumpled downward and landed squarely on top of Abbie, who made a valiant effort to remain standing. She nearly succeeded, too, until Grace's full weight came crashing down on top of her. Grace's downward momentum was enough to knock them both off the chair and send them sprawling across the ground.

That's gonna leave a mark, she thought.

Somehow, Abbie came to rest on top of Grace, who was lying half in and half out of the presidential herb bed. When she opened her eyes, Grace could see that Abbie's tousled hair was dotted with a few sprigs of dark purple flowers. In that perfect moment, she understood that win, lose or draw, she'd always associate this grand debacle with the heady scents of creeping thyme and night-blooming jasmine.

"Are you okay?" Abbie pushed herself up on her forearms.

"I think so. How about you?"

Abbie nodded. "I think you broke my fall."

"That would be a happy first."

"Grace . . ."

"I mean it. I guess I fucked things up."

"Well," Abbie said. "Climbing trellises really lost its romantic allure after Cary Grant perfected it in *To Catch A Thief*."

"That's not what I meant and you know it. I only came over here because you wouldn't answer your damn phone."

"So, you thought a spot of misdemeanor breaking and entering would soften me up? Make me want to talk with you?"

"Something like that," Grace muttered. "It was Rizzo's idea."

"So you said. You called her?"

"*No.* She called me—and ripped me about twenty-five new

146

assholes for being such an idiot and allowing you to get caught in the crosshairs with that anemic she-bitch, Lorrie."

Abbie dropped her eyes. "So, I guess you know I called her when I got home?"

Grace struggled to sit up. Abbie scooted back and took hold of her arm to steady her.

"Yeah," Grace said. "She told me, in ear-splitting decibels, that I needed to get over here and clean up my mess—by any means possible."

"Which mess was that?"

"Lorrie. I had nothing to do with her showing up like that, Abbie. You have to believe me. The woman is like a juggernaut who won't take no for an answer."

"Set her sights on you, has she?"

Grace shrugged and had to fight not to wince. She knew she was going to feel like shit tomorrow. "I guess so."

Abbie stared at her for a moment before leaning forward and kissing her softly.

"I've got news for St. Allie's resident poet," she said.

Grace's head was spinning. "What's that?"

"She's gonna lose."

Grace gave Abbie a big, goofy smile—which lasted until Abbie took hold of her hand and gave it a warm squeeze.

Against her will, Grace let out a tortured whimper.

"What's wrong?" Abbie's voice was filled with concern.

"It's my hands." Grace held one up so Abbie could see her damaged palm.

Abbie's eyes went soft. "Oh, honey."

Grace nodded. "Those damn vines of yours are a menace."

Wait a minute . . . did she just call me honey?

"Why don't we go inside," Abbie suggested, "so we can soak your wounds and put some ointment on them?" She scrambled to her feet and took hold of Grace's elbow to help her up.

"Okay." Grace grunted her way to a standing position. She met Abbie's eyes. "So, you're not still mad at me?"

"Not right now," Abbie said. "But the night is young and you are a woman of great invention."

They started walking slowly toward the patio doors, although Grace did more limping than walking. About halfway there, something occurred to Grace. She stopped and turned to face Abbie.

"Hey? Where *were* you, anyway? I just risked my life to break into an *empty* house."

"Oh." Abbie took hold of her elbows. "That's easy. I went back to your place."

"My place? Why?"

"Well, it would appear yours wasn't the only asshole Rizzo ripped to shreds this evening."

Grace smiled at her. "Did you leave the back porch door open for Grendel?"

Abbie bent forward to kiss her. "Of course I did."

Chapter Seven

Grace did finally get a chance to talk with Brittney—but not until Thursday morning, the day of the dinner at Abbie's. Since seeing Grace with Abbie at Burton Island, Brittney had skipped two classes, a *Borealis* meeting, and a scheduled office appointment—but she had still managed to turn her theme paper in on time. Grace had tried emailing her and even sending her a note through campus mail. No response. Nothing.

Grace was making a quick stop at the *Borealis* office on her way home to get changed for the pre-inaugural soirée. She needed to drop off some marked-up copies of two short stories for Bryce, and pick up three new submissions to read over the weekend.

She ran into Brittney in the foyer of the building.

When Brittney saw her coming, she tried to veer off down an adjacent hallway, but Grace called out to her. Enough was enough.

"Brittney. Wait up, please. I've been trying to catch up with you."

The young woman stopped and turned around. She watched Grace approach with what Grace thought was reluctance and trepidation. When she drew closer, Grace couldn't quite read the girl's expression. The only thing she was sure of was that Brittney was not meeting her with composure.

"I've been concerned about you," Grace said. "It's not like you to miss two classes in a row."

Brittney shrugged, but didn't say anything.

"Are you ill?" Grace asked.

"No." The girl shook her head. She didn't offer any other explanation for her absence—and she avoided making eye contact with Grace.

Grace decided to try another approach.

"Did you enjoy the holiday weekend, Brittney?"

"I stayed here," the girl said curtly.

"I thought I saw you out on Burton Island," Grace offered. "On Sunday."

Brittney lifted her chin. "I saw you, too. With Dr. Williams." Brittney threw out the words like an accusation.

Bingo.

"That's right, Brittney. Dr. Williams was visiting a friend on Butler Island. I offered to give her a ride back and save Captain Polly the trip."

Brittney looked unsettled, like maybe she hadn't expected Grace to own up to getting busted so easily.

"She's really pretty," she said. "But those sunglasses looked totally weird."

Grace tried hard not to laugh. "She's very nice, too. I hope you have a chance to get to know her. She's going to be a real asset to St. Allie's. We're lucky to have her."

"I got invited to a luncheon with her on Monday—after the inauguration."

"That's great. And a real honor, too. I hope you go."

"I'm not the only one," the girl explained. "There are a lot of students going."

"All the more reason for you to be there," Grace suggested. "Especially since you're so active on campus."

Brittney shrugged again. "Maybe I will go."

"Good. Perhaps you can take your friend along, too."

Brittney looked confused. "What friend?"

"The one you were with on Sunday—at Burton Island."

Brittney blushed. "She's not really my friend. She's just some girl I met out there."

"Oh. Well, I'm sure there'll be plenty of people you know."

"Will you be there?"

"On Monday? No. I didn't get an invitation to that event, I'm afraid." Grace glanced at her watch. "I need to run, Brittney. I want to catch Dr. Oliver-James before he leaves. I've got some pages to give back to him."

"He's still up there," she said. "I just met with him."

"Oh." Grace was nonplussed. *When you hear hoofbeats, think horses not zebras.* Sister Merry Larry was on overtime these days . . .

"Great," Grace said with more enthusiasm than she felt. "Well, I'll run this right up to him. You take care, Brittney. I hope I see you in class on Tuesday."

"Okay, Dr. Warner."

Grace headed for the stairs without looking back. When she reached the first turn and started up the next flight, she could see that Brittney was still standing in the same spot, watching her with that oddly blank expression.

It gave her the shivers.

The black suit was totally wrong for this evening. The jacket hung on her like a shroud and the pants made her look like a mobster.

She stared at her reflection in the mirror.

"I look like a rerun of *What Not to Wear*."

The classy invitation card read "cocktail attire." Grace had no clue what that meant. She thought about asking CK, who was also invited, but she knew CK would probably show up in flip-flops and tie-dyed yoga pants, no matter what caliber of dress was requested.

When in doubt, go to The Google.

She walked to her computer and opened her browser. "What is cocktail attire?" she typed. The screen filled with about twelve thousand links to retail stores and online shopping venues. She clicked on "images" and scrolled through the photos. Most were of rail-thin women who were scantily clad in sleeveless short dresses with plunging necklines.

Yeah. I don't think so.

It wasn't that Grace hated dresses. She didn't. She just didn't own many—and none of the ones she had were what you'd call chic. They were mostly classified as wedding or funeral attire. She actually did own one "party" dress. It was a fussy, flouncy something-something and tulle creation her mother had painstakingly and expertly stitched together for her to wear at her brother's second wedding. *Wait . . . third wedding.* They got married in Wilkes-Barre at the Moose Lodge because Dean couldn't get the church to annul his second marriage—or his first, for that matter. Her brother never understood why the diocese didn't accept his claims of spousal infidelity as an adequate basis to have those sacramental unions dissolved—not even when Grace took pains to explain that it was *his* infidelity that ended the relationships, not the unoffending spouses.

"So?" he declared. "Cheating is cheating—and the church makes it clear that cheating gets you out of a bad marriage."

"Dean," Grace tried again. "'Cheating,' as you call it, is not like a canonical 'get out of jail free' card—especially when you're the one doing the cheating."

He remained unconvinced, and, as the years and the spouses passed, he continued to file his petitions for declarations of nullity.

She looked over at her closet, where the puffy sleeve of what she called the "Moose frock" projected from her somber cache of dress clothes.

Yeah. That's not happening.

She closed her laptop. This was getting her nowhere.

Desperate times called for desperate measures. She picked up her phone before she could think better of it, and punched in a number.

Her mother answered on the second ring.

"Hello?"

"Hi, Mum. It's me."

"Well, my goodness. Is there an *R* in the month?"

Grace rolled her eyes. "It hasn't been *that* long since I called."

"Yes, it has. It was Shrove Tuesday. I remember exactly because I was baking the king cake for the altar guild, and I was so distracted by your call that I accidentally dropped five plastic babies into the batter. Vivian Makowski was unlucky enough to get the slice with the 'quintuplets,' and everyone teased her about taking fertility drugs."

"How is Mrs. Makowski?"

"She's doing pretty well, considering."

Grace knew it was a mistake, but she took the bait. "Considering what?"

"She had twenty-two polyps removed during her last colonoscopy. But that's nothing compared to what Kolby did while she was in the hospital."

Kolby was Mrs. Makowski's ne'er-do-well son. He was forty-three years old and still lived at home in his mother's basement. Grace had actually gone out with him a few times while they both were inmates at Bishop Hoban High. Her mother never missed an opportunity to remind Grace of how close her bad judgment nearly brought her to complete ruination.

"Do I want to know what that was?" Grace asked.

"Well, he stole her keys and took that floozy, Marlene Zink, joyriding. He's on his fourth DWI and isn't allowed to drive anything—not even the forklift at the Schott's plant. Of course, he totaled the Buick—hit a pothole and rolled it three times before it crashed through the plate-glass window at The Chicken Coop. I have no idea how those two escaped without serious injuries. Vivian said they were too drunk to realize what'd happened. I guess Kolby climbed out of the car and tried to order some ribs."

Grace closed her eyes and dropped the phone to her shoulder. *These are my people.*

"But that isn't why you called," her mother continued.

Eureka. It usually took the span of five or six more object lessons before Agnes allowed Grace to get to the point of her call.

"Yeah. I have to go to a quasi-fancy dinner party tonight and I don't know what to wear."

As soon as the words left her mouth, she regretted them.

"Fancy? How fancy?" She could hear the excitement in her mother's voice. "Is this a date? Because if it's a date, you really should ask your . . . *companion* . . . what he . . . *or she* . . . is wearing. You don't want to clash."

"It's not a date, Mum. It's a college event. Dinner at the new president's home."

"Oh. How nice. Have you met him yet? Is he single?"

"Mum. *He* is a *she*—and, yes, she's single."

Silence on the line.

"How old is she?"

Grace sighed. "I dunno—maybe forty-six or -seven? I didn't ask."

"So, you've met her?"

Grace had to hand it to Agnes—she had the prosecutorial instincts of a U.S. Attorney.

"Yes. I've met her a couple of times."

"Are you attracted to her?"

"Jesus, Mum."

"Do *not* blaspheme, young lady."

Grace took a deep breath. "I did not call to discuss Abbie. I need advice about what to wear."

"Her name is Abbie?"

Blood in the water. How could I be so stupid?

"Where are her people from?" Agnes was all over it now. "Has she been married before? Will I get to meet her at Thanksgiving?"

I want to die . . . Maybe I should just wear the fucking Moose frock and be done with it?

"Mum." Grace tried again. "*Forget* about Abbie. I need advice about what to wear. The invitation reads 'cocktail attire,' and I don't know what that actually means. That's why I called. You know my wardrobe choices—what should I wear? I don't wanna show up looking like a doofus. *Please.* I'm running out of time. The thing starts in half an hour."

Her mother sighed. "I suppose it's pointless to suggest you wear a dress?"

"I'd say the odds are about as good as they were for Kolby getting that full rack of St. Louis ribs."

"I take it that's a no?"

"That would be a no. Correct."

"Well." Her mother seemed to think about it. "Do you have black slacks—and a decent pair of shoes that don't look like work boots?"

Grace stifled her reflexive response. "Yes, to both."

"Are the shoes black?"

"One pair is."

"And they have heels?"

Grace walked to her closet and checked. "Little ones."

"Those'll work. Now, do you have a tailored shirt—preferably white? Something with a nice collar, long sleeves and decent cuffs?"

"I have that one you bought me on sale at Macy's last year."

"Perfect. Is it pressed?"

"Well," Grace demurred. "I've never worn it so it still looks pretty good."

Her mother let that one pass. "It's September, so you could get away with a jacket—as long as it's tailored and matches the slacks."

"Yeah. I don't have any that aren't too lived-in. They all make me look like one of the Blues Brothers."

"How about a vest—something short and colorful?"

Grace thought about it. "I have that Chinese-looking one I wore to cousin Serena's confirmation two years ago."

"That's just right. Now all you need are earrings and a nice bracelet."

Earrings? And the only thing she had approximating a 'bracelet' was a pair of gag handcuffs she and Denise wore one year to a costume party.

"I'll see what I can find," she told her mother.

"And, sweetie?" her mother asked. "It would be a very nice gesture for you to take Abbie some flowers. Nothing too ostentatious—maybe Peruvian lilies, if you can find them in orange or red."

"Right," Grace agreed, because it was easier. "Orange or red. Got it. Thanks, Mum. You *really* helped me out. I gotta run."

"Have fun, dear. And remember to work your silverware from the outside in."

Grace rolled her eyes. "Yes, Mum. I remember. Talk to you later, okay?"

"Bye, dear."

"Bye, Mum. I love you."

Grace disconnected.

Peruvian lilies? *What a ridiculous idea.*

She wondered if they had any at Howard's Florist . . .

CK was the first person she saw when she arrived at Abbie's. The cocktail reception preceding the dinner was being held outside, so Grace headed straight for the scene of her recent tenure as an owl job artist. She hoped her dismal failure at that pursuit wasn't a writ-large, flashing-light preview of the likely outcome of her other tenure pursuit, but she figured it probably was. Metaphors as great as that one were hard to dismiss—especially for her. She did her best to act blasé as she passed by reminders of events that had taken place there just a few nights ago. And she was careful to avoid the areas where the loose pavers were located. Although she was interested to see that all of the pots of geraniums she'd destroyed had been replaced with flowering plants that were more refined. She noted that they also were arrayed in heavy, cast-iron planters. She wasn't sure if that decision had been part of a staging plan for the event, or a concession to the new president's apparent penchant for breaking things. Probably both.

CK was immediately recognizable as she stood near the bar like a Technicolor tent pole. *Stood out is more like it,* Grace thought. Grace hadn't been wrong in her suppositions about what CK would choose to wear. The physicist was decked out in a tunic top and loud checked pants that looked as if they could double as evening wear for a curling team. Her only saving grace for the absurdity of her getup was the fact that her pants were in

St. Allie's colors. She wore a pair of what Grace liked to call her happy-ugly shoes—but she at least made a grand concession to the gravity of the event by opting for black ones. At least, they appeared to be black . . . mostly.

Grace made her way toward CK as discreetly as possible. She did her best to try and conceal the bouquet of lilies—and to avoid looking at the trellis, which seemed to have been rejuvenated since the other night. She wondered how Abbie explained *that* one to the grounds crew.

Of course, CK noticed the bouquet of flowers immediately. She gestured toward them with her tall glass of—something. There were several slices of lime floating in her drink—a clear indication that this wasn't her first round.

"What the hell are those for?" she asked, indicating the flowers. "Are we gonna lay something to rest after the dessert course?"

Grace was tempted to say, "Yeah. My prospects." But instead, she told the truth. "They're for Abbie."

CK raised a pierced eyebrow. "Are you asking her to the prom?"

"Give me a break, please?" she pleaded. "This is bad enough already."

She caught the eye of one of the bartenders. He was a tall, handsome man who looked more like a male model than a mixologist. "I'd like whatever she's having." She pointed at CK's glass.

The bartender looked at CK. "Does she mean that?" he asked.

CK faced Grace. "It's six ounces of Belvedere and a drizzle of fresh lime juice."

Grace blinked. "On second thought, I'd love a glass of red wine."

"Hit her with the burgundy, Derek." CK winked at him.

"Sure thing," he said. He picked up an unopened bottle of Domaine Dureuil-Janthial Rully Rouge. Grace gaped at the label. It was a 2013 Premier Cru.

"Damn," Grace observed. "I guess it's top-shelf everything at this gig."

"No shit." CK leaned closer and lowered her voice. "Although I will tell you that not everyone is getting the good stuff."

"What do you mean?"

"I saw them pour Lorrie's glass from a bottle of Smoking Loon."

Grace chuckled. "Her fame must precede her."

"No doubt."

Grace glanced down at her chest. "I wonder if these name tags are color coded?"

"It wouldn't surprise me—especially if Lucretia Fletcher had anything to do with it. Mine is probably emitting toxic doses of radon."

The bartender handed Grace her glass. It was a generous pour—at least a third of the bottle.

"Thank you." She beamed at him.

"No sweat, Dr. Warner," he said. "When you're ready for a refill, you come find me, okay?" He pointed at his name tag. "My name is Derek." He walked off.

"See?" CK commented. "Told you. Obviously, Abbie put you on a special list."

Grace didn't want to discuss anything related to where Abbie might 'put her'—especially not after the other night. She thought she should've won an Oscar for the practiced nonchalance of her predawn exit from the president's house the morning after.

Another bartender delivered CK's refill. She was blond, gorgeous and about eight feet tall.

"Thanks, Pamela," CK said. "Great will be your reward."

"Where'd they get this waitstaff?" Grace whispered after Pamela glided off. "They look like they belong on the red carpet at the Scandinavian Film Awards."

"Yeah," CK agreed. "It's clear they ain't homegrown. Lucretia must've hired out to impress her new boss."

"Where is our hostess, anyway?" Grace looked around the assembly of highbrow muckety-mucks and academic worker bees milling about the patio.

"Host, you mean," CK corrected. "This is Mitch's shindig. He's over there, schmoozing Abbie's parents."

Abbie's parents? Grace looked over at the small group CK indicated. Mitchell Ware, chair of the board of trustees, was holding forth in grand fashion—probably boring the Abbots to tears with his tired superlatives about the fabled history of St. Albans. M. and Mme Abbot looked like patrician pictures of polite disinterest. M. Abbot was tall and suave, with a slender build and wavy white hair. He was tastefully dressed in what had to be a Sartorialto creation. Grace recognized the distinctive cut because she'd once lucked out and acquired one of their hand-tailored jackets at an estate auction in Trois-Rivières. She'd had *no* idea how great her fortune was until she got home and researched the label. Since then, she'd become a true aficionado of the haute men's fashion gurus who custom-made all of their suits. She had a plan to make one of Ochre's captors an aspiring sartor, employed by the high-end Montréal house of couture. She had grand designs for how their multi-tiered dialogues about how shape, texture, color and the fluidity of form could breathe life into once inanimate rolls of fabric—transforming them into living works of art—and how it could mirror Ochre's own path to legend.

Yes. Grace studied Abbie's father. He stood with one hand casually inserted into the front pocket of his trousers—giving the appearance that he was comfortable—with himself, if not the circumstances. His poise reminded Grace of actor David Niven—a perfect gentleman who handled any situation with complete composure.

She decided she liked him.

Mme Abbot, on the other hand, was trickier. She looked more . . . formidable.

She was shorter than Abbie, and quite beautiful—like her daughter. She, too, was elegantly dressed. And she had stylishly cut, graying blond hair. That part was a surprise. Abbie's darker coloring must've hailed from her father's side of the family. But there was something else about Mme Abbot that differed from Abbie. Grace decided it was her dour expression—a shame really, since it distracted from an otherwise striking appearance. Unlike her husband, Madame did not look at ease or happy to be there. It led Grace to wonder if the disapproving set to her features was situational, or a more general feature of her disposition.

She reminded Grace of a classic Hitchcock woman—beautiful, but icy and aloof.

She took a deep breath and turned back toward CK. "Where is our honoree, then?"

"Right behind you," a low-pitched, made-for-late-night-FM-radio voice replied.

Grace started and turned around to face Abbie—who was jaw-droppingly, show-stoppingly, death-defyingly gorgeous in a form-fitting black dress and high-heeled pumps. Grace stood gawking up at her with all the refinement of a small-town doughboy, getting his first look at the Eiffel Tower.

"Hail to the chief," she croaked.

Abbie threw back her head and laughed. It made the tiny rubies that dangled from the ends of her Egyptian-patterned silver earrings dance and sway.

She was a perfect synthesis of high-class elegance and old-money refinement.

She also looked hot as hell . . .

Oh, yeah. She was all that and a bag of chips.

Grace thrust the bouquet of flowers at her. "My mother told me to bring these," she explained.

Abbie gave her a look Grace hadn't seen before. It made her insides go all soft and squishy.

"Thank you, Grace," Abbie said. "These are lovely. Lilies are my favorite."

Grace felt clumsy and awkward as she continued to stand there and stare stupidly up at Abbie like she was a magic obelisk that had just risen from the slate pavers. "Well," she lowered her gaze, "it was either these or a wrist corsage."

CK chuckled.

Grace shot her a dirty look. "What?"

CK stepped closer and lowered her voice. "Why don't you two blow this pop stand and go get a room someplace?"

Grace's eyes widened, but Abbie just laughed. "Believe me, CK," she said, "I'd like nothing better." She touched Grace on the arm. "Let me get these into some water and go make nice a bit longer. I'll see you shortly."

"Okay," Grace replied. Her mouth was suddenly dry.

Abbie squeezed her arm before releasing it. "I'm so glad you're here."

She moved on.

Grace caught a trace of her scent as she passed—an oddly intoxicating blend of nutmeg and cedar. She nearly lost it when she finally got a chance to steal an unobstructed view of Abbie's dress—and the provocative slit that extended halfway up one glorious thigh.

"This night is gonna kill me."

"You'll survive," CK said. "But you might wanna drink up. Here comes Lorrie."

Oh, great. Just what I need.

"Fuck," Grace said.

"My sentiments exactly," CK agreed. "If you ask me, somebody should put a canister of Tannerite up that bitch's ass."

Grace looked at her with disbelief. "Dude, I think you're spending way too much time with my brother."

Lorrie had now pushed her way through the crowd to join them.

"Hello, CK. Hello, Grace."

Lorrie's gaze raked CK up and down, then lingered longer on Grace. A *lot* longer. "Don't you look adorable?" she said. "Like a sexy, androgynous schoolgirl, hawking ivy-league hair gel."

"Is that a compliment?" Grace asked. She resisted an impulse to smooth her hair. It did tend to be unruly, especially when it was cut as short as she was wearing it for the summer.

"Duh," Lorrie replied. "Did you miss the 'sexy' part?" Lorrie reached out to tuck a few strands of wayward hair behind Grace's ear. "I love how the light catches these blond highlights. And the nerdy glasses are a perfect accessory for this evening."

Accessory? Grace had advanced presbyopia and she always wore "nerdy" glasses at night—they gave her better vision than her contact lenses.

"I'm glad you approve," she said. "I wasn't really going for any kind of fashion statement."

"Well if you had been, the message has been received—loud and clear."

Are you for fucking real? Grace wondered why Lorrie didn't just throw herself across a platter of canapés and shout, "Dig in, everyone!" The woman was a total horn dog.

She shot an anxious look at CK, who was watching their exchange with obvious amusement.

Will you please give me a damn hand?

CK finally took the hint. "So, are you having a good time, Lorrie?" she asked.

Lorrie immediately launched into her best, most invasive behavior—insinuating herself into the sliver of space between CK and Grace. "This party is simply the *best*. So many fascinating people. Have you met Abbie's parents yet?"

Grace shook her head, but CK stepped right into the batter's box.

"I have," she said. "Her father's kind of a Charles Boyer type, isn't he?"

"Oh, yes," Lorrie agreed. "That's a perfect analogy. I absolutely adored him in *Love Affair* with Irene Dunne."

"Funny," CK said. "I was thinking more of *Gaslight*."

Lorrie knitted her brows. "I don't think I know that one."

"You wouldn't," CK replied.

Grace cleared her throat. "What about Mme Abbot?"

"A flawless beauty," Lorrie gushed.

"A total douchebag," CK corrected.

Lorrie blinked at her. "Do you really think so?"

"Are you kidding?" CK continued. "She makes Gwyneth Paltrow look like Millie Dresselhaus."

Lorrie's look of confusion was so pronounced that Grace had to take pity on her.

"Lorrie? It looks like you're on empty. Let's get you some more wine."

Lorrie beamed at her. "Isn't this Burgundy just the *best?* Leave it to Abbie to serve such exquisite wine."

CK opened her mouth to comment, but Grace glared at her.

"It looks like they're rounding us up. Why don't you go inside and find our table, CK? Lorrie and I will be right along."

"Oh." Lorrie laid a restraining hand on Grace's arm. "No need. I've already checked it out. All three of us are at the *head* table." She beamed. "With Abbie, her parents, the dean of the faculty, and the board chair."

The head table? Grace shot a panicked look at CK.

"Now *whoever* could've predicted that?" CK chuckled.

"Oh, Abbie thinks of everything. And she just looks amazing, doesn't she?"

Grace nodded dumbly, unsure of what to say.

"That dress? Halston. *Classic.* And those Christian Louboutin shoes? Worth a king's ransom."

"I like the red soles," Grace agreed.

CK snorted.

"I saw those earrings she's wearing once in New York. Cartier—I'm *sure* of it." Lorrie fanned herself. "Her late husband must've been positively loaded."

"I wouldn't know," Grace said.

"Or maybe," CK offered, "Abbie made her money the old-fashioned way—by earning it herself."

Lorrie didn't make any reply.

CK took that as encouragement enough. She drained her glass. "One more for the road, ladies?"

"Don't mind if we do." Lorrie hooked arms with Grace and turned her around to face the bar. "I think we have just enough time before dinner."

Never in her life had Grace been more tempted to swap her place card with someone else's.

Not only was she seated at the head table—the hand-lettered

little card bearing her name sat proudly to the immediate left of the spot reserved for President Williams.

CK sat on Abbie's right. Lorrie was next to CK—followed by Luc and Solange Abbot, Board Chair Mitchell Ware, and Dean of the Faculty Edwin Meeker.

Grace began to feel queasy.

Why not just slap me in stocks on the quad and paste a big damn scarlet A on my chest?

"Will you just relax," CK whispered in her ear. "This is the safest place for you to be."

"How do you figure?" Grace pulled out her chair and sat down. It was only then she noticed the flowers on the head table—red and orange Peruvian lilies. *Her lilies.*

"Because," CK continued, "if Abbie feels confident enough to seat you right here, she must believe there is nothing to be worried about. You need to trust her."

"I guess so." Grace stole a glance at Abbie, who was moving through the room, touching base with all the guests at the other six tables. She also saw that Abbie's parents, Solange and Luc Abbot, were making their way toward the head table. Luc Abbot pulled out the chair for his wife, and then took pains to introduce himself to Grace and CK.

"Hello," he said, extending a slender hand to Grace. "I am Luc Abbot, Élisabeth's father."

Grace took his hand and shook it warmly. "Grace Warner, Dr. Abbot. It's a pleasure to meet you."

"And you," he said. "You are a teacher at St. Albans?"

"Yes. I teach English literature," she replied. "Badly."

His blue eyes sparkled. "I somehow doubt that. Élisabeth has spoken very highly of you."

"Oh. Um . . ." Grace was stunned. Abbie had spoken about her to her parents? "I'm flattered. But I fear she has exaggerated my . . . skill level."

"Your humility does you credit," he offered before moving on to CK.

Grace was moved by Luc Abbot's clear overture at friendship.

She began to wonder if maybe CK had been right. Maybe there *was* nothing to worry about?

Then she caught Abbie's mother glaring at her from the other side of the lilies. She looked anything but accepting. Solange Abbot was making no effort to talk with anyone—not even poor Mitchell Ware, who was doing his level best to converse with her in broken French.

Give it up, Mitch, she thought. This lady wouldn't give you the time of day if you were sporting a toque with one hundred perfect pleats. She'd be likelier to tell you to go suck an egg than ask you to explain how to cook one perfectly.

Lorrie and Edwin Meeker had now taken their places at the table.

The dean leaned toward Grace. "Thanks for coming, Grace. We really wanted Abbie to get to know some faculty who represent the future of St. Allie's. You and Dr. Greene were the unanimous choices."

Grace had no difficulty understanding why they included CK—even though she was teaching there on a temporary basis and would probably opt to leave as soon as her grant funding expired. She was certain the college would move heaven and earth to try and keep her, though. What CK would do was anyone's guess. Grace figured she'd have her pick of about two dozen offers—all at schools with greater prestige and whopping big endowments.

For her part, she wondered how expansive the dean's definition of "get to know" was.

Probably better not to think too much about that—at least for tonight.

"Thanks, Eddie," she said. "I'm honored to represent the department."

"Bryce tells me that you've got some stellar contributions to *Borealis* rolling in."

Bryce was talking with the dean? *Horses—not zebras,* she reminded herself. "We do. Don DeLillo, Dorothy Allison, two poems by Isobel Van Dyk—and another submission Bryce doesn't know about yet. Ann Patchett."

"Really?" Eddie looked impressed. "How'd you finagle that one?"

"She was my dissertation adviser at Vanderbilt." Grace shrugged. "I essentially blackmailed her."

He smiled. "I doubt it."

"Don't be so sure. I threatened to announce on Twitter that she is the ghostwriter of my unpublished novel. She caved immediately and overnighted a short story to us." Grace smiled at the dean. "Worked like a charm."

"I'm sure Bryce will be thrilled with this news."

Yeah. About as thrilled as he'd be to have his hemorrhoids excised.

"Thanks," she said. "I think so, too."

Eddie looked up as someone approached the table. It was Abbie.

"Forgive me for keeping you waiting," she addressed them all. "And thanks for saving my seat." She briefly rested a hand on Grace's shoulder.

Jeez, lady. Like to live dangerously?

"I can't take credit for that, Dr. Williams," Grace corrected her. "Whenever anyone got too close for comfort, Dr. Greene would belch."

"It's true," CK chimed in. "Belching on command is my real claim to fame."

Grace nodded. "Not a lot of people know that about our resident MacArthur genius."

Abbie took her seat. "I can see I got lucky with this seating arrangement." She glanced at Grace. "Very lucky."

"Ain't that the truth?" CK bumped shoulders with Lorrie. "Our esteemed artist in residence here has offered to regale us with bawdy limericks from the old country."

Lorrie looked perplexed. "What old country?" she asked CK. "I dunno. Pick one."

"How about Mongolia?" Eddie offered.

Grace looked at him. "Mongolia had bawdy verse?"

He shrugged. "It could happen."

CK raised her glass. "I say we consider only bastions of dead languages."

"You mean like St. Allie's?" Grace asked.

Abbie chuckled.

"I have no idea what you're all talking about," Lorrie lamented.

Across the table, Luc Abbot chanted, "There was a young lady of Niger . . ."

"Who smiled as she rode on a tiger," CK continued.

Eddie took up the charge. "They returned from the ride . . ."

"With the lady inside," Grace continued.

"And a smile on the face of the tiger?" Abbie asked.

Luc began the applause. *"Bravo. Merveilleux."*

"And to think I almost didn't come." CK clinked glasses with Abbie.

"I still don't get it," Lorrie sulked.

CK patted her hand. "Don't worry, dear. Carbs are en route."

White-coated servers arrived and began depositing perfectly bronzed, mini-brioche pastries on their plates.

"Poor little thing," CK mused, holding her roll between her thumb and index finger. "Cut off in its infancy." She looked at Abbie. "I think its mother was a bâtard, don't you?"

"Un émigrés, for sure." Abbie looked amused. "Based on those aspiring swirls, I'd say its father was an itinerant baguette."

"Qu'il faut se méfier des métamorphes."

It was Abbie's mother.

"Oui, maman," Abbie addressed her. "We should beware of shape-shifters. But tonight, we speak English—as a courtesy to our guests."

Solange Abbot waved a hand. *"Comme vous le souhaitez."* Abbie's father touched his wife's hand. "As you wish," she amended.

Grace noticed a slight tightening to the set of Abbie's jaw. She wanted to take hold of her hand, but she couldn't. She wanted to lean her head against her shoulder, but she couldn't. She also wanted to throw her down on top of the table and have her way with her, but she couldn't do that, either.

"Would you like my butter?" she asked.

Abbie looked at her strangely.

167

"I'm not going to eat it." Grace shrugged and gave her a shy little smile that she hoped no one else would notice.

Abbie's expression softened. "Yes," she said softly. "I'd love to have your butter."

Grace passed her plate over so Abbie could discreetly transfer the two small pats of butter to her own plate.

"Thank you," she said.

"I thought you could use it," Grace added. "Consider it combat rations."

"In that case, could I have your brioche, too?"

Grace laughed.

Abbie contrived to touch Grace's fingers when she handed the bread plate back. To Grace, her touch was like the jolt from a 220 line.

It was ridiculous.

Grace was going down for the count, and they hadn't even made it to the first course.

Handsome Derek was making the rounds. Grace noticed that he was artfully serving from two different decanters. She surmised that one contained the Rully Rouge, and the other the Smoking Loon. She waited for him to reach their table to test her hypothesis. Sure enough, she, Abbie and Luc Abbot were served from the same decanter—Lorrie from the other.

Statuesque Pamela followed behind Derek with a single decanter of white wine, proving that the special treatment must've been reserved for Lorrie.

Grace caught CK's eye.

"Told you," her friend mouthed.

"So, Abbie." The beleaguered visiting poet leaned forward to command the new president's attention. "I'm dying to learn more about your background. Why did you leave such a promising career in academe to pursue foundation work?"

Abbie sighed. "It was a pragmatic decision, actually. When my husband became ill, I needed a position with greater flexibility, to allow me to spend more time at home. It was a difficult decision, but really, the only one I could make under the circumstances."

"I am sure the administration at Princeton understood," Mitchell Ware added. "You were a real asset to the classics department there. I know they were sad to lose you."

"Thank you for saying that, Mitchell. But I think you dress me in borrowed robes. I was more of an acolyte than a leader—basking in the shadows cast by real scholars."

"You're too modest, Abbie." It was Eddie Meeker this time. "I read your first two monographs on Boccaccio and Petrarch. If those aren't seminal works, I don't know what are."

Abbie smiled that million-dollar smile of hers. "I'm amazed you made it through those, Edwin. I rather thought they were tomes, destined to become doorstops."

"I don't agree." Eddie raised an index finger. "You have a natural gift for exposition. The writing was excellent and the scholarship was superb."

Abbie shook her head.

"You don't have to flatter her, Eddie," CK offered. "She already accepted the job."

"I only speak the truth." He looked at Abbie's father. "You must agree, Monsieur Abbot?"

"Of course, I agree," he said. "Our Élisabeth can often be *timide* . . . shy," he corrected.

"*Il y a beaucoup de choses qui n'ont aucun sens,*" Solange added.

Grace's French wasn't all that great, but she got the sting of Abbie's mother's remark.

"You are right, *maman.* There are many things that don't make sense." Abbie regarded the rest of the table. "How about we make a pact to spend the rest of the evening focusing only on things that do?"

"Fine with me," CK said. "I'll start." She held up her wineglass. "This is just about the best wine I've had since coming to Vermont."

"Here, here." Lorrie raised her glass of Smoking Loon. "I'll second that."

They all raised their glasses.

Grace happened to catch a nonverbal exchange between Abbie and her mother. It didn't look friendly.

She glanced at her watch as discreetly as she could.

How many more hours of this did they have to endure?

After Father Beatty—everyone just called him Jimmy—delivered the invocation and Mitch Ware made his brief remarks welcoming President Williams, all attention shifted to the meal. There were four courses, all French and all superb. There was also enough ambient conversation and laughter to allow Grace and Abbie to exchange a few words.

They both took pains to speak in code, because Lorrie seemed especially eager to eavesdrop on anything they said to each other.

"How was your reentry from North Carolina?" Grace asked.

"It was touch and go," Abbie replied. "At first, I thought the transition was headed in a positive direction, then it took a turn for the worse."

"I'm sorry to hear that," Grace commiserated. "What do you think caused the change?"

Abbie looked at her. "It was a regrettable misunderstanding. I'm happy to say that order was restored fairly quickly."

"That's always a relief," Grace agreed. "It can be horrible when you think someone has mistaken your intentions."

"I agree. Tell me," she asked, "how are you feeling about the way the evening is going?"

Grace was surprised by the double entendre. "I think everyone is having a delightful time."

"Are you?"

Grace nearly dropped her salad fork. She had to parse her words very carefully.

"I'm . . . enjoying the . . ." she looked at Abbie, "view."

Abbie smiled at her. "Me, too."

"Abbie?" Mitchell Ware called out to her. "We need you to

settle a dispute. Your father says that France makes the best vodka. I say that Vermont does. What say you?"

"Oh, my," Abbie replied. "I don't know that I can settle this question. Anyone who knows me understands that I'm not a connoisseur of intoxicants." Beneath the table, she pressed her leg against Grace's. "With, perhaps, one exception."

"Maybe you should try a blind taste test?" CK suggested.

"Capital idea, Dr. Greene." Mitchell cast about for one of the Scandinavian stunt doubles. He caught Pamela's eye. She approached the table. "Pamela, could you please bring us two shots each of Grey Goose and Smuggler's Notch vodkas— straight up. Dr. Abbot and I are going to do a blind taste test."

"Of course." Pamela glided off.

How the hell does she do that? Grace wondered. *It's like she's moonwalking.*

"I have a feeling this will end badly," Abbie said in an undertone.

"Why?" Grace asked.

"Because my father hates to lose and he's a diehard Francophile. He'll never be willing to admit that Vermont makes a better vodka."

"I thought you didn't know anything about intoxicants," Grace teased.

Abbie pressed against her leg again. "Believe me," she said. "I know plenty."

Lorrie must've noticed their exchange. "Tell me something, Abbie. Why do men get up to these ridiculous contests?"

"I'm sure I have no idea, Laurel," Abbie replied.

"But surely, your late husband didn't partake of such foolery?"

Abbie took a moment to reply. "He was much too sick for most of our years together. The small bit of energy he could muster went into his legal work—not games."

Lorrie was either too stupid or too vindictive to back off. "It's too bad you weren't blessed with a longer life together."

"Son mari était trop vieux pour elle. Elle n'aurait jamais du l'épouser."

Abbie shot a stern glance across the table at her mother.

Solange addressed Lorrie. "My apologies. I said her husband was much too old." She shifted her sights to Abbie like she was lining up a kill shot. "Élisabeth should never have married him."

Grace could detect a subtle stiffening in Abbie's posture and knew she was about to get up from the table.

She knew she had one shot at defusing this looming gunfight at the not-so-okay corral. As casually as she could, she picked up her wineglass and unceremoniously dumped half of it down the front of her shirt.

"Oh, dear *god*." She noisily shoved her chair back from the table. "Look at the mess I've made."

A flurry of activity ensued, with virtually everyone offering Grace his or her napkin and an accompanying amount of homeopathic advice about how to immediately neutralize red wine stains.

"Use white wine," Mitchell Ware called out.

"Baking soda and vinegar," Eddie Meeker suggested.

"Take off your shirt and suck out the venom," CK cried.

Grace glared at her.

"Hey, it's an idea," she said.

Lorrie didn't miss a beat. "I volunteer to help with that one!"

Abbie shot a look at Lorrie before glaring at Grace. She was strangely silent in the barrage of helpful solutions. She just sat there, staring at Grace as if she wasn't really seeing her.

That can't be a good sign, Grace thought.

Somehow, Pamela, the blond Tutsi, appeared at her side. "Let me take you someplace where you can deal with that stain," she offered. Grace nodded, and shot a last, hopeful glance at Abbie before getting up and meekly following Pamela out of the dining room.

Grace was rubbing furiously at the stain, which had permeated a five-inch-wide swath down the front of her starched white shirt.

What kind of idiot am I? She rubbed more of the mysterious paste Pamela had given her into the stain. *I ruin my best damn shirt, and for what? So Abbie can just sit there and glower at me like*

172

I'm some alien life form? Maybe she should've gotten up and gone ten rounds with that harridan of a mother of hers. More paste. *It's no skin off my nose.*

Grace sat back and held her shirtfront out under the light to try and see if her efforts were resulting in any improvement. It was impossible to tell. The powder room Pamela had led her to was small and at the back of the house. The overhead light in here was amber-colored and of low wattage, and that made it hard to tell if she was making any headway.

This is ridiculous. I need to take the damn thing off.

She got to her feet and removed her vest, after first checking to be sure the adjacent sitting room was empty. She didn't really need to worry—nobody would be coming all the way back here tonight. She had been tempted to drop breadcrumbs en route just so she could find her way back to the dining room.

She folded her vest and placed it over the back of her chair and unbuttoned her shirt the rest of the way. Once it was off, she could do a better job of attacking the stain. She didn't know what she was going to wear the rest of the evening if she couldn't succeed in lightening this up a bit. Right now, her shirt looked like the last act of *Bonnie and Clyde*.

Hell, even if I do get the damned stain out, it's going to be soaking wet. Maybe I should just wear the vest? CK would without thinking twice about it.

And Lorrie would probably love it . . .

She rinsed the big globs of pulverized paste out and peered at the fabric. Maybe it was beginning to work a little bit?

She set about applying a fresh coat of the mystery glop and wondered what was going on in the dining room, and whether Abbie had killed her mother yet.

Dear god that woman was impossible. No wonder Abbie expressed ambivalence about the wisdom of taking a position so close to Québec. Grace wondered why she hadn't sought employment opportunities in Tierra del Fuego.

She was startled when she heard a door slam. Pictures on the wall in the powder room shook.

Oh, fuck . . . somebody just came into the sitting room.

She quickly reached out and snapped the switch to turn the overhead light off.

Maybe if I'm really quiet they won't know I'm in here.

Unless they have to use the bathroom . . .

Fuck.

Horses, not zebras. Horses, not zebras.

Whoever was in the next room started talking swiftly—and loudly—in French.

"C'est un vrai cauchemar! Je ne peut plus. C'est assez!"

Grace couldn't quite follow. "It's enough," was about all she could make out. Whoever the woman was, she was *pissed*—that much was for sure.

"Je devrais avoir ma tête examinée! J'etais fou de penser que ca passerait bien!"

Grace could tell by the way the sound kept coming and going that the woman was striding about the room. It also sounded like she was picking things up and slamming them back down.

"Comment qu'elle peut venir ici et m'humilier? Rien que je fasse est assez bon."

The angry voice was getting closer. Grace held her breath and tried to plaster herself against the back wall of the powder room, clumsily holding her shirt up against her bare chest.

Great. Just great.

"I don't know why I thought tonight would be any different. She's *always* this way."

Grace looked toward the doorway in shock. *Abbie?*

Oh, holy shit . . .

"Papa es un faible qui ne resistera jamais á elle. Ridiculous. Pathetic."

A hand reached inside the doorway and flipped the light switch.

Grace closed her eyes and waited for it.

"Oh! Mon dieu!" Abbie cried.

Grace held up her free hand and waved. "Hi there."

Abbie looked stunned. "What are you *doing* in here?"

Grace nodded toward her wine-stained shield. "Trying to be decent. As you can see, I appear to have failed miserably . . . again."

"Oh, dear god." Abbie raised a hand to her head. "This whole evening is a nightmare."

"Tell me about it."

"I honestly cannot endure very much more." Abbie was making no effort to calm down.

Grace tried to hush her. "Maybe try to lower your voice by a few decibels?"

"Why?"

"Because you probably don't want people out there to hear you?"

"You think I give a flying fuck at this point—after that delightful performance by Mommie Dearest?"

"Abbie . . ." Grace held out a hand to try and placate her.

Abbie ignored the offered hand. "And, *you*—carrying on with that anemic coquette, right under my nose."

"Hey, wait a minute. I did *nothing* to provoke or encourage that—the woman is like a hunk of Styrofoam. She can't do anything but float on the surface."

"Very clever, Grace." Abbie jerked her head toward the front of the house. At least, Grace *thought* it was the front of the house—Pamela had led her down so many hallways, she really had no idea where they were. "Maybe I should go fetch her so she can explore your . . ." her eyes dropped to Grace's chest, "verisimilitude?"

Grace had had enough of this bullshit.

"What the hell is the matter with you? I have *zero* interest in that faded sororitette, and you know it."

Abbie closed her eyes and leaned back against the vanity. She didn't say anything for the better part of thirty seconds—which was an eternity in the middle of an argument.

Finally, she gave a bitter-sounding laugh and opened her eyes. "You did that on purpose, didn't you?"

At least her voice was calmer . . .

"What?" Grace asked with feigned innocence.

"That." Abbie pointed at her shirt. "The wine. You spilled it on purpose, didn't you? To distract me from hurling a cheese knife at my mother."

"That depends," Grace said.

"On?"

"On whether you think it was a brilliant idea or an officious and inappropriate intrusion."

Abbie thought about it. "Do I have to make a snap decision?"

"Well, while you deliberate, maybe you can tell me who won the vodka throw down?"

"Oh, that." Abbie rolled her eyes. "My father complained that neither variety was appropriately chilled, so he was unable to make a clear choice."

"Speaking of things that are appropriately chilled," Grace indicated her bare arms and midriff, "it *is* getting kind of cold in here."

"I dunno." Abbie crossed her long arms. "I kind of like having you at a disadvantage."

Grace rolled her eyes. "Boy, you sure do rebound quickly."

"Meaning?"

"Meaning, one minute you're out there, spewing vitriol like a Sig Sauer on steroids—the next, you're in here—dispassionately torturing a half-dressed innocent bystander."

"Oh, I'm anything but dispassionate, I assure you."

Grace wasn't sure how to react to that one. "Torture is torture."

"I'm torturing you?"

Grace nodded. "Pretty much."

"How so?" Abbie asked.

"For starters, you're a bit too . . . alluring."

"I am?"

"I'd say so, yes."

"Any suggestions about how I might alleviate that?"

"Well." Grace thought about it. "You could consider leveling the playing field a bit."

Abbie raised an eyebrow. "How so?"

"It seems that I'm at a particular disadvantage, sitting here half dressed. So, as I see it, you have two options. You could either find me something to wear that isn't marinated in red wine—*or* you could remove some of your own clothing in a bold demonstration of solidarity."

Grace could see that Abbie was fighting not to smile. "These are the only options?"

"From where I'm sitting, yes."

"I have another suggestion. How about you change your seat?"

"I'm not sure what you mean," Grace replied.

"You're not?" Abbie reached out, took hold of Grace's arms, and pulled her up into a standing position. The powder room was small, so they were plastered against each other. "How's this for a show of solidarity?" Abbie asked from very close range.

'Solid' was definitely the right word to describe the sudden condition of Grace's . . . parts. She knew they were cruising toward certain disaster if they continued any further along this road. "We can't," she muttered against Abbie's hair. "I mean it. I'll get your dress wet."

"I don't care." Abbie kissed her.

"You need to care," Grace said, after they finally broke apart to breathe. "You have a house full of new employees—*and* bosses. I can't let you throw that away on a whim."

"This isn't a whim, Grace. You know that as well as I do."

"But we *can't*, Abbie. Especially not here, and not now."

Abbie leaned her forehead against Grace's. "I know."

Grace sighed. "I wasn't kidding about one thing."

"What's that?"

Grace pushed back and smiled up at her. "Could you maybe lend me something to wear?"

Abbie kissed her on the tip of the nose. "Stay right here and let me go see what I can find."

"Oh, I promise I'm not going anyplace."

Abbie laughed and turned toward the door.

"*Mon dieu!*" she took a step backward. "*Maman. Qu'est ce que tu fais ici?*"

"I came to speak with you." Solange Abbot stood in the doorway, blocking their exit. "To suggest we set our differences aside for the remainder of the evening. I see now it was a waste of effort."

"*Maman . . .*" Abbie began.

Solange stopped her with an upraised palm. "There is nothing to explain, Élisabeth." She gestured toward Grace, who stood there like a chippie, clutching her wadded-up shirt to her naked chest. "*Tu es juste comme ton père.*"

She turned on her heel and swept from the room.

Abbie and Grace exchanged miserable glances.

"*Merde,*" they said in unison.

The rest of the evening was a blur for Grace.

Abbie did manage to find her a tailored white shirt to wear, although the sleeves were about a foot too long. They both laughed at how many times she had to turn up the cuffs. If anyone suspected where the garment came from, no one asked her about it. Not even Lorrie, who seemed subdued for the rest of the night. Grace was relieved. She didn't have the stamina to care much about what caused the change in Lorrie's demeanor—but she suspected CK.

I'll have to find a way to thank her for this, Grace thought. *Maybe I should relax and let her keep hitting it with Dean in my guestroom.*

No. CK's act of friendship was great, but not *that* great.

After the meal, guests were invited to mill about outside and enjoy the warm evening before the dessert course. It was rumored there might even be fireworks on the quad after nightfall.

Hell, Grace thought. *They'd have to go some to beat the ones going off in that powder room about an hour ago.*

She had the good fortune to hook up with Grady outside. He was a guest at the dinner too, although he had been seated at another table for the meal. He looked very snappy in his light-weight suit and striped bow tie.

"How's your night been?" he asked. He was holding a glass of white wine with a couple of ice cubes floating in it—probably a spritzer. Normally, Grace would rag him for having such a candy-ass drink.

"You really don't wanna know," she replied.

"That sounds ominous." He looked at her with concern. "You not feeling well?"

"I'm okay. Just tired. You know how it is the week after a long break—the kids pretty much kick your ass."

"Things go okay on the island?" he asked. "I hated to bail on you like that."

Grace smiled at him.

"Things were great." Better than great, she thought. She wondered how Grady would react when the news got out—as it surely would. "How's the new baby?"

"Fat," he said. "And loud—like every other woman in Karen's family."

"Oh? She had a girl? That's great. What'd they name her?"

"Leaf." He rolled his eyes. "Karen's sister is a big Thomas Wolfe fan."

"Are you kidding me?"

"Nope. Her firstborn's name is Stone."

"*Look Homeward Angel?*" Grace asked.

He nodded.

"I hope she never has a third one."

Grady laughed. "I ran into your brother at Walmart. He said he dropped off some shiplap."

"He did—but I'd call it potential shiplap. It's maybe enough to do a small section of wall—like behind the dining table. That was Dean's thought, anyway."

"Yeah. Maybe." Grady sounded uncharacteristically unenthusiastic about the project. Normally he'd be all about discussing improvements to the cabin.

"What's up?" she asked.

He looked at her with a guilty expression. "What do you mean?"

"You're acting weird."

"No I'm not."

"Grady, come on. I know you. You're just like me. You live and breathe to get out there and work on that damn cabin. What's up?"

He took a drink of his spritzer. "Nothing's up."

"Dude."

"Come on, Grace. This isn't the place to discuss it."

So, there *was* an 'it' to discuss. She knew it. There was only one reason for him to be so cagey—and it had to have something to do with Karen.

"I don't agree. Besides," she said, "my week has been so shitty, I could use a good diversion."

He sighed.

"Are you and Karen okay?"

"Yeah." He shifted his weight from one foot to the other. "It's not about us. Not directly, anyway."

"Well then, what is it? Come on, man. You know you can tell me anything."

He met her gaze. His brown eyes looked wary.

"I got a job at St. Anselm. That's partly why I went along with Karen for the damn labor vigil. They made the offer on Friday." He reached out and took hold of Grace's arm. "I really didn't want to tell you like this, Grace. It was a long shot—and I never thought I had a chance at it. But it's a tenure-track position, and I need to think about my family. You know? I can't keep teaching here with no real job security. You know that well enough."

Grace nodded sadly.

Of course, he was leaving. How could it be otherwise?

Grady and CK were her best friends on the faculty. *Hell.* They were her best friends *period*—at least in Vermont. Losing him would suck. It would be a tremendous blow to her in just about every way. There were few things she enjoyed more than her days out on Butler Island with Grady, working to transform that indifferent fishing shack into something worthy of HGTV.

"I'll really miss you, man," she said. "More than you'll ever know."

His eyes softened. "There are a lot of things about leaving here that'll be hard for me—but leaving you, and all our times together at the cabin—that'll be the hardest."

Grace was doing her best to keep her focus on Grady and not herself. She was also trying hard not to cry. What she most wanted to do was go find a dark corner where she could sit down and wail about the cascading injustices in her life. "When are you gonna leave?"

"As soon as finals are over. Eddie said he could hire an adjunct to pick up my spring classes. I hated doing that to him, but they need me to start teaching a winter-term seminar in January."

"Are you looking for a place in Manchester?"

"Karen is," he said. "But I'd rather find something out toward Concord. Away from her mother."

Grace squeezed his arm. "You'll let me know how I can help? I mean it."

"Sure." He looked down at his shoes. "You can maybe help me clear out the cabin?"

Grace felt her heart sink. "You aren't keeping it?"

He shook his head. "Karen wants to sell it. She thinks we can get a pretty penny for it if we put it on the market right away—before the season ends. Our hope is that it'll give us a decent-sized cash down payment for a house. You know we've been living in college-owned housing here. The rent's been so high we haven't been able to save much toward buying a home."

The last thing Grace wanted to do was make Grady's news about herself. But it was becoming impossible not to feel like god's favorite whipping post. Losing the cabin was just about the last off-ramp on her joy ride along the highway to hell.

"I know how hard this is gonna be for you, Grace," Grady said apologetically. "It's gonna suck for me, too. And I don't think even I love it half as much as you do."

She had a thought. "There's no one in Karen's family who wants to keep it? As a weekend place or a rental?"

He shook his head. "We already asked. I think family enthusiasm for the place waned once they learned the truth about how

Uncle Martin used it as a trysting place." He touched her on the arm. "I wish you could buy it."

She sighed. "I do, too. But there's no way. I'm up to my eyeballs in renovation expenses on the house. I nearly lost my shirt when Denise departed the pattern—it depleted most of my savings. Besides, there's no guarantee I'll get tenure—and if I don't, I won't be far behind you getting out of here."

"Come on, Grace. You're a shoo-in for it. Everybody knows that Blowjob is nothing more than a self-important wind-bag."

Grace had to smile at Grady's use of CK's nickname for Bryce.

"I wish I could count on that, Grady. But you never know how things might turn out. I have to be prepared for any outcome." *Especially these days,* she thought.

"Well, I just don't see them letting you go. You're practically a poster child for the new St. Albans 'Integrated Instruction Module.' They'd like nothing more than to clone you."

Grace shrugged. She wasn't sure how news of her getting caught, half-naked, in a clinch with the new president—*by the president's mother*—would go over with the dean. And that was only if Abbie's vindictive *maman* decided to make mischief. She also had Brittney to worry about. And Bryce—if Brittney chose to enlighten him about Grace's cozy, weekend boat tour of the islands with Abbie. And then there was Lorrie—as crazed a loose cannon as she'd ever encountered. Not to mention anyone else who might have seen her doing the walk of shame when she snuck out of Abbie's house at dawn the other morning.

Oh, yeah. She'd teed this one up nicely. By these calculations, she'd be packing up her own shit by midterms.

"Come on, Grady." Grace squeezed his arm. "Get rid of that and let me buy you a real drink to celebrate your good news."

He looked down at his wineglass. "I thought the drinks here were free?"

"Okay, then. Let's allow the new president to buy us *both* a drink."

When they reached the bar, Grace wagged a floppy sleeve at Derek.

"Hey, handsome," she called out. "Hook a sister up?"

The event planners had to bail on the fireworks when a light rain began to fall. It hadn't been predicted, of course. But in Vermont, weather predictions had the forecast integrity of fortune cookies.

Grace wasn't really sorry. She knew she probably wouldn't have any more private time with Abbie—not after getting busted by her mother. For her part, Solange Abbot disappeared and didn't return for the rest of the meal, or the dessert. Her husband made apologies for her and said she had come down with a migraine— an effect of traveling down from Québec City that same day.

Abbie seemed to relax once her mother was subtracted from the equation. She moved among the guests with grace and ease, charming everyone with her keen intellect, personal warmth and good humor. When Grace could manage to step back and view her without the distortions added by her twin lenses of anxiety and attraction, she had to admit that Abbie truly was an exceptional choice for St. Allie's—or for any top tier college. It was easy to imagine that under the leadership of President Williams, the little college that *could* might actually *do*—and by doing, accede to greater academic heights and more lucrative advancement prospects than anyone had reason to believe. Already, the normally cantankerous faculty was standing up a little taller and talking in guarded, although hopeful terms, of what all *might* finally be possible with a real academic at the helm.

Grace just wished—as she always seemed to be wishing lately—that she could find a way to remove herself as a variable in Abbie's potential for success.

Damn you, Rizzo, for throwing us into each other's paths.

But that wasn't fair. Whether she'd first met Abbie on a plane bound for San Francisco, or in the parking lot at Price Chopper in Alburgh—the outcome would've been the same. At least, it would've been the same for her. She knew that now. She was in love with Abbie. That was the truth—plain and unvarnished. She had felt stirrings of it within about five minutes of meeting her—but she understood it without a doubt when she opened that cabin door and saw Abbie standing there in the rain—looking uncertain and undaunted at the same time.

Abbie's bravery was a behavioral poser for Grace. She wasn't used to it. She'd certainly never had much experience with it in her own adult life. Bravery had always been the provenance of other parts of the relationship domain—remote areas that Grace never had occasion to visit. But Abbie? Abbie was different. Abbie inhabited a realm where bravery was a first response—not a last resort.

It took some getting used to. It was an acquired taste—like learning to appreciate things that didn't naturally occur together. Salt and chocolate. Vinegar and French fries. Grilled cheese and fig jam. Grace and Abbie.

Yeah. They were a walking paradox, all right—an explosive collision of diametric opposites. There was no earthly reason why they should work together.

And yet?

And yet, they did. In all those gloriously confounding ways that should have been celebrated as an eighth wonder of the world—next in line to the Lighthouse of Alexandria. Hell. They should be able to sell tickets. And offer concessions—comestibles that were testaments to all the other unlikely combinations that somehow worked.

She felt the familiar chafing of her spiritual hair shirt. None of this would ever happen. The hoofbeats were growing louder. And this time, they were zebras—not horses.

She glanced at her watch. It was nearly nine. She needed to make her goodbyes and head home.

Tonight, she would join Grendel on the back steps and howl in the rain.

Chapter Eight

On Saturday morning, Grace decided to indulge herself and walk to the Catalyst Coffee Bar on Main Street. She was an early riser, and she figured if she got there before eight, she'd luck out and snag a table in a quiet corner of the normally bustling establishment.

She was right. There were only three other patrons when she arrived—a retired professor from the religion department, Dr. Something-Slavic, and a couple of sweaty coeds in running clothes. Grace ordered her large siphon coffee and retreated to an obliging corner with her copy of *The Burlington Free Press*.

The Saturday paper was usually a quick read. It always amazed Grace that the 24-hour news cycle more or less ground to a halt at midnight on Fridays. She prepared herself to be inundated with tales of whatever petty larcenies had occurred overnight, previews of live music concerts, obituaries, sensational pet stories, and rumors of what was likely to unfold in season eight of *Game of Thrones*. So, it surprised her when she opened the local news section of the paper and saw an interview with some of the headlining speakers at a UVM-sponsored #MeToo rally planned for the next day at City Hall Park near the Church Street mall. The three women profiled hailed from different ethnic and socioeconomic backgrounds. Two of them came from retail and banking backgrounds, one had been a high school teacher. None of them were native Vermonters.

She read the article's profiles of the three women with interest.

April Gagnon worked second shift in the grocery department of a Target store for more than five years. One night, the shift supervisor cornered her behind the walk-in cooler and threatened her with termination if she refused to perform oral sex on him. April was an unwed mother who was barely making ends meet, and she was terrified of losing her coveted job in a small town with few employment opportunities. As the abuse continued night after night, April became more traumatized, fearing disclosure as much as termination. She knew from experience that no one would believe her if she came forward. It was only when April discovered by accident that the supervisor was similarly abusing two other female employees that she summoned the courage to report him to the store manager. Predictably, he denied the allegations and April was terminated. The growth of the #MeToo movement gave her the courage and the community to finally tell her story without fear of censure or reprisal. After April's public disclosure, five other employees of the Target store came forward to share their own stories. It took more than two years, but eventually, the offending supervisor was fired and faced charges in civil court for his crimes against the women.

Former teller Ja'nelle Hopkins worked for many years at a large, suburban Boston bank. Because she was a woman of size, Ja'nelle endured a constant barrage of lewd comments about her body shape and was subjected to boorish patterns of behavior from three male managers, who frequently made her the brunt of crude sexual innuendos. She described a locker room culture that rewarded men who delivered consistently weak and inferior performances with bonuses and raises that far outstripped the advancement pace of any of the harder working women employed at the bank. Ja'nelle and eight other employees banded together and filed a group grievance with the HR department at the bank's headquarters in Boston. Their courageous and unflagging efforts attracted the attention of local media outlets, igniting a broader investigation, which ultimately exposed an entrenched corporate culture that had suppressed and concealed similar complaints by female employees for many decades.

Activist and outspoken LGBT rights advocate Mary Lawrence was a former member of the Congregation of the Sisters, Servants of the Immaculate Heart of Mary, who taught for many years at a parochial high school in Wilkes-Barre, Pennsylvania. She left the Catholic Church in 2007 to become a . . .

Grace lurched forward and set her table rocking, spilling about half of her six-dollar siphon of coffee.

"Shit!" She leapt to her feet before the spreading sea of liquid could run off the table and stain her only remaining white shirt. The entire tabletop and her newspaper were completely soaked.

What the hell? Sister Merry Larry? No longer a nun? And she's appearing in Burlington . . . tomorrow?

It was impossible.

One of the skinny baristas rushed over with a wad of towels.

"I'm sorry," Grace apologized. "I'm just clumsy."

"No sweat." The young woman proceeded to wipe up Grace's mess. "Do you want another coffee?" She asked.

"No. I'm fine. Thanks. I think I've done enough damage for one day."

"Do you wanna keep this?" The barista indicated Grace's soggy newspaper.

"No. I think I'll give this one a Christian burial."

"I'll take care of it." The barista carefully folded up the pages, wiped the tabletop beneath them, and walked off toward a big trashcan beside the counter.

Well shit fire. Grace collected her messenger bag and made her way to the door. On her way out, she stopped by the register and dropped a couple of bucks into the tip jar.

She'd make sure to snag another copy of the newspaper from a rack on the corner.

Sister Merry Larry was now an outspoken LGBT activist?

What the fuck? Was there some new world order that conspired to put everything in Grace's orbit on perpetual tilt?

She still couldn't believe it. She had to talk with someone about this—someone who would appreciate what an incredible, completely unlikely turn of events this was.

She reached for her phone.

Dean answered on the first ring.

"*What?*"

He sounded pissed.

"Gee, bro. Nice greeting."

"Grace? I thought you were Frank, from the store in Vergennes. He's trying to assemble a gas grill and he's called me five times in the last half hour. Stupid fuck couldn't find his ass with two hands and a GPS."

"First-world problems," she said.

"What's up?"

"Did you happen to read the Burlington paper this morning?"

"Hell no. I don't read the paper."

That much was true. Dean got all his news from Trump TV.

"There's an article I think you'll find interesting," she explained. "A profile of three women who are the speakers at a #MeToo rally tomorrow in Burlington."

"Why would I give a shit about that? If you ask me, those bitches are all out for a fast buck and fifteen minutes of fame."

And CK was hitting this on a regular basis? Seriously?

Grace sighed. "Well you might want to expand your consciousness a tiny bit. One of the women is Sister Merry Larry."

"They let nuns do that shit?"

"Work with me, Dean. For starters, they don't 'let' any women participate—it's voluntary. And the point here is that Merry Larry is no longer a nun. She's left the Church."

"No shit?" He sounded surprised. "What happened?"

"I honestly don't know. In her case, the article doesn't cite any particular kind of incident. But get this—she's now a leading LGBT advocate."

"No shit? She's a dyke?"

Grace no longer bothered to try and raise her brother's level of consciousness. It was a lost cause.

"Maybe. She could just be a sympathizer."

He laughed. "I doubt it."

"Why do you say that?"

"Come on, Grace. Why do you think she was always hanging around the girls' locker room?"

"Because she was the *gym* teacher?"

"Exactly. And she probably got her rocks off watching you all shake your wet booties in the shower."

"You're really a pig, Dean."

"Hey, ask her if I'm wrong."

"What do you mean, ask her?"

"What do you think I mean? You're going to see her tomorrow, right?"

"I hadn't thought about it."

"Bullshit," he scoffed. "You'll be there—in the front row, wearing your Argents t-shirt."

Was she going? Maybe she would like to see Merry Larry—and hear her story about whatever happened.

"I might go," she said.

"Take CK. She gets off on that feminist crap." He chuckled. "She gets off on just about everything."

"I'm hanging up now, Dean. Thanks for fixing the yard."

"Later alligator. Lemme know how it goes." He disconnected.

—————

Grace decided not to ask CK to go with her to the rally. For one thing, if she did get the chance to meet with Merry Larry, she wanted to do it in private—without being subject to CK's discriminating eye and penchant for sardonic observation.

Besides, nothing said she'd be able to summon enough gumption to approach Merry Larry after the event, and she wanted to have the latitude to lay a patch getting out of there if she chickened out.

The crowd at City Hall Park was impressive. Grace hadn't seen so many women in one place since some renegade student health advocates at the Vandy wellness center celebrated the anniversary of Roe v. Wade by passing out free condoms. The wide array of women crowding into the park had to number several hundred. She hadn't gotten there early enough to nail a seat in front of the stage, but she managed to stake out a spot on the fountain, which gave her a slightly better vantage point.

She recognized Merry Larry right away—even without her habit. There was just something so familiar about her bearing and her gait as she took the stage—nobody else walked with that much authority. She was as tall as Grace remembered, too—topping the other women on the platform by several inches. She looked older, of course—but, then, so did Grace.

She wondered if Merry Larry would remember her—and would recognize her if she did. Maybe Dean was right and she should've worn an Argents jersey. God knew, she had enough of them stuffed into a box on the floor of her closet.

The speeches were about to begin. Grace made herself as comfortable as possible and strained to see over the sea of pink pussy hats. She checked her watch. It was nearly two. The rally was only scheduled to last for ninety minutes, so she should be comfortably back in St. Albans by five-thirty or six . . .

Two earsplitting hours later, she found herself pushing her way through the dispersing crowd to head toward the stage. She had no idea if any of the speakers were hanging around, or whether they'd already departed for the buses headed to the next rally, which she heard was taking place at Middlebury College later that evening. She didn't see Merry Larry or either of the other speakers when she finally made it to the platform, which organizers were already starting to tear down.

"Hi there," she addressed a buxom young woman in a tie-dyed tank top who was busy wrapping audio cable. "Do you know if any of the keynote speakers are still around?"

The woman cast about before answering. "If they are, they'd be over there." She pointed to an area full of vehicles. "Where they hold the farmer's market. That's where the buses are."

"Thanks." Grace started walking in that direction and was startled to realize that Merry Larry was walking just ahead of her. She hurried to catch up with her.

"Excuse me," she said when she drew abreast of her. "I hate to bother you, but I knew you back in Pennsylvania."

Merry Larry stopped and eyed Grace with curiosity. Her eyes crinkled. "Well, I'll be damned. Grace Warner. How the hell are you?"

Merry Larry wrapped Grace up in a bear hug. Grace was surprised, but gratified by the response.

"I'm okay," Grace said when Merry Larry finally released her. "I saw your name in the newspaper yesterday and I was intrigued— so I came out today to see you. You gave a stirring speech," she added.

"Intrigued?" Merry Larry smiled. "I just bet you were *intrigued*. Did you think I got kicked out?"

"Well, no . . . not really. Although I called my brother Dean to tell him about you and that was his first thought."

"I just bet it was." Merry Larry laughed. "Tell me, did that boy end up in prison?"

It was Grace's turn to smile. "Not yet."

"Damn. Well it looks like I took that one in the shorts. Sister Monica gave me four to one odds."

"Maybe you shouldn't tell her?" Grace suggested.

"Maybe I won't." Merry Larry was giving Grace a good once-over. "How are you Grace? Has life turned out the way you hoped it would?"

191

"Not yet," Grace repeated. "But hope springs eternal." She quoted one of Merry Larry's favorite aphorisms.

"Hope schmope." Merry Larry waved a hand. "I gave all that bullshit up for Lent. You want a certain outcome?" She bent closer to Grace. "You get off your ass and make it happen. There's no higher power that's going to step in at the eleventh hour and arrange everything for you. The universe just doesn't work that way, kiddo."

"You don't believe in God anymore?"

"I still believe in god, Grace—but god with a little *g*."

Grace was nonplussed. "But all the things you taught us . . ."

"I thought of it as a calling, but it was a job, Grace. Pure and simple. Something I signed on to do before I was even old enough to understand what it all meant. And I did it well—at least, as well as I could as a know-nothing recruit in The Lord's Army. And all of us who went through that novitiate together? We were like lambs being led to the slaughter. Night after night, I'd lie on my hard, little cot in that big, cold room at the convent—shivering with fear and shaking with longing for the girl on the cot beside me. When I dreamed, I didn't dream about glorifying the blessed Virgin who became the mother of Christ—I dreamed about all the carnal ways I could glorify the blessed virgin who lay awake next to me, keeping her own silent vigil. Finally, I met someone who could no longer be consigned to the realm of dreams. And everything about my life changed—beginning with my vocation."

"So, you fell in love?" Grace asked.

"I did. With myself." Merry Larry chuckled. "Of course, getting my first bit of snatch was a fast second."

Grace's head was reeling. Merry Larry thought everything she'd done—everything she'd said—was a lie? None of it was true? None of it had meaning for her? All of it was a ruse—a mistake? A long trip down a spiritual rabbit hole that led to nothing?

"I don't know what to say." Grace looked at her with wonder. "I'm speechless."

Merry Larry placed a bony hand on Grace's shoulder. It was

dotted with age spots. "You've always had a good voice, Grace. You were just never brave enough to trust it. Don't listen to the ones that keep you pinned down or lead you astray."

Grace didn't know how to tell Merry Larry that the voice she heard most often was *hers*.

"I'm confused."

"There's nothing wrong with that. Hell. Anyone who isn't confused isn't paying attention."

"I guess so." Grace wasn't sure what she had expected from this conversation, but this wasn't it.

"Tell me something, Grace." Merry Larry was still holding onto her shoulder. "What have you done with your one life? What profession have you landed in?"

"I teach English literature. Here in Vermont, at St. Albans College."

"Nicely done." Merry Larry looked pleased. "And are you in love?"

"Well . . ." Grace blushed.

"So, that's a yes."

"It's a yes," Grace agreed. "But it's complicated."

"So?"

"So?" Grace repeated.

"Sooooo," Merry Larry drew the word out. "Go and *un*-complicate it. Neither of us is getting any younger."

Grace looked at her with confusion. "It's not that easy."

"Oh, horse hockey. The act of *un*-complicating things is *very* easy. And once you get the hang of it, you'll know the truth. And remember," she laid her warm palm against Grace's face, "the truth shall make you free." She smiled. "Go and teach all nations."

The woman who was and wasn't Merry Larry walked off to join her fellow advocates at the bus that would carry them on to their next rally.

Grace watched her go in silence. She felt like a volley of cannons had just discharged inside her head—initiating a sequence of aftershocks that threatened to lay waste to their phalanx of scriptural counterparts.

"Things fall apart, the centre cannot hold . . ."
Grace shook her head with wonder.
Yeats must've been writing about Sister Merry Larry . . .

Grace made sure that she'd never again get caught without decent booze in the house—especially since she was cycling through so many occasions lately that called for it.

Like tonight.

So, she'd made a trip to the Beverage Mart on Saturday to load up on what she considered to be her staples: Smuggler's Notch vodka, Rémy Martin cognac, Jameson Irish whisky, and wine. *Lots* of wine.

She made it home from the #MeToo rally by shortly after six. She had no plans for the evening other than grading papers and trying, with any gray matter she had to spare, to process the collateral damage from every hand grenade Merry Larry had summarily lobbed into the middle of her wounded psyche.

She fed Grendel and fixed herself a big fruit salad topped with toasted almonds and goat cheese.

Tomorrow was going to be a long day—and a tough one. Abbie's inauguration was slated to begin at 10 a.m. That meant Grace and the rest of the faculty had to be robed up and on-site no later than nine-fifteen, so they could process in and be seated behind the board of trustees before the president-elect entered, accompanied by the roster of luminaries who would make up the platform party.

The board had assembled quite a list. Joining Abbie on the stage would be the Lieutenant Governor of Vermont, the Bishop of the Roman Catholic Diocese of Vermont, the Chairman of the St. Albans Board of Trustees, and the President of the St. Albans Alumni Association. There would also be remarks by the President of the Student Government Association. When it was all said and done, Abbie would be sworn in as the fifteenth president of the college, and a new era would begin for St. Albans, for her, and for Grace.

It was a lot to take in—and even though she felt as though she'd been preparing for it for weeks, she still didn't feel equal to the task.

She tried to read papers from her four sections of English 101, but it became clear in short order that she didn't have the stamina or focus to do them justice. She decided that she'd set them aside and pick up her GAN. A lack of focus had never presented too much of an obstacle to working on that. Besides, it wasn't as if anyone else would ever get the chance to actually read it.

Grace was anal retentive when it came to writing. One of her idiosyncrasies was a determination to fully review whatever she'd written last before she moved forward with any new content. She believed it made her a cleaner and more careful writer, and however much it slowed the overall process down, she was convinced it would result in a better final product. That being the case, she started this evening by poring over the handwritten pages she'd crafted on Sunday at Butler Island. She hadn't yet made time to type them into her MS Word file. Since she was reading handwritten copy, she didn't bother to boot up her computer—she simply carried the loose-leaf pages, along with a printout of the entire manuscript, to her screened porch. She was going over her newest addition with a toothcomb, questioning every word choice and nuance and thinking seriously about carrying the pages outside and burying them in one of the remaining holes of Grendel's that Dean's men hadn't filled yet.

Something in the new copy caught her eye. It didn't seem quite right, and she wasn't exactly certain why. She thought it had something to do with how the saga began—before Ochre was stolen from the museum in Arizona. Normally, she would simply type a keyword into the search window in her Word document. But since she was sitting on the porch, with Grendel asleep on her feet, she decided to ferret out the inconsistency the old-fashioned way, and search the hardcopy manuscript.

Grace actually liked thumbing through the book this way. Handling the printed sheets of paper was almost cathartic for her. It made the book feel real in a way that scrolling through the pages on a computer screen didn't. She knew it was the worst kind of brazen arrogance to be impressed by how heavy the full document was—by how tidy and regular the prose looked when the pages were all stacked up together in their perfectly sized box.

She wondered if Abbie had ever felt this way when she was working on either of her two published works.

Scratch that. Thinking about Abbie was a sure way to guarantee that she wouldn't make progress on this enterprise, either.

She dug out the first quarter of her printout to begin looking for clues to determine whether her newest prose conformed well enough to the original story. It didn't take her long to realize that something was wrong with the manuscript. Badly wrong. Grace checked the box multiple times. It didn't make any sense. There were pages missing. The first fifty were MIA—and another twenty-seven were missing from chapter four.

She sat back in her chair and tried to puzzle it out. Had she lent the printout to anyone?

No. No one was reading *Ochre* besides her. Well ... and CK. And, of course, Abbie had read a lot of it on Sunday morning before Grace got up and joined her outside. There'd be no reason or opportunity for either of them to take sections of the book.

Had she accidentally left the printout anyplace where the pages might have become separated from the rest of the manuscript?

The only thing that occurred to her was the night Abbie showed up on the island and the pages got knocked off the sofa when they ... became otherwise engaged.

But that couldn't have been it because Abbie picked them up and re-collated them in the morning before she started reading the book outside. She remembered because Abbie told her about it. So, she knew the pages had been present when she came home from Butler Island on Monday.

So what had happened to them?

Dean?

There was no way. Dean could barely read a *TV Guide*. And no one else had access to her house. Unless ...

No. CK would have no reason to snoop around in Grace's office after her trysts with Dean. That would *never* happen.

But if not CK, who?

Grace bit her lip in frustration. *Only one way to find out.*

She picked up her phone and punched CK's number from her contacts list.

"Hey," CK said when she answered. "How was the rally? Did you meet her again?"

"I did, actually," Grace said. "It wasn't at all what I expected."

"Really? What were you expecting?"

Grace thought about it. "I honestly don't know. Maybe for her to be more like she was?"

"That's an interesting idea. Are you like you were?"

"No . . ."

"Then why would you expect her to be as she was?"

"I'm not saying it made sense, CK." Grace was glad to have this confirmation that her instinct for not asking CK to go along with her had been correct.

"Okay," CK said. "So, how was she different?"

"You mean, apart from her not being a nun anymore?"

"Yeah."

"I think the biggest change is her attitude toward God and the church." Grace tried to think about an expeditious way to frame everything that Merry Larry said about her new path. "She wanted the latitude to explore her sexuality in ways the church didn't allow or sanction. I can understand that part—no problem. What's a harder leap for me is to get a handle on why she felt she had to abandon all the things that formed her moral compass— things that, for me, exist in a place outside doctrinal definition."

CK was quiet for a moment. "So, you're saying she's now an agnostic?"

"I'm not really sure. In fact, I don't know if *she's* really sure what she is. She said she still believed in God—but in God with a little *g*."

"Well, that's a difference without a whole lot of significance."

"Maybe to you. But, then, you weren't raised Catholic."

"True," CK agreed. "I sometimes think my parents were raised by wolves."

"That would explain a lot."

"Did your apostate ex-nun have any other pearls of wisdom to impart?"

"Yeah." Grace wasn't sure about how much to reveal. "Essentially, she eschews wishful thinking and blind adherence to any belief that things will just work out the way they should."

"Meaning, you should take life by the balls and go after what you want?"

"Damn. You're pretty good at cutting through the chaff to find the wheat."

CK chuckled. "Makes you rethink what I see in your brother, doesn't it?"

"Not really."

"And you think I'm a tough nut to crack."

"I'm not kidding, CK. The revolution in this woman's character has rattled me to my core. It's not that I've lived my life according to her precepts—I haven't. But she was a seminal figure in my upbringing, and she functioned like a touchstone for me. I learned to understand the world and my place in it by defining things in relation to her—like an infant who struggles to learn the difference between me and not me."

"That's a self-actualization process that each of us goes through," CK explained. "If we're lucky," she added. "It always amazes me to confront how many unexamined lives are swirling around out there. Plato must've read Camus."

"I think you have that in the wrong order."

"You know what I mean. What was Camus' immortal epitaph for modern man? Something about fornication?"

Grace rolled her eyes. Of course CK would go straight to the basest summation of human frailty. "'He fornicated and read the papers,'" she quoted.

"Bingo. That's the one. Genius in my view."

"Apropos of Camus, I have stumbled upon a narrative mystery of my own."

"What's that?" CK asked.

"I got home from the rally intending to grade a section of theme papers from one of my 101 sections. But the new heights of linguistic mutilation they presented killed any energy I had for the enterprise. So I thought I'd try something else."

"Binge drinking?" CK offered.

"Close. I hauled out my manuscript and started reworking the chapter I wrote last weekend."

"So what's the problem? You run out of ideas for ways to keep rewriting the same scenes? Or are you finally taking my advice and putting some skin in the game?" She chuckled. "Skin *on* skin, if you get my drift."

"CK, a painting cannot have sex."

"Grace, a painting can't engage in Socratic dialogues, either. So, if you're going down this whole magic realism road, why not extend the metaphor and let Ochre get horizontal with a few of her captors? I'm telling you—it would sell, like, a zillion more copies."

"At this rate, it's not going to sell any copies."

"What are you talking about? The book is fabulous."

"I appreciate the vote of confidence, but I called to tell you that about seventy-five pages of the printout are missing."

"So?" CK was unfazed. "Just open the Word file and reprint them. You do save backups, right?"

"Of course. But this is unsettling to me. I've only allowed two people to read the hardcopy—and you're one of them."

"Who's the other?"

It was clear to Grace that CK was dodging her implied question. "That's immaterial."

"No, it isn't—not if you're suggesting that I stole the pages."

Grace considered belaboring the point, but knew it would be a meaningless exercise. "It was Abbie."

"Of *course* it was. And have you asked her about the missing content?"

"No. I thought I'd start with the usual suspect."

CK sighed. "I appreciate the vote of confidence, Grace. But

what the fuck would I do with seventy-five pages from your lugubrious work in progress? Send them off to a literary agent who represents other wanna-be authors like Julia Alvarez and Lorrie Moore?"

Grace closed her eyes. This was not happening.

"Please tell me you're being anecdotal."

"Hmmmm. Not so much."

"CK . . ."

"Don't get your knickers in a knot." Grace could hear CK typing something into her computer. "Here it is. I was gonna wait and regale you with this later on, after the canonization But, hey. No time like the present. Let's see here . . . email received on Thursday at 10:24 a.m. Lemme read it to you:

Dear CK,

Thanks so much for putting Grace Warner's manuscript in front of me. Very captivating and innovative story. I agree that she has an engaging style and should get a welcome reception at the right press. I passed it on the same day to Kathy over at Algonquin Books, thinking they'd be the best fit for a first-time author. Their submissions editor is generally quick at saying yay or nay, so I'll let you know what I hear back. If they take a pass on it, I have a few other places in mind. U. of Wisconsin is making a name for itself in the literary fiction market, so we could give them a go. I'll be in touch soon.

And are you ever going to let me shop that monograph of yours around? Ira at Simon & Schuster keeps asking me about it. Heard you're presenting at the NY Innovators in Science Awards in October. Maybe we can connect while you're in town?

Best,

Stuart

CK paused before continuing. "Oh, he also added a postscript related to the small matter of actually getting you to *sign* with him, since he got you a gig. No escaping that part, I suppose."

Grace was speechless. "CK, I don't need a literary agent. I don't have anything worth shopping around."

"Yeah? Well you might need to reconsider that because I heard back from him this afternoon, while you were off doing your whole dark-night-of-the-soul thing at that pussy hat shindig. To put it bluntly, it looks like Algonquin wants the book."

"*What?*" Grace didn't think she'd heard CK correctly.

"Yeah. Some dude named Brunson is going to be calling you within the next couple of days, so I suggest you pick up the phone. I gather he's going to offer you a decent-sized advance and an option on your next book."

Grace's head was spinning. "What next book?"

CK chuckled. "The one I told him you were writing."

"CK—the first one isn't even finished yet."

"Yes it is. You've written about *fourteen* endings—just pick one and be done with it."

"I'm going to fucking kill you . . ."

"I doubt it. Why are you so bent out of shape about this? It's what you wanted, right?"

"No. It's what *you* wanted."

"You say potato . . ."

"I don't fucking believe this."

"Well," CK exhaled dramatically into the phone. "You'd better start wrapping your head around it—which means you first have to pull it outta your ass. Opportunities like this don't come along all that often—so don't fuck it up."

"I don't know what to say."

"Lemme give you an idea. How about, 'Hello, Abbie? You won't believe what just happened.'"

"Go to hell, CK."

"Way ahead of you," she cackled. "You can thank me later, home girl." She disconnected.

Grace sat holding the phone against her ear for so long her hand grew numb.

Ochre was going to be published? *By a real press?* And they were going to pay her for it? *In advance?*

Shit like this didn't happen to her. Now . . . falling off a damn garden trellis? Or falling in love with her boss? *That* was the kind of shit that happened to her.

But CK said it was for real.

She really was going to kill CK for doing this. How dare she make such a brazen assumption?

Who was she kidding? *It was CK.* She probably did shit like this a dozen times a day.

God, I need a drink. She got up and headed for her kitchen.

And I guess I'd better tell Eddie that I was just blowing smoke about Ann Patchett ghostwriting my novel . . .

Chapter Nine

In the morning, Grace needed to make a quick stop at her office on her way to the St. Allie's convocation center. Bryce had called her at 7:30 and said he had something urgent to share with her and asked if he could meet her at her office at nine, before the inauguration. She felt like an idiot dragging her academic regalia with her, but she knew she wouldn't have time to run back home to fetch it. All faculty members were expected to be garbed-up and in line by half past nine. She was going to be marching in beside Bryce, so she wondered why he couldn't just talk with her then, while they waited to enter the great hall after the board of trustees, and ahead of Abbie—who would enter the hall last. He told her he would only need a few minutes of her time, and that he preferred to speak to her in private.

Grace was smart enough to see through his subterfuge. Besides, Bryce had a tell: his grammar became even more imperiously precise when he was nervous—or excited. She wasn't positive about what drove him to ask for a private audience, but she suspected it probably had something to do with Abbie. At this point, she felt things were coming down so fast and furious she didn't have the stamina to waste time worrying about whatever he was going to hit her with. Besides, she had more than a slight hangover skirting around her frayed edges after last night's dalliance with a new bottle of Rémy.

So, Blowjob could *blow* her . . .

She smiled at her own wit. Pretty amazing, considering the world, as she knew it, was turning upside down or inside out or in any direction that was exactly opposite to how she normally experienced it.

And she was still pissed at CK . . .

She'd barely finished her first cup of coffee when her phone rang. The caller ID read Chapel Hill, North Carolina.

She stared at the phone as it continued to ring.

One guess who this is . . .

In fact, the editor in chief at Algonquin Books was . . . wonderful. She seemed unfazed by Grace's customary self-deprecation, and spoke in glowing terms about the book, its quirky subject matter and innovative narrative structure. And she was a good friend of Ann Patchett's who, she said, spoke very highly of Grace's work at Vanderbilt.

That led Grace to an entirely new level of panic. *This shit was getting real.*

By the end of the call, they had a virtual handshake agreement, and Grace had an assurance that the relevant paperwork would be transmitted later that day via a secure e-sign document service. The editor told Grace to take as much time as she needed, and to feel free to have the terms of the contract reviewed by her personal legal counsel—assuring her that they were offering her an industry standard contract with a rider that gave them an option on Grace's next book, if she chose to stay on with them.

And they were paying her a *very* handsome signing advance.

Grace said she'd like until the end of the week to think it over, and the editor said that was just fine.

But Grace knew she was taking the offer. She had to. And given whatever Bryce was about to hit her with, she'd likely need this contract—and its handsome advance—to make ends meet until she could cobble together another teaching arrangement someplace else. That part wouldn't be too hard if she were willing to swallow her pride and pick up adjunct courses at Champlain College or UVM. Losing her health insurance would be the worst part—along with having to start over, teaching multiple sections of 'Intro to Anything.'

But she checked the employee manual, and she could stay covered under COBRA until she found a way to get coverage that was more affordable. And she'd just have to work something out with Dean to slow down the renovation work on her house. She loved her house, and she had too much invested in it to give it up. And, frankly, she didn't want to be too far away from Abbie.

Assuming, of course, that Abbie would even want her to remain nearby.

She passed several other faculty members headed across the quad with their gowns slung over their shoulders. Inaugurating a new president was a big event in the life of a college and today, Abbie was pulling off a whole slew of firsts. First president under age fifty to take the oath of office. First president to hold dual citizenship in the US and Canada. First president to have a PhD in classics—not religion. First president to be a woman.

And first president to be gay . . .

That last one was perhaps the most remarkable. And it was the one milestone not generally known by the community.

At least, not yet.

It was her hope that if push came to shove, she could make a graceful exit before it *did* become public knowledge. That way, Abbie could roll the news out in any way that suited her—if ever she chose to roll it out at all.

Bryce was waiting for her when she reached her third-floor office in Ames Hall. He was striding up and down the hallway, taking anxious looks at his watch about every five seconds. The monogrammed garment bag containing his regalia was neatly draped over a chair outside her door. His blue cap sat atop the bag. Bryce always wore an eight-cornered velvet tam, and that fact always amused Grace because she found it to be fussy and ostentatious. Her own tam was a circa 1932 castoff she'd found more than a decade ago at a thrift store in Nashville. It had the initials C.C.V. embroidered inside its headband. She loved to manufacture stories about how it had originally belonged to either Commodore Cornelius Vanderbilt—or to the person who invented the three-digit code on the backs of most major credit cards.

"Hi, Bryce. I hope I haven't kept you waiting?"

"Grace." He turned to face her. "No. You're actually right on time."

Grace unlocked her door. "C'mon inside."

Bryce followed her into the office and carefully closed the door once they both had entered. He sat down without waiting for Grace to invite him to do so.

"So." Grace took a seat behind her desk because her office only had two chairs. "Your request was awfully mysterious, Bryce. Don't keep me in suspense any longer. What's up?"

"Since you seem to be so eager, I'll get right to the point." He leaned forward on his chair. "Brittney McDaniel came to see me last week—and she was very upset."

Here it comes . . .

"I'm sorry to hear that, Bryce. Why was she upset?"

"It seems she had the misfortune to see you last weekend at Burton Island, gallivanting on a boat with our next president."

"Gallivanting?" Grace saw no reason to deny it. She was certain it would be in the public domain soon enough. "That doesn't sound like a word Brittney would use, Bryce. And, believe me, I've read enough of her tortured prose to be certain."

"I'm glad you think you can make light of something so serious, Grace. I daresay the dean won't share your casual approach to considerations of what constitutes professional conduct when I meet with him tomorrow morning."

"I'm intrigued, Bryce. Why would Dr. Meeker care if I offered a boat ride to Dr. Williams—in public—ten days before she became our new president?"

Bryce smiled at her. It gave her the creeps.

"I think when he evaluates that event in concert with the revelation that the president-elect made a late-night visit to your home—followed shortly after by a sighting of you, sneaking out of her residence at dawn—he'll be inclined to view the matter more seriously."

Grace took a deep breath and held it for a moment. She wasn't really surprised that Brittney had busted her by pouring her tender heart out to someone who pretended to be interested. But the *only* way Bryce could've known about Abbie's visit to her house that night was if Lorrie had blabbed about it. But to whom? Lorrie didn't give two shits about Bryce—so why would she want to do anything to help advance his prospects at St. Allie's?

Unless Lorrie was pissed at Grace for rebuffing all her advances.

And anyone could have seen her leaving the president's home at dawn that day—just like anyone could have seen Abbie walking through town on her way to Grace's house the night before.

CK would call this mess a big old-fashioned goat fuck.

"Well, Bryce. It doesn't look like there's much left for us to discuss."

He sat back against his chair. "I agree."

Grace looked at the wall clock above her desk. "I suppose we should get going. We don't want to be late for the inauguration."

Bryce stood up. "You'll forgive me if I don't accompany you? Under the circumstances, I think it would be in my best interest to go on ahead."

Grace laughed.

Bryce looked confused. "You find that amusing?"

"No, Bryce. I find it wholly consistent. Forgive my descent into the vernacular, but you're a spineless worm with the moral compass of a cockroach."

Bryce's face turned beet-red. He all but snarled at her before he yanked open her office door, picked up his garment bag, and hurried down the hallway toward the stairs.

Fucking chinless maggot.

Grace sat taking deep breaths to try and steady her heart rate. She gave Bryce a five-minute start before grabbing her things and making her own way across campus to the convocation center.

She found it oddly appropriate that her farewell performance at St. Allie's would coincide with Abbie's debut—and that both would be surrounded by so much pomp and circumstance.

Abbie looked resplendent in a dark purple robe with crimson velvet panels and four crimson bars on each sleeve—the ecclesiastical colors of St. Albans. The lining of her doctoral hood from Princeton was bright orange with a black chevron. The hood seemed to vibrate as she walked down the center aisle to take the stage. Her long hair was pinned up and she wore an eight-sided, black velvet tam with gold bullion trim.

She took Grace's breath away. And Grace was certain there were next-to-no people in the crowded hall not sharing that reaction. Abbie was impressive and prodigiously beautiful.

Most of the ceremony was a blur for Grace. Abbie's formal installation as the fifteenth president of the college didn't take more than a few minutes. Once Mitchell Ware administered the oath, hung a huge medallion bearing the college seal around her neck, and handed her the college mace, it was pretty much a wrap. There were cheers, waves of thunderous applause, and even a few catcalls—mostly from the student body.

Abbie's speech was short but remarkable for its expressions of humility and insight, and her grasp of the unique place St. Albans held in the life of the church, the community and the honored traditions of academe. She concluded by pledging herself—her industry, her love for scholarship and her lifelong commitment to the enduring ideals of the liberal arts—in service to the mission and continued vitality of St. Albans College.

"I make this solemn promise to each of you," she said as her gaze swept the hall, finally coming to rest on Grace. "I will always care more about doing this job, than keeping it."

She held her gaze on Grace a moment longer, until the hall erupted in applause and the St. Allie's orchestra commenced a spirited performance of Purcell's Trumpet Voluntary.

The entire assemblage got to its feet and stood while the

newly installed President of St. Albans College left the stage and exited the hall between rows of cheering faculty, students, trustees, distinguished alumni and friends.

The entire community was invited to a reception immediately following the inauguration, so Grace connected with CK and the two of them walked together to the big atrium where the after-party was being held.

CK looked outstanding in her scarlet gown lined with gray silk. She'd been a Rhodes Scholar—of course—and was the only Oxford University PhD on the St. Allie's faculty. Her latest ink—a phoenix tattoo on her neck—blended beautifully with her vestments.

"So, what do you think?" CK asked. "We can either claim a spot in line behind all of the other enterprising suck-ups to wait our turn to shake our new leader's manicured hand—or we can head straight to the wine bar."

"Is this a rhetorical question?" Grace replied.

CK took hold of Grace's arm. "Good girl. I knew you weren't dead yet."

They pushed their way through the maze of people. Grace caught a glimpse of Abbie, surrounded by equal numbers of well-wishers and brown-nosers. She knew the odds were slim to none that she'd get an opportunity to say anything privately to her. There were just too many people determined to claim prior privilege. So, she resolved to content herself with stealing glances at her when she thought no one was paying attention. Like right now.

"Busted." CK nudged her elbow. "Quit looking at her like she's a steak and you're a bottle of A.1. Sauce."

"I wasn't doing that." Grace gave her a guilty look. "Was I?"

"Give me a break, Warner. You're so fucking transparent."

"Thanks."

They edged forward a few inches in the queue at the wine bar. "Well, if it's any consolation, she spent a fair amount of time looking at you the same way."

Grace shot her an anxious look. "You noticed that, too? I thought it was just wish fulfillment."

"Nope. Fortunately, most of the people at this joint are so self-important they probably thought she was speaking directly to them."

"This is a mess, CK."

"No it isn't. A mess looks nothing like your predicament."

"How do you figure?"

"Okay. Take a look over there at Blowjob, waiting his turn in line. He probably shoved about twenty octogenarians out of the way to gain a better spot. Now—the unlucky person who has to go home at night and crawl into bed with him? *That's* someone with a mess on their hands. Your problem? It's a blip on the radar."

"Yeah, well about our friend, BJ." Grace lowered her voice. "He asked me to meet him at my office this morning before we got over here to line up. He knows about . . . *things*. And he made it clear that he's taking it straight to the dean and the department chair."

CK scoffed. "Even if that were true, which I doubt, why the hell would he *tell* you about it?"

"Beats me. Maybe he couldn't resist the opportunity to gloat about his good fortune?"

"He's an idiot," CK said with contempt. "Does he sincerely think that being the giddy bearer of catastrophic news will endear him to the hearts of an administration basking in the heady afterglow of a legendary hire? Williams is a fucking rock star and everybody on three continents knows it. Blowjob would have to waltz in there with hi-def video of her in bed with Beelzebub before the board chair would even consider batting a grizzled eyelash."

"I wish I had your confidence."

"I wish you had my fashion sense." CK laughed. "That yellow fucking robe is a menace. But in the meantime, let's not ruin a day we should be celebrating." She snagged two glasses of what masqueraded as red wine. "Here's to a long and happy life with the woman of your dreams."

Grace's eyes grew wide.

"Not *that* one," CK amended. "The other one, who's about to make her explosive debut in stunning shades of ochre."

Grace rolled her eyes. "I still want to kill you."

They clinked glasses.

Grace stole another glance at Abbie. The initial crush of people around her had thinned out. She was now talking one-on-one with someone. Grace did a double take when she realized it was Grady.

She felt a twinge of jealousy. *I wonder how in the hell he finagled that?*

"Don't sulk," CK chastised her. "Get your ass over there and take advantage of the lull." She gave Grace a little shove.

Grace handed CK her wineglass and made her way across the atrium to where Abbie stood.

Dear god, the woman was spectacular.

Abbie saw her coming. The smile that illuminated her face was something Grace knew she would never forget.

"Okay if I crash this party?" she asked Grady when she joined them.

"Hey, you'll have to ask the boss," he said. "If you're lucky, she'll even make you stay after school."

Grace thought that was an odd observation from him, but she decided to roll with it.

"Oh, yes please, ma'am," she said to Abbie. "I'd love to clap your erasers."

Grady positively guffawed and Abbie raised an eyebrow.

"That has to be the most original thing I've heard so far today," she said.

Grace fixed Abbie with her most apologetic look. "That didn't really come out the way it should have."

"Yeah," Grady agreed. "Not so much." He extended a hand to Abbie. "I enjoyed our chat. I'll be in touch with you later on."

Abbie smiled and shook his hand. "We'll miss you around here, Grady."

"I think I'm leaving you in good hands." Grady looked at Grace. "See you around the chaparral, sister."

"Later, Grady." Grace watched him walk off.

"I didn't think I'd get to talk with you today," Abbie said. "Thank you for coming over."

"Are you kidding? I've pretty much had you staked out since you walked in here."

"So," Abbie began. "About those erasers . . ."

"Oh, good god—I'm sorry. I don't know where the hell that came from."

"Don't you? I have a few thoughts."

"I just bet you do." Grace stifled a laugh. "By the way . . . nice bling. It really suits you."

Abbie regarded the huge gold medallion around her neck. "You think so?"

"Absolutely. I think it would be too gaudy for most women to pull off—but on you, it works."

"Is that a compliment?"

"Oh, yeah. I think you should wear it all the time."

Abbie raised an eyebrow.

"Well . . . maybe not *all* the time," Grace corrected.

"I'm glad you like it. I plan to wear it for quite a while."

"In for the duration, then?"

Abbie nodded. "I hope both are."

Grace knew she had to talk with Abbie about Bryce—and about the book. But now was not the time and here was certainly not the place.

"So, when you can work it out, I need to talk with you. I know it may have to wait a bit until things settle down for you."

Abbie looked concerned.

"Don't worry," Grace added quickly. "It's nothing bad." She hoped Abbie would forgive her for the lie. She didn't want to do anything to blemish such an important day.

"I'm going to be tied up for most of today," Abbie apologized. "But my parents are leaving after dinner."

"Maybe you can give me a call later on, if you're not too done in?"

"I have a better idea. How about I give you a call when the

coast is clear and you can come by the house?" She smiled. "I think you know the way . . ."

Grace thought it was an insane idea. But on the other hand, what did she have to lose? And she really did need to talk with Abbie—soon.

"I suppose I can always try the trellis again. I bought a pair of new work gloves at Tractor Supply."

"I have a better idea," Abbie whispered. "How about I leave the patio door unlocked?"

Out of the corner of her eye, Grace could see Lorrie Weisz approaching. *Great timing, as always.*

"You're on," she said to Abbie.

Lorrie rolled toward the two of them like a speck of flotsam at high tide.

"Just look at the two of you," she gushed. "Abbie in purple, Grace in yellow. All of these brilliant colors. You're like a couple of kaleidoscopes."

"You're nuts, Lorrie," Grace said. "We look like a meltdown at a Peeps factory."

Abbie stifled a laugh. "I have to agree with Laurel, Grace. Your gold robe makes quite a statement."

"Yes," Grace agreed. "It's a bold reminder of the thousands of dollars in student loans I still owe Commodore Vanderbilt's University."

"The things we do for love," Lorrie agreed.

Grace and Abbie exchanged glances.

"Apropos of that," Grace said, "I need to go schmooze the hands that feed me. I hope you enjoy the rest of your day, Dr. Williams. It was a moving ceremony."

"Thank you, Dr. Warner. I appreciate you coming by to speak with me."

"See you around, Lorrie."

Grace beat a hasty retreat and headed back toward the bar. She hoped CK was still saving her wine.

She was halfway there when she heard someone call out her name. It was Luc Abbot.

"Hello, Grace," he said cordially. "I was hoping I'd get to see you today."

"Dr. Abbot." She shook his hand. "You must be very proud, sir."

"I am," he said. "We always knew our Élisabeth was meant for *grandeur* . . . greatness. It is gratifying to see her so happily installed in a place where she can achieve that."

"I can imagine it is," Grace nodded. "She is an exceptional woman."

"As her father, I wish most for her to be happy. A career as consuming as this is—how do you say it? *Solitaire?*"

"Lonely," Grace agreed.

He nodded. "I do not wish that for her. A life of solitude—*loneliness*. I wish instead for her to find happiness with an equal. A partner she can respect. And love."

He was looking at Grace so intently it made her feel exposed—like he could see through the veneer of impartiality she was trying desperately to present.

She decided to take a chance. "Does Madame Abbot share your concerns?"

He gave Grace a sad smile. "My wife is a complicated woman with an unforgiving spirit. She loves her daughter—but on her own terms. That has been Élisabeth's cross to bear—and my own."

"I am sorry for that," Grace said with feeling.

"I believe you are, Grace." Abbie's father held out his hand. When Grace extended hers, he took hold of it and raised it to his lips. *"S'aimer l'un l'autre,"* he said.

Then he bowed and walked away.

Grace made her way across the atrium like she was in a trance. Luc's words reverberated in her head as if they were bouncing around in an echo chamber. Her French was shitty, but good enough to understand his benediction:

Love each other.

As soon as she could do so without attracting notice, Grace beat a hasty retreat from the all-star reception and headed for home. She was chagrined when she saw Brittney McDaniel heading straight toward her on the sidewalk that led away from the convocation center. Grace hoped the girl would veer off—as she had been doing lately—but no such luck. Brittney stopped dead in her tracks and waited for Grace to approach.

"Hey, Dr. Warner," she said.

Grace sensed that Brittney was trying to be cordial—also a departure from the recent norm.

"Hi there, Brittney," she said. "You on your way to the luncheon with the new president?"

Brittney nodded. "I wanted to be sure to get there on time—especially after you said getting invited was a big deal."

"It is a big deal. I'm very proud of you for getting an invitation."

Brittney shrugged. "She seems really nice."

"She?" Grace asked.

"President Williams. I met her yesterday at Twiggs. She came in for lunch with her parents and some other people."

"Oh. That's nice. I'm glad you liked her. She's going to be very good for St. Allie's."

"I think so, too." Brittney kept shifting her weight from one foot to the other. Grace could tell she was uncomfortable. She was nicely dressed today, and she was wearing makeup—both departures for the normally taciturn young woman. "Dr. Warner? I'm really sorry I was unfair to you about Dr. Williams. I didn't think it would be such a big deal. Honest."

"What do you mean?" Grace asked—even though she already knew what it meant.

"When I told Dr. Oliver-James about seeing you with President Williams on the boat. I didn't mean for that to get you in trouble."

"Oh. Why do you think it would get me into trouble, Brittney?"

She looked down. "He seemed pretty upset about it. He said it needed to be reported to the dean, and he thanked me for telling him. I knew right then I'd made a mistake. I wish I could take it back. Honest."

"It's okay, Brittney. Try not to worry any more about it. I'll take care of any misunderstanding that might arise. Okay?"

"Okay." Brittney did not sound convinced. Grace actually felt sorry for her.

"You go on and have a great time at the luncheon." Grace reached out a hand and squeezed Brittney's shoulder. "Do *not* worry about me. I am just fine." Grace smiled at the girl. "I'll see you in class."

She continued walking toward home. She was still wearing her doctoral robe, which billowed around behind her like a parasail. She knew the bright yellow-gold vestment made her look like a crazed clone of Big Bird—but she didn't really care.

CK always called her a "dirty bird." The irony of the nickname always amused Grace—but lately, it seemed to fit how she'd been feeling about her prospects with Abbie.

Grendel was waiting for her at the gate when she reached her house. Grace marveled at the way the little mutt had already become so integrated into her life. She was like a fixture these days. She kept Grace company at night when she sat in her study or on the back porch grading papers. She hovered around Grace's feet in the kitchen when she made coffee in the mornings or cooked her dinner at dusk. And she now slept at the foot of Grace's bed—on her own fleecy blanket, festooned with colorful little paw prints.

She still made time, however, for her sacred ritual every twelve hours. Grace suspected that this proclivity of Grendel's would never change.

Grace shucked her regalia and sat down to check her email messages. There were two new ones since that morning. One was from Grady, asking if she'd like to use the cabin the upcoming weekend. He offered her the boat, and said he wanted her to have another shot at staying out there before they cleaned the place out and got it ready to sell. He also asked her to collect any of her personal belongings and bring them back with her. "I know how hard this is going to be for you, and I'm sorry to ask you to do this," he wrote. "But Karen wants to move on this as quickly as possible, and you know how she is when she gets how she gets and has her mind set on something. Let me know for sure if you want to head out there, okay? See you around, G-diddy."

Grace smiled at Grady's use of his wishful nickname, and sat for a minute, staring at the computer screen.

Damn. This whole thing was a serious drag. She really had no right to be as upset about it as she felt. It made sense for Grady and Karen to want to maximize their resources and buy a house. They weren't getting any younger—and they had small children to raise.

But to lose access to the cabin on Butler Island—permanently?

That sucked. And it especially sucked coming on the heels of so many other losses.

She shot a quick note back to Grady, telling him that yes, absolutely, she'd take him up on the weekend offer. In fact, she'd find a way to blow off her Friday morning classes so she could get an extra day out there.

Why the hell not? She was going to be quitting tomorrow, anyway . . .

The second email was from her new editor at Algonquin Books. She'd followed up and sent Grace copies of all the contract offers. Grace had already written back to CK's buddy at Artist Management to formalize her relationship with him. It looked like his efforts would net him a solid 15 percent of any royalty money *Ochre* earned after publication.

That sucked, too—but she understood that this was the way things worked in the book trade. Without his contacts, no one at Algonquin would've looked at her pages twice. Hell . . . *once.* Like most mainstream publishers, Algonquin did not accept unsolicited manuscripts.

Her editor also forwarded a link to a *New York Times* article Grace hadn't seen yet. "You might find the attached interesting," she wrote. "Looks like your girl's whereabouts is no longer a mystery. This makes your book especially timely, and we may want to get with our catalog people to try and expedite publication. This can sometimes happen if the manuscript is clean, as I suspect yours is, and doesn't require many rounds of changes. Be thinking that idea over, and we'll discuss once you return the e-signed documents."

Grace clicked on the link to the article and about fell out of her chair when the story displayed on her screen. "A de Kooning, a Theft and an Enduring Mystery," the headline read. Below the byline was a photo of a security guard at the University of Arizona Museum of Art, posing with "Woman Ochre," which had finally been discovered hanging behind a door in the bedroom of a modest ranch house in New Mexico. The painting, which had been missing since its theft in 1985, had been positively identified, and returned to its rightful owners at the museum.

Grace's head was spinning. *Ochre had been found?* And not as she had imagined—languishing in the subterranean salon of some moneyed, off-the-grid collector in Milan or Paris. But in suburban New Mexico—hidden behind a door in a ranch house on a mesa.

It was an incredible and unlikely end to one of the art world's greatest unsolved mysteries.

And it was an outcome that took her thoughts about how she'd end her *own* epic tale about the painting and its captivity, and blew them to proverbial kingdom come.

What the hell would she do now? And why wasn't her editor reacting to this news the way she was?

It didn't make sense.

She read the rest of the story and shook her head in amazement.

The article about the painting's discovery provided a few more details about the initial theft. After "Woman Ochre" had been slashed from her frame on the day after Thanksgiving in 1985, the security guard at the museum recalled that the couple deemed responsible for the theft seemed *odd*—and commented that one of the two perpetrators appeared to be a man dressed as a woman.

To Grace, the discovery of "Woman Ochre's" whereabouts was a paradigm shift. What did this revelation mean for Grace's Ochre, and her fictionalized sojourn with so many imagined captors? Was Ochre's entire journey now just the product of simple illusion, writ large? Did the truth now revealed make her story cross over from the realm of magic realism to skirt the edges of fantasy or science fiction?

She really had no idea. She was going to have to live with the information for a while and see what would shake out from what she knew would be countless hours of thoughtful rumination.

Correction. *Not countless.* She had to solve this puzzle, and soon—especially if Algonquin now wanted to try and expedite publication of the book.

It was ironic, really. Ochre was like the antithesis of T.S. Eliot's wayfarer in *The Four Quartets*. At the end of *her* exploration, she would arrive where she started and know the place—*not at all.*

Grace had an inkling that she was on to something.

Perhaps *that* was the key for Ochre? To understand that being returned to the sterile environment of a cold museum hall constituted a captivity greater than all the others?

Yeah. She closed her email browser and opened the manuscript file.

It was time to write.

Day morphed into night faster than Grace could've imagined. Grendel's escalating complaints about wanting her dinner finally succeeded in distracting Grace from working on the novel. She also knew she needed to set the book aside and prepare to make her clandestine way to Abbie's house.

After she fed Grendel, she grabbed a black jacket from the hall closet.

Do people dress in dark clothing for this kind of thing?

Why did they even bother to sneak around? It wasn't like half the campus didn't already know about their trysts.

"C'mon, girl. Let's go outside and go pee-pee." She clapped her hands to get Grendel to follow her to the back yard. Once they were outside, she gave Grendel a good scrub of the ears and a big Busy Bone.

"See you later on, pal."

She left the porch door ajar for Grendel, just like before.

Just like before? Good god . . . I've become a real floozy. Agnes would be so proud.

But this time, Grace was resolved not to spend the night with Abbie. Until her status at the college was resolved, she had no desire to toss any more kerosene on the flames of her failed career prospects.

The walk to Abbie's along back streets took only about ten minutes. Grace was fortunate not to pass anyone she knew. And it was easy for her to cross the quad and head toward the college library, which was conveniently located behind the president's residence. All Grace had to do was veer off the brick sidewalk and duck unseen behind a conveniently placed hedgerow—and voila! She was on the patio at the side of Abbie's house.

Sure enough, Abbie had left one of the big patio doors unlocked, and Grace stepped inside with far less ceremony than her last nocturnal visit to the house. She was trying to decide which way to head to find the stairs that led to the upstairs apartment when she heard Abbie's voice call out to her.

"Grace? I'm up here. Turn right at the door and head to the end of the hallway. You'll see the stairs on the left."

"Okay," Grace replied. She followed Abbie's directions and made her way to the second floor of the big house. Abbie was in her small but nicely appointed kitchen, standing at a countertop cutting up raw vegetables.

"Are you hungry?" she asked. "I got next to nothing to eat all day and I'm famished. I very nearly ordered us a pizza."

Grace walked over to where she stood and hesitated only a moment before kissing her on the cheek.

"I'm famished," she said. "And why not order a pizza? You don't have to defend your culinary peculiarities to anyone now. You be the boss."

"Really?" Abbie stopped chopping. She looked down at her mound of what Grace knew were locally sourced veggies. "Screw nutrition," she said, and dropped her chef's knife. "Where's the phone?"

"Beats me," Grace said. "I've never had the privilege to breathe this rarified air before."

"Well that's *not* true." Abbie rolled her blue eyes. "As I recall, you breathed quite a bit of this rarefied air the other night."

"Yeah, but that doesn't count. You never actually *gave* me a tour. Besides—if memory serves, I was doing a lot more gasping than breathing."

"Whose fault is that?"

"Oh, it's no one's *fault*," Grace clarified. "And I'm certainly not complaining—so don't draw the wrong inference."

"Uh huh." Abbie wiped her hands on a dishtowel. "I just hope that like most scientific experiments, it's replicable."

"I see you have the entertainment portion of the evening figured out."

Abbie laughed. "The phone is on the small desk behind you. If you would kindly hand it to me, I can call Mimmo's and order our dinner before giving you the grand tour of my pied-à-terre."

Grace gave her the phone. "Great idea—but Mimmo's doesn't deliver."

Abbie plucked a card off the side of the refrigerator. "Yes, they do. It seems that rank has its privileges. What do you like on yours?"

"Anything but onions," Grace said.

"Okay." Abbie began to dial the number.

"Or olives. I really hate olives," Grace added.

"No olives," Abbie said. "Okay."

"Oh, god—no anchovies."

Abbie dropped the phone to her shoulder. "Anything else?"

"Well. I don't really eat banana peppers, but I can pick them off if you like them."

Abbie sighed. "Hello," she said into the phone. "This is Dr. Williams at the college. I'd like to place an order for home delivery. That's right—for my residence. I'd like a medium pizza with extra cheese. No. No other toppings. Right. You have my credit card information? Great. Thank you. Forty-five minutes is perfect. See you shortly." She hung up.

"Extra cheese?" Grace asked.

Abbie glared at her. "If you tell me you hate cheese, this relationship is over."

"Oh, no. I *love* cheese."

"Well, thank god." Abbie put the phone down on the countertop. She eyed Grace with suspicion. "You'd better be telling the truth."

"I promise," Grace insisted. "I love cheese almost as much as I love you."

Abbie looked surprised by Grace's casual declaration—but nowhere near as surprised as Grace felt at just blurting the words out like that. The problem was—she meant them. Literally.

Well. Not that part about the cheese . . .

"I just said that, didn't I?" Grace asked her.

Abbie nodded.

"Oh, god, Abbie. *I'm sorry.* I know that makes me sound like a real loser. Don't let it scare you off, okay?"

"So, you only meant the phrase anecdotally? Is that what you're saying?"

"Yes. *No.*" Grace closed her eyes and took a deep breath. When she opened them, Abbie was still regarding her with an odd expression. "What's the right answer?" she asked. "You tell me."

"I can't tell you what's right for you," Abbie said. "But I *can* tell you what's true for me."

Grace could feel her heart pounding

Abbie took a step closer and bent toward her. "I *love* cheese," she whispered.

Grace socked her on the arm. "Asshole."

Abbie laughed merrily.

Grace sulked.

Abbie ended their standoff.

"Buck up, *amoureux*," she said. "I love you, too."

Grace tried not to smile like an idiot, but she couldn't help it. Abbie was smiling, too.

Grace closed the distance between them and pulled Abbie into her arms.

"So, about this tour . . ." she began.

"We have forty-five minutes," Abbie said.

Grace kissed her. "Then we'd better work fast."

When Grace got home early the next morning, she was greeted by an email from her department chair, Sharon Glaspell. Sharon asked if she could meet her at the academic dean's office on Thursday at 2 p.m., after Grace's one o'clock class finished. Grace wasn't at all surprised to hear from Sharon—although she was impressed by how quickly she and the dean arranged to meet with her so soon after Bryce's salacious allegations.

No flies on them.

She'd thought long and hard about whether to tell Abbie about all that was likely to transpire in a few days, but she decided against doing so. For one thing, she knew Abbie would try to talk her out of resigning—and, Abbie being Abbie, would probably threaten to resign herself, as a means toward salvaging Grace's career.

She couldn't let that happen. Especially not after going through the ceremony yesterday and gaining an even profounder sense of what all Abbie was bringing to the college and its broader community. Losing Grace would be a blip on the college radar. Losing Abbie at this juncture? That event would be cataclysmic for the burgeoning morale of the place—not to mention, a blow to its improved academic standing.

Grace would land on her feet. She always did. And now with the offer from Algonquin, she had a world of new opportunities to explore.

Besides, she'd have precious little opportunity to exchange two words with Abbie between now and the end of the week. The board of trustees was on campus because of the inauguration, and they were holding their biannual summit meetings with campus leadership over the course of the next two days. Abbie would essentially be under lockdown for the duration.

Maybe that would end up being a good thing. It would allow each of them the chance to get some emotional distance and clarity—something in short supply lately. Especially for Grace.

She was meeting CK for breakfast at Maple City Diner. Grace had suggested the place because it was outside the town limits on Swanton Road, and that meant there'd be less chance they'd run into students or other members of the faculty. She wanted to fill CK in on her plans, and she didn't want to risk being overheard—or having CK overheard when she erupted and told Grace to have her fucking head examined.

As usual, CK was already there. She was reading a magazine article and was most of the way through her obligatory maple shake when Grace joined her. There were also two mugs of coffee on the table.

"How can you drink a milkshake first thing in the morning?" Grace asked, tossing her messenger bag onto the seat in their booth.

"How can *you* drink that bland, six-dollar coffee water that's sucked through a vacuum tube?" CK replied before taking another loud slurp of her shake.

"*À chacun ses goûts.*"

"Seriously?" CK rolled her eyes. "It's clear you're spending too much time with our new President."

Grace picked up a menu. "Isn't that what you wanted?"

"I didn't say it was a bad thing, did I?" CK closed her magazine.

Grace noticed the title. *Helix.* "You got an article in there?" she asked.

CK made a face. "In this piece of sophomoric pablum? Hell, no. I was previewing some content to see if it were dumbed-down enough for my 101 students. Sadly, the articles contain too many three-syllable words. I wonder if *Highlights Magazine* has any issues devoted to the principles of quantum mechanics and its relationship to relativity?"

"Probably." Grace shrugged. "*Highlights* was always my go-to resource growing up. It taught me to understand that my mind would *always* betray me—and that horrible things would last forever."

"See?" CK brightened up. "Perfect. Those are precisely the driving principles behind my work."

"Who knew quantum physics had so much in common with the Roman Catholic Church?"

"Oh, good god. Are you still in sackcloth and ashes over Sister Maury Povich, or whatever in the hell that lesbo activist ex-nun's name is?"

"*Mary Lawrence*," Grace corrected. "And, so what if I am? Being an unrepentant apostate doesn't give you the right to throw stones at people of faith."

CK looked at her with incredulity. "That has to be the stupidest thing you've ever said."

"I'm glad you think so," Grace said. "Because that'll take the sting out of what comes next."

CK narrowed her eyes. "What's that?"

"I'm meeting with Sharon Glaspell and Eddie Meeker on Thursday—at their request. Care to guess why?"

"Oh, lemme see. Does it involve a walking asshole with no dick and three first names?"

"That's a big ten-four," Grace replied.

"That fucking waste of skin. So? He did it? He ratted you out?"

"It would appear so."

Their server appeared and deposited two big platters heaped with pancakes, home fries and bendy bacon.

"Thanks, Jessamyn," CK said. "Did you heat up the syrup?"

"You bet, CK." Jessamyn waved and wandered off. "Give me a holler when you need more coffee."

Grace gaped at the mounds of food.

"Whattsamatter?" CK asked. She was already liberally dousing her pancakes with the thick, amber-colored syrup. "You know I *always* order for you. It saves time because you're incapable of commitment."

"It would take me the rest of my natural life to eat all of this."

"Well, that's the beauty of pancakes. They expand to fill the time allotted. Besides," CK added, "I only need one more purchase on my Pancake Punch Card."

"What the hell is that?"

CK dug a couple of dog-eared white cards out of a side pocket in her wallet and showed the top one to Grace. "See? Buy four orders of pancakes, and get a fifth order free. It's a marvel of free enterprise."

"And I can see that this card occupies a sacred place, stashed covertly in a secret compartment with your ACLU membership card." Grace picked up her fork. "Apropos of your snide comment about commitment, I think I may have reformed."

"Oh, yeah? You finally thinking about putting a ring on that hot piece of presidential boo-tay?"

"*No.* I think she does a fine job picking out her own jewelry."

"Well, what is it, then?" CK asked. "Don't keep a girl in suspense."

"I'm quitting."

"Quitting? Quitting what?"

"St. Allie's," Grace said. "Thursday, when I meet with Sharon and the dean."

CK put her fork down. "Please tell me you're joking."

Grace shook her head. "I'm not joking."

"Grace." CK leaned forward. "You cannot quit. That's an *absurd* idea. It helps nothing. It solves even less."

"I disagree. Under the circumstances, I think it's the wisest course of action."

"For whom?"

"For everyone."

"That's a ridiculous hypothesis," CK scoffed.

"It's not ridiculous. It's the best thing I can do to ensure a just outcome."

"Just for whom? *Blowjob?*"

"Of course not," Grace insisted. "For Abbie."

"So, now it's your responsibility to manage outcomes for Abbie?"

Grace shrugged.

"Listen, Grace. There are no right or just outcomes. There are only *outcomes*—and they occur as they occur—with or without any interference or attempts at direction by us. To believe otherwise is to indulge in a dangerous and delusional exercise in grandiosity."

"So, you're saying there are no moral imperatives?"

"Of course not," CK replied. "And as much as those implied imperatives may direct *our* actions, they do not engineer pre-scribed results."

"I don't believe that for a second—and I'm pretty confident that you don't either."

"You're mistaken." CK held up an index finger. "I absolutely believe it."

Grace was unconvinced, and she allowed her expression to show it.

"Okay." CK tried another approach. "Let's consider Ochre. She could just as easily have been a paint-by-number creation—although, I'll grant you that her boobs would likely have been more symmetrical."

Grace rolled her eyes. "What's your point?"

"Well—if everything about Ochre remained the same, except for her humble origin, would anything about her subsequent history have greater or lesser value?"

"Probably everything," Grace replied. "For starters, she wouldn't have been stolen—or even sitting in an art museum to become a candidate for theft."

"True," CK agreed. "But that wouldn't make any aspects of the journeys she *did* have be of greater or lesser importance—they'd just be different."

"What's your point?"

CK sighed. "Let's say you approach an intersection and at the last second, you turn right instead of left. That one spontaneous action could change the entire course of your life."

"Ah," Grace countered. "But was the action truly spontaneous? Was it not influenced and informed by a hundred things that factored into the choice? A traffic backup on the other side of the street? You were in the wrong lane to make a left turn? Or maybe you were paying attention to the car ahead of you, and you inadvertently followed it? Wouldn't those catalysts seem to argue that there are no accidents? That everything happens for a reason, or because of a sequence of events?"

"Of course it does."

"Then what are we arguing about?" Grace asked. "This is like an exercise in navel gazing."

CK smiled. "Welcome to my world."

"I don't know that I want to be in a world where life is nothing more than a cosmic game of Mousetrap—and once the ball is set in motion, there is no stopping it or changing its path."

"But that's not the case, because any slight or subtle deviation will change its path and lead to a different result."

Grace squinted at her. "Because we create our own deviations?"

"No, Grace. Because we *are* our own deviations. The universe is the mousetrap—we are the marbles."

Grace flopped back against the booth. "I have even *less* clarity now than I did before."

"Welcome to enlightenment." CK speared a big forkful of pancake. "Please drive carefully, and obey the speed limits."

Chapter Ten

The rest of the workweek was a blur for Grace. She kept her nose to the grindstone, taught her classes, held her office hours, edited *Borealis* submissions, and spent her evenings at home with Grendel—fighting her way through the tower of theme papers that rose like stalagmites from the floor beside her favorite chair.

Why didn't I make it easier on myself and just let them watch the damn movie?

The idea had some merit. Although *Beowulf*, the movie, left much to be desired with its dramatized depiction of the Anglo-Saxon epic. Angelina Jolie's steamy and seductive portrayal of Grendel's mother did manage to liven up an otherwise benign and gratuitously violent film.

Angelina Jolie. *As if...*

Joile's interpretation of the legendary hag was a ridiculous departure from the original text, in which the slimy, swamp-like creature reeked of salt water and burning coal—and presented a horrifying visage replete with horns, fangs and the bilious scales of an amphibian.

Too bad Guillermo del Toro hadn't gotten the option on this one... he'd probably have nailed it.

But as it was, Grace's newfound ambition to press on and finish grading the accumulated papers from all four sections of her survey classes was long overdue. *A day late, and a dollar short*, as Sister Merry Larry said. *Would* have said, Grace reminded herself.

Grace was determined to complete her grading marathon before she left on Friday for her last weekend at the cabin.

When she finally tossed the last paper onto the completed pile late Wednesday evening, it was nearly nine o'clock—time for Grendel to head outside and sound her warning.

Grace decided to accompany her on the commission of her sacred duty. Why not? It wasn't like she didn't have her own cascade of impending disasters to bemoan.

She made herself a steaming cup of Lemon Zinger and walked out back to join Grendel on the steps. Against her better judgment, she took her cell phone along, hoping against hope that maybe Abbie would get a few minutes to break free and give her a call.

Not very likely.

They'd been missing each other with maddening consistency the past two days. Grace would call and leave a message. Abbie would return her call while Grace was teaching or being held hostage by a student after class. It never failed. The most contact they'd had since that memorable Monday night was a protracted text exchange that took place while Abbie was between meetings, and had a few minutes to retreat to the back of the room to pretend she was responding to email messages on her phone. Grace lucked out and managed to see the first text because she'd dashed home between classes to grab some lunch. She was just getting the jar of extra-crunchy peanut butter out of the cabinet when her phone nearly vibrated itself off the counter. She snapped it up and smiled when she saw the message was from Abbie.

Abbie: Hello! Are you there, by chance?

Grace: Bless Babel, I am!

Abbie: How'd I get so lucky?

Grace: I'm not sure—but I think we can rule out clean living.

Abbie: Hey!

Grace: Am I wrong?

Abbie: I hope so.

Grace: Why waste any more of this precious time on an exercise in rhetoric? How are you?

Abbie: Tired, and ready for these infernal meetings to be over.

Grace: How much longer?

Abbie: The rest of today, and then a dinner tonight.

Grace: Your place?

Abbie: Unfortunately, yes.

Grace: Please tell them all to avoid that downstairs powder room.

Abbie: Oh? Because?

Grace: It's quasi-sacred ground.

Abbie: I suppose I could insist they remove their shoes first?

Grace: Hey. That reminds me . . .

Abbie: Of?

Grace: Whatever happened to my shirt?

Abbie: What shirt?

Grace: Cut me to the quick! You don't remember?

Abbie: Do you mean the wine-soaked garment you employed (unsuccessfully) to conceal the fact that you were partly undressed when I burst in upon you in the aforementioned powder room—during my pre-inaugural meltdown?

Grace: Yes. That would be the one.

Abbie: Sorry. I don't remember it at all.

Grace: Oh, nice one, Rita Rudner! You should do stand-up.

Abbie: I've been told I perform better lying down.

Grace: This IS your personal phone, right??? The one with the cute little *Beverly Hills, 90210* cover?

Abbie: Of course, it is. This isn't my first roundup.

Grace: You mean rodeo?

Abbie: Excuse me?

Grace: The phrase. It's, "This ain't my first rodeo"—not "roundup."

Abbie: You are such a stickler when it comes to these idioms.

Grace: Somebody's gotta keep you straight.

Abbie: Really? If that's the case, it appears you're failing miserably.

Grace: Again, with the jokes! Do I know you?

Abbie: Not as well as you're going to.

Grace: Aren't we optimistic?

Abbie: It seems one of us needs to be.

Grace: I know. I pretty much suck at that. I blame the Church.

Abbie: And how is that working out for you?

Grace: Well, since the person who's served as my moral compass for the lion's share of my life decided to do a 180, cash in her vows, and flip the Church the bird—I'd say not so great.

Abbie: Should I know what you're talking about?

Grace: Not really. I haven't had the chance to fill you in on any of this yet.

Abbie: That sounds ominous. Is there anything else you're not telling me about?

Grace: Of course.

Abbie: Grace . . .

Grace: It can all wait until we see each other again.

Abbie: Now I'm worried.

Grace: Don't be. It's good news. I promise. Mostly. At least, I think it's good news.

Abbie: Grace? This isn't helping to allay my concerns.

Grace: Trust me. It will all keep until we're together.

Abbie: I hate this, Grace. I won't have two seconds of free time until Sunday, when all this meeting madness is concluded.

Grace: It's okay. I'm heading out to Butler Island on Friday morning. Grady and Karen are selling it, since they're leaving the area. I need to get my personal stuff boxed up and out of there.

Abbie: That breaks my heart. I know how much you love it out there.

Grace: True. But all good things must end, right?

Abbie: I'm going to have to trust you on that one.

Grace: I'd say turnabout is fair play on that one, sister.

Abbie: Okay. Then we'll have to trust each other. At least until Sunday, when we can be together.

Grace: You know, I'd have an easier time at that if you'd clear up one pesky thing . . .

Abbie: What's that?

Grace: What'd you do with my shirt???

Abbie: That's easy. It's in my closet.

Grace: YOUR closet? Why???

Abbie: If you have to ask me that, I clearly need to do a better job telegraphing my intentions.

Grace: I do tend to miss a lot.

Abbie: So, I've noticed. Oh, damn!

Grace: What is it?

Abbie: They're all coming back into the room—I've got to go be presidential.

Grace: Okay. Do your best to keep your pantyhose on. I'm told it helps.

Abbie: I don't wear pantyhose.

Grace: I know. Lucky me.

Abbie: Nutjob. I'll try to call you later if it isn't too late.

Grace: I'll be right here, howling at the moon with your dog.

Abbie: <3

And that had been that. Smart. Sweet. Clever. Provocative as hell. And never lasting long enough.

All the things Abbie was.

Grace checked her phone. Tabula rasa.

Wishful thinking. Abbie said she'd be tied up most of the evening.

She looked down at Grendel. "What do you think, girl?"

Grendel looked up at her with an implied question.

"I was just wondering if we should put on our night vision goggles and go engage in some second-story work?"

Grendel stared at her a moment like she was considering it, before shifting her gaze back to continue scanning the perimeter of the yard.

Okay, I'll take that as a 'no.'

Grace glanced at her phone again.

This is ridiculous. I've gotta get a grip.

On the stair beside her, Grendel stiffened before getting to her feet and assuming what Grace now called "The Position."

It was the crack of nine. *Time to boogie . . .*

Grace had back-to-back classes on Thursday morning. She was consistently faced with waves of grim and unhappy faces when she handed back the theme papers.

"Okay, okay," she said to her eleven o'clock Lit Survey class. "Calm down. It's not as bad as you think." She paused. "Well, for some of you it probably *is* as bad as you think—but none of these grades are mortal wounds."

"Dr. Warner?" Carrie Forbush was wildly waving her arm from her seat near the back of the classroom. Carrie's treatise, "How Themes in Beowulf Foreshadow *The Lord of the Rings*," was actually one of the more thoughtful attempts at exposition Grace had suffered through. It was unclear to her whether Carrie had ploughed through Tolkien's iconic trilogy—or just opted to see the movies. Either way, her thesis was at least an interesting one with some merit.

Grace gave her effort a B+.

Apparently, that assessment didn't sit well with Carrie.

"Yes, Carrie?" Grace recognized her.

"Dr. Warner," she began. "I worked really hard on this paper and I think it was a good concept about a comparison not many others have made. I checked that part out when I was doing my research. I don't understand why you didn't like it."

Grace perched on the edge of her desk. "I did like your idea, Carrie. Quite a bit, in fact. It was insightful and unique—and it highlighted universal themes that have contemporary parallels in many great works of literature. And I gave you a grade reflecting that."

Carrie looked down at her paper. "You gave me a B," she said.

"B+," Grace corrected. "That's a very good grade, Carrie."

"An A- is better," another voice quipped. The rest of the class laughed.

"Okay, okay. Stow the commentary." Grace waved a hand to settle them down. "You all understand that your grades are not solely based on how creative or innovative your arguments are. They're also based on how well you *present* them—including accurate bibliographic citation, correct spelling, appropriate use of grammar *and* proper format." There was a chorus of moans. "Hey? Them's the breaks. None of this is a surprise to you, guys. There's a reason this class is referred to as 'Freshman English.' Part of its purpose is to prepare you not only to think critically— but to learn to express your ideas with proficiency *and clarity*, preferably in a mode that is at least vaguely reminiscent of proper written English." She pulled a red pen from her jacket pocket and held it aloft. "That part be where my little best friend, here, comes in. Get it? So, if any of you would like to join me for a delightful and searing exposition of what factors contributed to the grades you received on your papers, I'd welcome your company during *any* of my regularly scheduled, but woefully ill-attended, office hours." She scanned the room. "Thoughts?"

"I still think I deserved a better grade," Carrie muttered.

Grace tapped her red pen on her thigh in agitation. An idea occurred to her.

"How many of you would like the chance to raise the grades on your theme papers by an entire letter—meaning D to C, C to B, or B to A?"

Hands shot up all over the room—belatedly at first, but then with more energy.

"Okay," Grace continued. "Here's what I have in mind." She crossed her arms. "There is a literary convention coined by *Lord of the Rings* author, J.R.R. Tolkien. It's called *eucatastrophe*. Eu from the Greek for good or well, and catastrophe, also from the Greek, meaning ruin or misfortune. Okay. Write this down." Grace waited for her students to open their notebooks. "Eucatastrophe is a term akin to its literary precursor, *deus ex machina*—a Latin translation of the Greek phrase. Anyone care to explain what *deus ex machina* means?"

There were no takers.

"Come on, guys," Grace prodded. "This is a *Catholic* college ... take a wild guess."

"Could you spell that?"

It was Franny Magill, a legacy admit from Philadelphia. Her grandfather had once been headmaster of a prestigious girls' boarding school in Chambersburg—Penn Hall. Grace's mother had been a reluctant student there—years before marrying Johnnie Warner, and moving to Wilkes-Barre to start a family.

Grace sighed. "Sure."

She hopped off the desk and walked to the chalk board. This building was one of the oldest on the St. Allie's campus, and the college's growing endowment hadn't yet expanded its tentacles to up-fit the teaching aids in these classrooms. Grace picked up a broken bit of chalk.

EUCATASTROPHE, she wrote in big, block letters. Followed by DEUS EX MACHINA.

She faced the class. "*Deus ex machina* means 'god from the machine.' It's a term describing a literary device employed to bring about an unexpected or unlikely resolution—generally happy, but not always—to a dire or impossible situation. It was originally a theatrical convention that allowed the gods to intervene in human affairs and sort out the messes they created. But it was always a plot convention that was foreshadowed in the text. We've all observed it in literature—and in film. Tolkien was talking about a twist on the same idea. Only in his parlance, eucatastrophe was *always* a turn from a bad to a good outcome—and it was *not* always predicted or set up in advance. For Tolkien, eucatastrophe was not the product of divine *intervention*—it was an effect of divine *involvement*. Eucatastrophe may be *deus ex machina* by this reasoning, but for Tolkien, God is *not* a machine—or a device." Her eyes swept the classroom to see if her students were following. "Make sense?"

Mostly nods. That was progress.

"So, here's my idea. Any one of you who would like a shot at improving the grade on your theme paper can write a fifteen-hundred-word examination of the use of *either* eucatastrophe or *deus ex machina* in *Beowulf*—because informed arguments can be made for each. I want you to make a case for the author's use of one versus the other, and discuss the overarching merits of each—with direct—and proper—citations from the text. Clear as mud?"

"How much time do we have?"

Pragmatists to the last . . .

"How about two weeks? That seem reasonable?" Grace asked. More nods.

"Cool. Okay then." Grace checked the wall clock. "Looks like we're about outta time. I'm gonna let you go a few minutes early so I have time to grab lunch before an appointment. Try to control your sorrow," she quipped. "Okay?"

Her students immediately began to close their notebooks and check their cell phones.

"And don't forget my office hours if you want to discuss your papers—old or new," she added as they continued to gather up their backpacks. "Otherwise, I'll see you all next Tuesday."

Grace had just enough time to run home and make a quick sandwich before she had to head back across campus for her showdown with Sharon and the dean. As she approached the house, she was surprised to see Dean's truck in her driveway.

There were several large appliance boxes on her back porch—all empty. Nothing about that made any sense. Dean knew she was a long way off from having enough money saved to swap out her old fridge and dishwasher. They'd been able to replace the stove at Christmas, and it was a doozy—a dual-fuel gas range with two ovens. That indulgence set her budget for the companion items in the suite back a bit. She didn't want to go into debt on the renovation project, so that meant Dean was doing the work as Grace had the money saved to pay for it. The rest of her kitchen was in pretty good shape. The new cabinets and flooring were in—and apart from the remaining appliances, she just needed new countertops and a glass brick backsplash. Then this room would be finished.

Seeing the flattened boxes on her porch alarmed her. *What the hell was Dean up to?*

She hurried inside to find him checking the position of the big, French-door fridge with a level. A new dishwasher and an under-counter wine cooler sat out in the middle of the floor. Grendel was perched at Dean's feet, watching him work with interest. She was plainly mesmerized by all he was doing because she paid no attention to Grace until she heard her call out to Dean from the doorway.

"What in the world are you doing?"

Grendel dashed over to greet her. Dean whirled around.

"Don't sneak up on me like that," he chastised her. "You scared the piss outta me."

"Dean . . . what the hell are you *doing?* I don't have the money for all of this right now."

"I know," he said. "But word on the street is that you're getting that book of yours published. So, I thought I'd help you celebrate."

Obviously, CK had talked with him.

"Well, that's a sweet thought," she said. "But my advance isn't big enough to cover these *and* put food on my table for the next six months."

"Hey, no sweat." He finished with the fridge and closed its massive doors. "Like I said, we're celebrating. Besides, your old fridge was for shit and my beer was never cold enough. So, it's as much for me as it is for you. So, cool your jets and say, 'Thank you, Dean,' or I'll rat your ass out to Agnes for being rude."

Grace was amazed. "*You* bought these? *For me?*"

He nodded. "Why are you so surprised? I'm not a total asshole, you know."

She crossed the room and threw her arms around his meaty neck. He hugged her back.

"Take it easy," he said. "I own the fucking store . . . it's not that big a deal."

"It is a big deal," she said into his shoulder. "And yes, you *are* a total asshole—but you've also got about the biggest, softest heart on the planet."

"Yeah, well don't tell anybody, okay?"

Grace stepped back and rubbed a hand across her wet eyes.

"When were you gonna tell me about this book deal?" he asked.

Grace sniffed. "It's not like I was keeping it from you. It only just happened over the weekend."

"Does Mum know?"

Grace shook her head. "I thought I'd wait until the ink was dry on the contracts. That way, if it goes south, I won't have to live down her expressions of disappointment."

He nodded. "Grady was on the ferry with me today. He told me about the cabin. I'm really sorry about that. I know how much you love that place."

"Yeah. It pretty much blows chunks."

"Well." He looked around the kitchen. "We get this room squared away and you'll at least have one place in your house that's not ripped to shit. That oughta be worth something."

"True." Grace didn't disagree with him. It would be fabulous to have her new kitchen finished and back online. "What was Grady doing over in Plattsburgh?"

Dean shrugged. "Beats me. He said something about meeting with a real estate attorney. I figured it was about getting the cabin ready to sell."

"Probably," Grace agreed. "They're going to be moving at the end of the semester. I'll miss him a lot."

"I wish I could help you buy that place, Grace. If I could run it through the business, it'd be a no-brainer."

She smiled at him. "I know that. Don't worry about me. I'm going to be so busy soon that I won't have any spare time to miss being out there."

"With the book, you mean?"

"That and other stuff."

"What other stuff?" he asked.

Grace wondered if CK had talked with him about Abbie, too? Probably not. It would be unlike her to blab about something so personal.

She decided to tell him herself. He'd find out soon enough, anyway.

"Do you want some coffee?" she asked.

"Sure, why not." He walked to the table and pulled out a chair.

Grace got the pot of coffee started before joining him at the table.

"So, I have some other news that you're probably not going to like," she began. "I'm resigning from my teaching position here this afternoon."

She saw no reason to beat around the bush.

Dean was shocked. "Why the fuck would you do that? Aren't you up for a big promotion this year?"

"I was," she agreed. "But that's not going to happen now."

"Why the hell not?"

Grace sighed. "I managed to get myself caught up in something that's guaranteed to ruin my shot at getting tenure. So, the best thing for me to do is quit before they terminate me."

Dean's eyes clouded over. "What the hell did you do? Get caught screwing a student?"

"*No.*" She reached across the small table and swatted him on the arm. "Of course I didn't."

"Well what the fuck did you do, then?" He rubbed his arm. "Shack up with the new president?"

Grace could feel herself beginning to blush. And the more she tried to avoid it, the worse it got.

Dean noticed immediately. "*No fucking way?* You're hitting the president?"

She sighed. "I wouldn't describe it quite *that* way, but, yeah . . . that's pretty much the gist of it."

He laughed. Loudly. "Well, I'll be goddamned. You go, little sister. That's one hot commodity. I'm proud of you."

"Proud of me? For doing something that's going to cost me my teaching career?"

"Hey. Jobs come and go. But a woman like that . . ." He shook his head. "I'd do her."

"You'd do a hole in a tree."

"Hey." He held up his hands. "Insulting me doesn't minimize the mess you got *your* ass into."

She had to agree with him. "I know."

"So, what's this chick's name? Annie?"

"Abbie."

"*Abbie*," he repeated. "That's it. Mum was asking me if I knew anyone over here named Abbie. Now I know why."

Grace was incredulous. "When did she ask you that?"

"Sunday morning when she called."

Grace rolled her eyes. *Good ol' Agnes. She really had a nose for it.*

Hell. Grace ought to just start calling her "Agnes ex machina."

"I'm really in over my head this time, Dean."

"You mean like with Denise?" he asked.

"No. Not like Denise. Not like anyone before."

"In so far you're willing to give up something you've worked seven years for?"

She nodded.

"Well, I'll be damned. She must be something else."

"She is."

It was his turn to sigh. "Wish I could find somebody like that."

Grace smiled at him. "Maybe you'll have a shot now that you're branching out to other letters of the alphabet."

He looked confused. "What do you mean?"

"CK?"

Dean still looked clueless.

"Her name doesn't start with a *D*," Grace explained.

"Yes, it does," he said. "Her first name is 'Doctor,' right?"

Grace sighed and started to respond, but before she could, the coffeemaker beeped.

Thank god . . .

Bryce Oliver-James was coming out of Franklin Hall just as Grace was climbing the outside steps to enter it. As usual, he threw the door open so hard it made the glass rattle. She was glad he didn't see her before he roared down the steps and hurried away from the building.

What an asshole.

Grace entered the building more sedately and made her way to the dean's office on the first floor. She had her neatly typed letter of resignation tucked inside her messenger bag. She hoped the meeting would be short and sweet. She didn't want to belabor the point. She just prayed that Eddie and Sharon would be understanding enough to allow her to be the one to tell Abbie.

That conversation would be a lot of fun. *Not.*

She passed Lucretia Fletcher on her way to Eddie's office.

"Hello there, Lucretia," she said.

The prune-faced woman nodded coldly, and kept walking.

What a mean-spirited old battle-axe. I wonder if Abbie will keep her on?

She didn't see how the two women could possibly work together. Lucretia was an old-school, old guard, dyed-in-the-wool, by-the-book, capital C-conservative Catholic. She was a charter member of what the newer and younger staff at St. Allie's called the "papal mafia." Abbie, the college's first woman president—and a lesbian, to boot—represented everything Lucretia feared. And that collision of values would be especially pronounced once the news of Abbie's relationship with Grace leaked out—as it surely would, no matter how hard Eddie and Sharon tried to keep it under wraps.

Sharon was already in with Eddie when Grace arrived. Eddie's assistant told Grace to go on in, after asking if she'd like anything to drink—which seemed like an odd request, considering the purpose of the meeting. Grace thought about asking for a cup of coffee laced with hemlock, but opted not to. She thanked the young woman, and said she was fine. Then she tapped on Eddie's door.

"Come on in," he called out.

Grace opened the door and stepped inside. Eddie and Sharon were both seated in comfy chairs around a small meeting table. They each had cans of Diet Coke. Eddie indicated that Grace should join them.

"How are you, Grace?" Sharon asked. "I've heard good things about the next issue of *Borealis*. Is it true you got a piece by Ann Patchett?"

Sharon was a great department chair. She was an actual alumna of St. Albans, who had gone on to get her master's and PhD degrees at Cornell before coming back home to Vermont to teach at her alma mater. Grace liked her a lot, and she understood that Sharon was probably not enjoying the errand she was forced to undertake today. That being the case, Grace didn't understand why Sharon was bothering to make small talk instead of getting right down to the point. But she decided just to roll with it.

At least, Sharon was being cordial.

"It's true," Grace explained. "I'd like to say she did it as a favor to me, but that'd be a lie. The journal has a good reputation, and she's wise to want to appear in it."

"Well, I think you get a lot of the credit for that, Grace," Eddie said. "You've done an exceptional job as editor these last several years."

Grace was beginning to feel like this was an awfully strange run-up to getting canned.

"Thanks, Eddie," she said. "I love my work on the journal, and I'm glad you think it's gone well the past few years."

"That's partly what we wanted to discuss with you today, Grace," Sharon said. "That, and your standing in the department and community at large."

Here it comes, she thought.

"As you know," Eddie continued," the board of trustees are meeting here this week. And tenure recommendations were part of their agenda. The committee presented its recommendations to me on Friday, and those have since been presented to the board. You're also aware that one of the decisions concerned an open tenure-track position in the English department."

"I'm going to stop you right there, Eddie," Grace said. "I know what you're about to say, and there's really no need for you to go to any lengths to defend the board's decision. I accept it. In fact,

I've already anticipated it." She reached for her messenger bag and withdrew her letter of resignation. "Here you go." She handed the letter to the dean.

He seemed surprised. "What is this?" he asked.

"My letter of resignation," Grace explained. "It's effective at the end of the semester—unless you'd like me to leave sooner. In which case, I can redraft it to reflect that."

"What are you talking about, Grace?" Sharon was looking at her with concern. "You're resigning?"

Grace nodded. "Isn't that what you wanted to discuss with me today?"

Eddie and Sharon exchanged glances. Eddie cleared his throat.

"Grace, I think you may be under some misapprehensions about a few things."

"I don't imagine I am," Grace replied. "You are both aware of my . . . *personal* . . . relationship with President Williams, I suppose?" she asked.

"Well . . ." Eddie began.

"I assumed as much," Grace said. "Isn't that why you asked me to meet with you today?"

"Wait a minute," Sharon interrupted. "Grace, we asked you to meet with us to tell you the board has formally accepted our recommendation that you be awarded tenure in the English department."

"*What?*" Grace was stunned.

"That's right, Grace." Eddie handed the unopened letter back to her. "Under the circumstances, I think you may wish to keep this."

"And, hopefully, put it into the shredder," Sharon added.

"I don't understand. Bryce Oliver-James told me he was meeting with you to shed light on the inappropriateness of my interactions with Abbie—*President Williams*," Grace corrected. "I assumed that meant you'd need to take—*corrective* action. It matters to me that Dr. Williams does not have her reputation or her prospects tainted by any hint of scandal."

"That's very noble of you, Grace." Eddie nodded. "If the circumstances were different, I'm sure the board would've appreciated your sacrifice. Don't you agree, Sharon?"

"I do," she said. "But the circumstances weren't different in this case, thankfully—so there was no reason or motivation for us—or the board—to act differently."

Grace's head was spinning. *What was happening here?*

"I don't know what to say," she said, for lack of anything more coherent.

"Let me try to clarify things for you." Eddie got up and walked over to his desk. He opened a drawer and withdrew a file folder. "I'd like to share something with you, Grace." Eddie rejoined them at the table. He withdrew a small stack of papers. "I think this will set your mind at ease." He lifted the top sheet. "This is a copy of the acknowledgment that Élisabeth Abbot Williams made to the Chair of the Board of Trustees, the Chair of the English Department, the college general counsel, and to me on the morning of the day after she was introduced to the community as the President-Elect of St. Albans College. I won't bore you by reading it aloud—the gist of it is that she disclosed the existence of a prior romantic relationship with a current member of the St. Albans faculty. She offered immediately to recuse herself from any role or involvement in decisions related to that faculty member's evaluation, compensation, reassignment, promotion or tenure discussions. Additionally, she offered to resign her own position immediately if the board or senior academic officials, after consideration, felt her role or effectiveness as president would be compromised or viewed as illegitimate in any way by the community at large." He lowered the paper. "She hand-delivered these letters to each of us, Grace." He shook his head. "It was quite a demonstration of integrity and leadership—and, might I add—attachment to the individual with whom she hoped to continue a relationship."

Grace was finding it hard to breathe.

"You *knew* about this?" She looked from Eddie to Sharon. "You *both* knew about this?"

Sharon nodded.

"I have to say," Eddie chuckled, "it would've been kind of hard *not* to know about it—after that whole dinner party fiasco. Abbie's mother was rather—*loquacious* with her indiscretion when she returned to the table after her daughter disappeared."

Grace ran a hand over her face. "Do I want to know what she had to say?"

"Probably not," Eddie replied. "Just be glad that most of the other diners had already finished their meals and ventured outside."

"Of all nights for me to take one for the team and volunteer to sit with the alumni association officers," Sharon added. "I missed all the good stuff."

Good stuff? Dear god. Sharon knew? Eddie knew? Mitchell Ware knew?

And Abbie knew that they knew . . . the entire time. *Because she had told them.* Well in advance of her trip to Butler Island— and well in advance of Bryce coming here, to try and submarine her career by ratting them out to the dean and her department chair.

And now she had tenure and Bryce had . . . *what?* A pink slip? *It was incredible.*

This was one paradigm shift she never saw coming. All along, she had been convinced that her tenure at St. Allie's would end in a way that was consistent with how most tragedies ended— she'd make a grand sacrifice to the greater good, sustain a mortal wound, and then limp away to die alone on some remote fjord.

After all, the real test of a hero wasn't whether she could prevail in a fight; it was how she'd behave on the day she *lost*— and what account she would give of herself when she finally understood the certainty that she was destined to die.

That was the head space Grace had been living in ever since she saw Abbie that day on the stage. And it made sense for her to retreat to that bleak vision of her prospects. Why wouldn't she? It was how she'd spent the better part of her last seven years at St. Allie's— drilling those ancient precepts into the minds of her students.

Now this?

It was surreal. Unlikely. Unpredictable. A completely unfore-seen end to what had been shaping up to be a Grade A textbook tragedy.

Grace felt a tingling sensation. It started at the top of her head, spread out behind her eyes, ran down her spine, and fired across every synapse to travel along every nerve ending in her body.

Nothing about it made any sense, but she understood without a doubt what was happening.

And there was even a word for it . . .

Eucatastrophe.

Grace was at home, packing her things for the trip to the island so she could get an early start, when her cell phone rang. She grabbed for it anxiously, hoping it might be Abbie, but it wasn't. It was Lorrie.

"I heard the good news," she gushed. "Oh, Grace, I'm just so happy for you."

Grace had to take a second to figure out which good news Lorrie was referencing. Was it her book getting picked up by Algonquin? Or was it the tenure decision?

She decided to make it easy.

"What good news?" she asked.

"The tenure, silly. It's so wonderful when a place gets it right."

"Thanks for that, Lorrie. How did you hear about it? I only just left the dean's office an hour ago."

"Oh, that's easy," Lorrie explained. "Bryce called me."

"He did?" Grace was shocked. "What did he say?"

"I don't really wish to repeat all those expletives. I am sure you can imagine."

"Yes," Grace agreed. "I probably can."

"He did hint at something intriguing, however."

Grace could sense she wasn't going to like what was coming. "What was that?"

She giggled. "He said St. Albans might be getting a new first lady. Know anything about that possibility, Grace?"

Grace closed her eyes. "No comment," she said.

"I have to tell you that as soon as Bryce made his absurd suggestion, I realized what a fool I'd been. Of course, I noticed the obvious charged atmosphere between you and Abbie whenever you were together, it just never occurred to me that there would ever be any kind of there, there—if you know what I mean."

Grace sighed. "I'm not sure I'd say there *is* any there, there, Lorrie."

"Oh, honey—don't kid a kidder. I'm just sorry I made things . . . *uncomfortable* for you. Had I known you were already committed, I wouldn't have behaved like such a bitch in heat."

Grace's eyes widened. "I wouldn't go quite that far, Lorrie . . ."

"Oh, don't worry about it, Grace. All's well that ends well, right? The two of you make such an adorable couple."

"Lorrie? I appreciate that you're being so kind and supportive—but it would mean the world to me if you would keep all of this under your hat for now. Nothing is fixed or certain between Abbie and me . . . *nothing*. And if and until there is anything to discuss, I'd like to nip any conversation about this in the bud." She chose her next words carefully. "Being the accomplished and insightful woman you are, I know you will appreciate that."

"My lips are sealed, Grace."

Just like Mata Hari's . . .

"Thanks, Lorrie. I knew I could count on you."

"Did you hear the other good news from the board meeting?" Lorrie asked.

Grace was afraid to ask. "No."

"It looks like CK got offered an endowed chair in physics."

"What?" Grace was incredulous. "Really?"

"According to Lucretia. And she should know—she sits in on all those meetings."

"Did she take it?"

"CK, you mean?" Lorrie asked. "I don't know. Lucretia said they just offered it to her today."

Holy shit. This was huge news. CK could have her pick of positions at any top-tier college or research university. Grace had no idea how she'd respond to an opportunity like this. One thing was for sure: St. Allie's was playing hardball to try and keep her.

"Lorrie, I can't tell you how much I appreciate your call. But right now, I'm on the hook to make about a hundred phone calls to family members who will disown me if I don't tell them the news. Will you forgive me if I cut our conversation short?"

"Of course," Lorrie said. "I just wanted to be among the first to offer congratulations."

"You certainly were," Grace said. "Let's meet for coffee soon?"

"Count on it," Lorrie said in her most upbeat voice. "Talk with you later, Grace."

"Bye, Lorrie."

Grace disconnected and stood staring at her phone. She was trying to decide whether she wanted to call CK or simply head straight over to her house when Grendel started barking—followed immediately by the sound of someone knocking loudly on her back door.

She wasn't at all surprised when she saw CK standing outside the door to her porch.

"The woman of the hour," Grace said, holding the door open. "I was just gonna call you."

"Oh, yeah?" CK entered the house and patted a dancing Grendel on the head. "I could say the same. But then I thought, what the fuck? Just go over." She shrugged. "So, here I am. Frankly, I wasn't sure if you'd be here or off celebrating with your *inamorata*."

Grace rolled her eyes. "I see you heard the news?"

"Yeah. How about it? I guess one of those little marbles hit a deviation along its path toward destiny. Go figure."

"Fuck you. Why do you always have to be right?"

"Probably because I generally am, so it's counterintuitive to argue with me."

"Do you want a drink?" Grace led the way to her kitchen.

"It's four o'clock in the afternoon."

"What's your point?"

CK thought about it. "Got any Smuggler's Notch?"

"Just got a new bottle. Want any ice? Lime?"

"Both, if you have 'em. Otherwise, just give me the bottle."

Grace laughed. "Sounds like you had a day like mine."

"Yeah." CK pulled out a chair and sat down. "Do tell? I understand you have news?"

"God, what is it with this place? Why don't they just project a news crawl across the pediment of Franklin Hall?"

"Beats me. I'd imagine gossip took longer to travel in the old days, when all the little monks had to illuminate the reams of handwritten rumors before dissemination. Now they just rely on text messaging."

"Or Laurel Weisz," Grace added.

"Oh? You heard from her?"

Grace handed CK a tumbler full of ice and the bottle of vodka. "You might say that. She called me with congratulations about twenty-five seconds after I walked in the door after my meeting with Eddie and Sharon."

"So, I take it, you didn't resign?"

"I tried." Grace grabbed a lime from her fridge. "But they wouldn't let me. Some weirdness about getting tenure? It was all kind of a blur after that."

CK smiled. It was a big, wide, happy smile that lit up her entire face. Grace had never seen her look quite that—*unencumbered*. It was nice.

"And I understand that you have some news to share, too?" Grace asked her. She took a couple of thick slices of lime to the table and dropped them into CK's glass.

"Yeah." CK sighed and sipped her drink. "It appears the powers that be at this joint just decided to sweeten the pot for me."

"So I heard. An endowed chair? At your age?" Grace shook her head and poured herself a glass of wine from an open bottle she had saved from the other night. "That's a pretty damn big carrot."

CK nodded. "It is. And they added summer research stipends and a generous travel allowance to facilitate continued access to professional development conferences and speaking engagements."

"Well, shit, girlfriend. What'd you say?"

"I didn't say anything."

"CK?" Grace looked at her with disbelief. "Don't tell me you aren't going to accept it? That'd be crazy."

"I didn't say I wasn't accepting it—I just said I didn't *say* anything when they offered it. I needed to gather some other information that was germane to my decision making."

"Well, did you get it?"

"Not yet." CK took another sip from her drink. "That's why I came over here."

"I don't get it."

"I wanted to find out what you were going to do first, idiot. Whether you were going to stay or leave."

"Me? What difference would my decision make?"

"Seriously, Grace? Have you never played connect the dots? Grady's already bailed. If you left, it would only be a matter of time before a broken and heartsick Williams left, too. And if Williams leaves? There goes my best shot at direct connection to a wealth of seriously deep foundation pockets." She shook her cropped head. "Do you think I wanna be stuck here alone, pushing Lucretia Fletcher and the fucking Sister Adorers of the Divine Wrath around in their wheelchairs?"

Grace smiled. "I see your point."

"A breakthrough."

"Hey. Give me a break. I haven't exactly been firing on all cylinders recently."

"You think I don't know that?" CK asked. "I've kind of been your wingman lately, you know? Fending off enemy aircraft?"

"I *do* know it. The truth is, I don't want to do this job without you, either. So, your decision about going or staying matters just as much to me as mine does to you." Grace smiled. "Foundation dollars, notwithstanding."

"Hey. I never said I wasn't *equally* motivated by pernicious self-interest."

"It is one of your more endearing qualities," Grace agreed.

"So. Whattaya say? Should we stay or should we go, now?" CK

chanted the last question in a perfectly wretched, atonal rip-off of The Clash.

Grace lifted her glass of day-old Barolo. "Stay. For realsies."

"Done." CK clinked rims with her. "Now that we settled that, we need to mature our plans for how you get to plant your flag on the summit of Mount Abbie . . ."

Grace was beyond disappointed that she never managed to connect with Abbie before heading out to the island on Friday morning. She knew that getting through to her had been a long shot at best—Abbie had been sincerely apologetic, but clear about how impossible her schedule would be until the trustees decamped. Grace tried calling her several times Thursday night, but to no avail. The phone rolled immediately to voice mail. Finally, Grace sent her a text message, saying how sorry she was they hadn't been able to connect before she made her final trek out to Butler Island to clear out her things. She promised to get back to St. Albans early on Sunday—the day Abbie said she'd have more freedom and greater latitude over her schedule. Grace resigned herself to having to wait until then to talk with Abbie about all that had transpired—*and* to hear her much-anticipated explanation for why she'd kept her recusal from Grace's tenure decision—and her revelations about their relationship—a secret all this time.

That part remained a conundrum for her. Abbie *had* to know how much Grace had been torturing herself with her catalog of dire prognostications about all the calamitous ways their story would be certain to end. From the outset, Grace had been persuaded that her banishment from St. Allie's would make Napoleon's retreat from Moscow look like a weekend junket to the Mall of America.

Not that winter weekends in Minneapolis were any picnic . . .

Still, it was no secret that Grace had been living with a toxic flood of angst that threatened to overrun its banks faster than the Susquehanna in April.

She didn't understand Abbie's silence.

But neither did she doubt Abbie's intent. She was sure there was a good reason for her lack of disclosure on the matter—it was just that, right now, she couldn't imagine what it was.

There was the other issue, too—her contract offer on *Ochre*. Grace had determined not to tell Abbie the news about the publication deal until after the tenure debacle had been resolved. Now, it had been—and more happily than she'd ever had reason to hope.

Yes. They would have a lot to discuss.

Maybe it was good she had the Butler Island trip to keep her mind off it all.

As she slowed the pontoon to approach the dock Grady shared with Roscoe, she knew it would take her a while to come to terms with how much the loss of this place would mean for her.

Probably forever. Grace couldn't remember ever feeling at home in a place the way she felt at home here. It was uncanny. If she'd finally managed to find her soul in Vermont, her heart resided on Butler Island.

Grendel stood proudly on the bow of the pontoon, like she was an experienced deckhand. She was wearing a blaze orange life vest that made her look chunky and comical—like an animated fire plug. Grace regretted that the thing had not been available in a spring tone that better matched the dog's natural palette.

Agnes would be so proud of me for even knowing that . . .

Grendel was watching their halting approach toward the dock with so much intent, Grace was half tempted to shout for her to toss the bumpers over and hop off to tug the boat in closer, so mooring it without crashing into something would be easier.

There was no sign of Roscoe's boat today. That meant he must be off on one of his scavenger junkets. She regretted that they'd never get the chance to make use of that stash of shiplap Dean had delivered. She had plans to build a screen to conceal the battery bank—something on a track that could roll aside like a cargo door when they needed access to the equipment.

Oh, well. Maybe the next owners would finish the place?

It didn't surprise her that there was no "for sale" sign near the water's edge. Most of the properties out here moved very fast, and almost always through word of mouth. Somebody would know somebody who had a neighbor or cousin who always kept an eye out for good deals on lucrative seasonal rentals.

She could see glimmers of the cabin's bright mustard exterior through the shifting leaves on the cottonwood trees. She loved how it shimmered in the sun and hugged that rise like it had staked a claim, and was stubbornly determined to stand there and bear witness to life on this lake forever. It reminded Grace of Ochre. Its history was etched in fits and starts, defined by periods of alternating care and neglect at the hands of a hundred accidental proprietors.

Grendel leapt to the dock as soon as Grace drifted in close enough to tie off, and roared ahead up the path toward the cabin with her tail whipping around in circles. Grace didn't worry about her veering off and getting into mischief. She knew the little dog well enough now to understand that Grendel was motivated too much by caution to engage in reckless behavior.

Grace unpacked her gear and the small stack of flattened boxes she'd picked up behind Price Chopper on Thursday. She hadn't bothered bringing anything aspirational or even especially interesting to cook. She decided it made more sense to concentrate on using up what stores of food they had in their small pantry. She made her way up the path a bit more slowly than Grendel. As much as she tried to suppress it, she couldn't shake an escalating sadness. It surged up from her feet like hammer blows and grew more pronounced with every step she took along the inevitability of her final stay at the one place where she truly felt at peace.

Why do I have to dramatize everything like this? It only makes me feel worse.

It had to be all the hours she'd just spent, consumed by the marathon grading of all those damn *Beowulf* papers. It was hard to yank her head back from its sojourn through the swirling fog of myth, where legendary heroes waged epic battles against monstrous foes—and the bleak hopelessness of winter was an enduring state of mind.

It all seemed to mesh perfectly with the somberness of her sentiments about today.

Grendel was nowhere in sight when she reached the cabin. That seemed odd. And it looked like the grass had just been cut. That seemed odder—unless Karen had already hired someone to keep the place spiffed-up and ready to show potential buyers.

But there was something else off-kilter, too. The door was open.

Grace felt a little surge of panic. Surely, she hadn't been so distracted the last time she was out here that she forgot to lock up?

Unlikely—even with her level of preoccupation over Abbie.

But if she had managed to forget, there was no telling what family of wildlife squatters might have taken up residence inside the house.

Only one way to find out . . .

She was halfway up the steps when she heard the music.

Joni Mitchell?

Yeah. She listened for a few seconds. It was Joni, all right—softly crooning jazz lyrics in her signature dulcet tones.

"The more I'm with you pretty baby . . ."

Joni was slowly unreeling the Lambert, Hendricks and Ross classic, "Centerpiece."

What the hell?

She took a tentative step inside. Still no Grendel in sight. And not only was there music playing, something smelled terrific—like sautéed leeks and fresh thyme.

Grace looked around the room to be sure that, in her distraction, she hadn't stumbled into the wrong cabin. All she needed was to have Edward or Mrs. Simpson bust a cap in her ass for breaking and entering.

And it wouldn't be her first offense, either . . .

Nope. This was the right place, all right. There was the same sofa, the same rug, the same table and chairs. The front windows were all open and a glorious breeze was blowing in off the lake. The music was playing from Grady's stereo—which meant someone had fired up the bank of batteries. The wonderful smells were coming in from the kitchen. Grace took a few quiet steps closer to try and peer past the doorway without being seen. That's when she saw it. It stopped her dead in her tracks.

Ochre.

There she was, in all her irreverent glory—full-sized and beautifully framed—dominating the back wall of the cabin.

Grace stood staring at her for so long she failed to notice that Grendel had rejoined her. She looked down at the excited dog and realized she was no longer wearing her life vest.

"What happened to your donut, girl?" she asked.

"I took it off," a voice from the kitchen answered. Abbie appeared in the doorway, holding the orange vest. "I hope you don't mind."

Grace dumbly shook her head.

"I felt she was pretty safe from drowning up here," Abbie continued. "Unless we get another tsunami like last time."

Tsunami? Yeah, that seemed entirely possible . . .

Grace finally stopped gaping at Abbie like an imbecile and found her voice. "What are you *doing* here?"

"Right now? Making a quiche. Are you hungry?"

"Am I . . ." Grace was tempted to pinch herself. "Is Rod Serling here, too?"

"Of course he is," Abbie laughed. "He's my sous chef."

"That figures." Grace dropped her load of boxes and gear and sat down on the arm of the sofa. "I'm gonna need a minute to process. How the hell did you pull this off?"

Abbie folded her long arms. "Pull what off?"

Grace waved an arm to encompass their surroundings. "*This.* All of this." She pointed at Ochre, who posed confidently against the far wall, staring back at them with amusement. "*That.* How'd you do *that?*"

Abbie shrugged. "Amazon Prime?"

Grace rolled her eyes. "I doubt it."

"Okay. I had a bit of help. CK had a contact on the board at the Arizona Museum of Art."

"Of course, she did." Grace shook her head in wonder and pointed at the reproduction. "She's beautiful." She looked at Abbie. "You're beautiful. Have I ever told you that before?"

Abbie didn't reply. Grace thought she detected a slight blush spreading across her neck.

"I'll never make that mistake again," Grace said. "I plan to tell you every day."

"I don't know about all that," Abbie said. "But I do know that I like the promise of every day."

"You do?" The simple declaration thrilled Grace.

Abbie nodded.

"So, I guess that means you know about my tenure decision?"

"I do," Abbie replied. "But only because I read the minutes from that part of the meeting last night."

Grace was confused. "You didn't attend?"

Abbie shook her head. "Remember the other day when we had our texting bonanza?"

"Sure."

"That's when the tenure committee was presenting its recommendations. I excused myself and went into the main meeting room until they concluded."

"And you never asked about the results?"

"Not right then, no."

"I was going to quit." She met Abbie's eyes. "I *tried* to quit—but they wouldn't let me."

"Thank *god*."

"That's when Eddie told me about what you'd done—the morning after they announced your appointment." Grace shook her head. "I couldn't believe it. He said you offered to resign if recusal wasn't good enough. Why'd you do something so crazy?"

"It wasn't any crazier than your offer to quit, Grace."

There it was again—that infernal coin with faces on both sides. *Janus*—their talisman. The god of beginnings and endings.

"I guess that's true," Grace agreed. "Why didn't you tell me? You had to know I was practically digesting my own organs worrying about the likely prospects for you—and for me."

Abbie crossed the room and perched on the edge of the coffee table, facing Grace.

"I *couldn't* tell you, Grace." Abbie took hold of her hand. "Please understand that. Even hinting at my recusal to you would have been a gross violation of the conflict-of-interest policy. I was honor bound not to discuss any aspect of this with you until the tenure decision was reached, and the dean informed you about the board's decision—whichever way it went. The outcome for both of us was too important to jeopardize. All I could do was hope and pray that you'd trust me—*trust us*. You'll never know how hard it was for me not to say anything to you—not to tell you that you didn't need to be so worried."

"I guess that makes sense." Grace gave Abbie a small smile. "Besides, every time I got too moribund, CK would shove her Birkenstock-clad foot a little more firmly up my ass."

"I do love that woman," Abbie said.

"By the way," Grace gave Abbie's warm hand a gentle squeeze. "Nice job on that whole endowed chair thing. Your idea?"

Abbie shrugged. "I may have suggested something about it to Mitch."

Grace chuckled. "Nothing quite like dangling that fat Duke Endowment Rolodex in front of her. Her eyes were pretty much rolling back into her head."

"Really?" Abbie seemed excited. "You talked with her?"

Grace nodded. "Last night. I think she's gonna do it."

"Well, I'll be damned."

"She said some pretty nice things about you, too. I think she wants to hang around St. Allie's for a while—see how things shake out."

"That certainly makes two of us," Abbie agreed.

"Three of us."

Abbie smiled and leaned forward. Grace met her in the middle. The whole damn thing was bliss. The cabin. The painting. The soft jazz. The warm breeze blowing in from the water. The aroma of Abbie's quiche. Even the paranoid little dog, nosing about their feet to demand her share of the action.

Grace didn't want any of it to end—not today. *Not ever.*

"I love you," she whispered against Abbie's fragrant hair.

"You'd better," Abbie said, before kissing Grace's ear. "Otherwise, I just made a serious error in judgment."

Before Grace could ask her to explain, a timer in the kitchen went off.

"That's breakfast." Abbie gave Grace a last quick kiss before getting to her feet. "Come and open the cava for me?"

"I'd love to." Grace stood up and followed her into the kitchen.

Abbie's quiche tasted as wonderful as it smelled. Every bite was like a little explosion of flavor.

"What all is in this?" Grace asked.

"Eggs. Cream," Abbie replied. "The usual."

"Nuh uh." Grace lifted another forkful to her mouth. "There's nothing *usual* about this delightful panoply of edible contradictions."

"Panoply?" Abbie asked. "Have you been binge-watching *Iron Chef* reruns?"

"Not lately. I've been too busy writing my own epitaph."

Abbie reached across the small table and patted her hand. *"Mon pauvre bébé."*

Grace smiled at her shyly. "You're gonna have to cool it with the French . . . every time you unreel one of those damn phrases, I turn into Gomez Addams."

Abbie looked at her with feigned innocence. "Is that a problem?"

"Maybe not for you. But keep it up, and I'm gonna have to start sitting on a towel."

She'd never seen Abbie cut loose and laugh like that. The waves of mirth rolled on and on—more like outright guffaws than laughter. Grace was captivated by it—and she resolved to find ways to ensure it would happen again. Often.

"Okay, come on." Grace tried to calm her down. "Give. What all is in this wonderful thing? It's amazing."

Abbie made a concerted effort to compose herself.

"It's a recipe from my grand-mére," she explained. "She would modify it with anything in season. Her base was simple. Cold butter and lard for the short crust. Crème fraiche. Eggs. A single grate of nutmeg." She shrugged. "After that? Add whatever herbs or cheeses strike your fancy. Today, I used leeks, fresh thyme, sundried tomatoes and gruyère. Simple."

Grace disagreed. "Simple—*not*. I had no idea you could cook."

"You mean you thought my only culinary skill was ordering pizza?"

"The thought did occur to me." Grace took another glorious bite. "I'm going to have to renew my Planet Fitness membership."

"Don't worry. Today is special. We're celebrating."

"You'll get no arguments from me on that."

Grace took a sip of her cava. It was cold, dry and perfect. It tasted like summer strawberries.

Abbie's music was still playing—Carmen McRae, now. "The Very Thought of You."

"So, you like jazz?" Grace asked. "I wouldn't have guessed that."

"No? Why not?"

"It seems so . . . *provincial* for you."

Abbie smiled. "If by 'provincial,' you mean *American*—you'd be right. I started listening to it as a teenager, precisely *because* it annoyed my mother. She hated anything that smacked too much of American culture."

"So, you did your best to provoke her?"

Abbie nodded energetically. "Of course, I did. And I was a great success, too. But, probably, based on my mother's sterling performance at dinner last weekend, you figured that much out."

"It's fair to say I had an inkling."

"Her behavior was outrageous. I can't think of it without mortification."

"Yeah. About that . . ." Grace took care to phrase her next

262

question carefully. "Eddie hinted at something your mother may have said when she returned to the dining room after discovering us in . . . an unguarded moment."

"Unguarded?" Abbie laughed. "That's *one* way to put it."

"Well? How would you describe it?"

"I'd probably say *authentic*—because, for me, it certainly was. I'd never actually said anything directly to my parents about my sexual identity—although I'm certain they suspected the truth about it. Especially after I married Harlan."

"Why then?" Grace asked.

"Harlan was a fine man—many years older than me. Old enough to arouse my mother's latent suspicion that I was marrying him to avoid the possibility of having children."

"Were you?"

She nodded. "But that wasn't the only reason. I genuinely cared for him. We were more like best friends than lovers."

"How did you meet? And I hope it's okay for me to ask these questions about him," Grace added. "I don't want to pry if you'd prefer not to talk about it."

"Of course it's okay for you to ask about my marriage to Harlan. I have no desire to conceal anything from you."

"Thanks," Grace said. "Really."

"He was a trustee at Princeton while I was teaching there. I first met him because he'd done his undergraduate work in classics and was involved in some of our departmental initiatives. I found him to be charming and erudite. He was a colorful figure, too— rumpled, gray and irreverent. An archetypal Southern gentleman with a penchant for Faulkner and Belle Meade bourbon. Of course, my mother disdained what she called his folksy, affected airs, his colloquial speech and his humble origins. Harlan was the eldest son of low-country tobacco farmers in the Pee Dee region of South Carolina. He attended Duke on an American Tobacco Company scholarship, then got his JD at Princeton."

"He was an attorney?" Grace asked.

"Judge," Abbie replied. "Fourth Circuit. For the first two years after we married, we commuted between Princeton and Richmond. But we moved to Harlan's home in South Carolina together, after he became ill and retired from the bench. In Greenville, Harlan introduced me to longtime colleagues of his who were trustees of the foundation—which is headquartered nearby, in Charlotte. You pretty much know the rest."

Grace was moved by Abbie's simple story of her marriage, and the fondness with which she spoke of her late husband. "He sounds like quite a man," she said. "I know you were heartbroken to lose him."

"I was," Abbie agreed. "You'd have liked him. He had so much innate goodness. And he was always so kind and deferential to me—to everyone, really. He never allowed my mother's churlish behavior to ruffle him or get under his skin." She looked at Grace intently. "I hope you won't, either."

Grace raised an eyebrow. "You think I'll get another opportunity to find out?"

"Count on it."

"At least your father seemed to tolerate me." Grace smiled. "He sought me out after the inauguration."

"He did?" Abbie sounded surprised.

"Yeah. He kind of spoke in riddles—which I'm beginning to learn is an Abbot family characteristic."

Abbie laughed. "They do tend to cherish obfuscation."

"When he said goodbye, he shook my hand and delivered what felt like a benediction . . . in French, of course—another charming proclivity of your family."

"What did he say?"

"Love each other."

Abbie didn't comment, but she slowly raised a hand to her mouth. It was clear she was surprised by the content of her father's charge.

"I hope it's okay with you if I plan to hold up my end of bargain?" Grace asked.

"Oh, yes. More than okay."

"Good." Grace cleared her throat. "Because there's one other piece of shocking news I need to share with you."

"Shocking?" Abbie narrowed her eyes. "*How* shocking?"

"It concerns our friend here." Grace pointed at the framed print of Woman Ochre. "It seems that during one of her afternoon trysts with my Cro-Magnon brother—*in the guestroom at my house*—CK decided to liberate some hundred-odd pages of my manuscript. She then took it upon herself to ship them off to a literary agent in New York. The long and the short of it is that I got a publication offer from Algonquin in Chapel Hill."

Abbie's eyes grew wide. "Grace . . ."

Grace tried hard not to smile. "Yeah. They're going to publish it—and they even gave me an option on a second book."

"*Oh, my god.*" Abbie jumped up from her chair and rounded the table to grab hold of Grace so she could haul her to her feet and fling her arms around her neck. "I'm so proud of you, I'm so proud of you," she gushed. "This is wonderful news. *Wonderful.*" She hugged her even tighter. "I *knew* this would happen. It *had* to—the book is so damn good."

Grace hugged her back. "I'm glad you think so. I wanted to kill CK when she told me about it."

Abbie drew back. "Why on earth would you do that?"

Grace shrugged. "I just didn't think the book was ready—that the time was right for the story. But now? Now that they've finally discovered her and know where she's been hiding for the last thirty-three years? Well. I suppose now the time *is* right to share some magical tales of what might have been."

"Oh, honey, this is such wonderful, happy news."

Abbie kissed her—which in turn led to Grace kissing her back. Which in turn led to Grace getting the same old idea she always got whenever Abbie was this close.

"Wanna mess around?" she whispered.

Abbie didn't reply right away, and after what felt to Grace like a ridiculous interval, she concluded that Abbie was taking entirely too long to consider her proposition.

"Hey?" Grace gently shook her tall frame. "Yea or nay, lady—we only have the use of this joint for another forty-eight hours. Then it's back to our late-night frolics with your satanic garden trellis."

"Yeah," Abbie took Grace's face between her warm hands, "about that. Remember I told you there was a chance I may have made a serious error in judgment?"

Grace was beginning to know Abbie well enough to smell a rat.

"What about?" she asked. "And am I going to like it or hate it?"

"You tell me," Abbie said, tugging her closer. "It could go either way."

"That doesn't exactly inspire confidence," Grace offered. Although, she did have to admit that the way Abbie was holding on to her was inspiring all kinds of other ideas.

"After our first few ill-fated attempts at trying to be alone together," Abbie explained, "I decided that we needed to adopt a bolder strategy to ensure we could have uninterrupted time together."

"That makes sense, I guess." Grace was having a hard time concentrating because Abbie had started to add more . . . *empirical* emphasis to her explanation.

"When I heard about Grady selling the cabin," she kissed along Grace's neck, "I decided it was a no-brainer." She blew lightly on Grace's earlobe. "So, I bought it."

Dear god . . . Abbie felt so damn wonderful. Grace was lost in sensation. Her head was swimming and she was losing focus. She knew she wouldn't be able to remain standing much longer. Not if Abbie kept doing what she was doing with her hands and mouth.

"*Je t'aime,*" Abbie whispered.

It was all so luxurious. Everything Abbie was doing. *Everything she was saying.*

Wait a minute . . .

Grace's eyes snapped open. She pushed away from Abbie's exploring mouth.

"Hold on," she said. Her voice was husky. "What did you say?"

"That I love you." Abbie repeated.

"*Before* that," Grace prompted.

266

Abbie smiled at her. "The cabin," she said.

"What about the cabin?"

"I bought it, Grace. For us."

The words were enough to tip the balance of Grace's tenuous hold on reality. In one dizzy and explosive moment, she surrendered her battle with gravity—and with everything else she'd fought so hard to resist throughout her life. Faith. Happiness. Outcomes that were fair and just. A belief that one day, life would offer up something permanent—an enduring connection that would thrive and grow stronger, instead of withering on the vine of indifference. And love. Love that would last and stand with her through the rest of time.

Here it was. Here it *all* was—hers for the taking.

In her freefall of surrender, she spread her arms and welcomed them—Abbie, Grendel, and a lifetime of wayward, prodigal dreams that had come home at last.

About the Author

ANN McMAN is the author of eight novels and two short story collections. She is a two-time Lambda Literary Award finalist, a two-time Independent Publisher Award (IPPY) medalist, and a five-time winner of Golden Crown Literary Society Awards. In 2017, she was awarded the Alice B. Medal for Outstanding Body of Work. Ann and her wife, Bywater Books Publisher Salem West, live in Winston-Salem, North Carolina, with their two dogs and an exhaustive supply of vacuum cleaner bags.

Acknowledgments

My love affair with Vermont began nearly two decades ago when I had the great fortune to discover a place called Shore Acres. Because it was the height of the tourist season, they had no room at the inn (literally), but still found a way to accommodate me after my arrangements for lodging at another place fell through. So, I stayed. And I have returned to Shore Acres every year—sometimes multiple times—to write, research, and replenish my soul. It truly is the place I feel most at home—and I would be remiss if I did not acknowledge the enduring debt of gratitude I owe to Susan and Mike Tranby, and to my entire Shore Acres family. You've enriched my life beyond imagining, and I thank you all from the bottom of my heart.

This book came into being because of the prodding, encouragement, and downright nagging I received from an army of readers who loved a short story called "Falling from Grace," originally published in 2012 as part of the story collection *Sidecar*. There is not enough space here to reprint all the email exchanges I had with folks who asked, "Will you ever tell us what happens to Grace and Abbie?" If we did, this book would be longer than *War and Peace*—and have nearly as many battle scenes. Who knew those two characters had so many legs? Four of 'em, to be exact—and taken together, long enough to flesh out a bona fide, book-length story.

Enter *Beowulf for Cretins*, in which Grace and Abbie get all the

269

ink they need (or as much as time and reason would permit) to resolve the mess they managed to create in their shorter prequel.

You'll have to let me know if you think their story is well and truly sorted out now . . .

I have many people to thank for their help and insight.

Captain Holly of Driftwood Tours—best charter service in the Champlain Islands—introduced me to Butler Island, a place of wonders, and an out-of-the-way spot for really great hot dogs. She was even (mostly) patient in the face of repeated entreaties to pilot her trusty pontoon past Bernie Sanders' North Hero Island house . . . twice.

No one writes in a vacuum—not unless they work for Oreck. None of this book would have been possible without the keen insight, collaboration, participation, determination, and steadfast encouragement (often delivered in the form of an Adidas-clad foot up the wiz wang) of my beloved Salem West, aka Buddha. You make everything I do better, and I never want to learn what it would be like to write a book—or live a life—without you. That is truer than ever after the horrors of the past year—which I never would have survived without you. Thank you for being my person.

To my Bywater family—Slumdog, Hot Lips, SKP, Stef, Fay, RaLo, and Radar (who cleans up my verbal messes)—I don't ever want to leave home without you. In fact, I pretty much don't want to leave home *period*—unless it's to go back to Vermont. And even then, I want you all along for the ride. Thank you all for keeping our little beacon of light shining on the best books in the bidness.

Nancy Squires—you improve everything you wave your red pen over, and I thank you for your superb job editing this book. Okay, so is this where I ask, "Hey?" I never can remember . . .

Thank you, Christine and Lou Lou, for taking time from your already impossible schedules to read early drafts of the book, and to plow through the whole shootin' match as soon as it left my hot little hands. Since neither of you suggested I enter a witness relocation program, I guess that means you think it turned out okay. If not, please don't tell me . . . not unless you toss a really BIG steak in first.

Eternal love and adoration go to Christine "Bruno" Williams—The Voice That Launched a Thousand Subarus™. Thank you, Bruno, for agreeing to be the voice of Ann McMan. You always make me sound taller . . . and better looking. Since your fan base is now about nine million times larger and more devoted than mine, I think this means our partnership has worked out pretty well. Through you, I got amazing audiobooks and a beloved friend for life. What a coup!

Merci to the amazing (and decorative) Québécois, Pam Roberts for translating Abbie's meltdown into comprehensible French. I hope you enjoyed your cameo.

As always, I am humbled by the starring role Carole Cloud plays in my life. Thank you, dear friend, for being my personal Rizzo.

Lynn "Skippy" Ames? I will always be grateful to you for giving me a mantra that kept me sane near the grueling end of this project: *Focus on content, Thumper. Not word count.* I met my incremental little goals every day—and you deserve the credit. You know I love you dearly.

I offer thanks to our late, beloved, sweet, and totally paranoid little dog, Gracie, for being the inspiration for Grendel. Implied threats *still* abound, Gracie. Thanks for keeping us vigilant—and for sending Dave and Ella our way to take up the slack.

My own personal Nurze, Jeanne Barrett Magill, kept me far from sober when the going got rough. Keep on pouring, Nurze. Your friendship (and strict enforcement of Lodge protocols) make me better in every way.

Thanks to Biz, who is more than a dear friend and adopted niece—she is frequently the only adult in the room. Biz? Please continue this activity.

Father Frank and Flora taught me (with great indulgence for my profound ignorance) about the marvel of *eucatastrophe*. Thank you both for standing fast at the helm of my moral compass. If my personal journey lands me anyplace worth the effort, you'll get most of the credit.

I would be in violation of a solemn promise made to my dear friend, Sandra Moran, if I failed to make mention of how her mother, Cherie, lost her best shot to set a world's record for FreeBASEing the Eiger while nine months pregnant. Sadly, when Cherie's water broke, it lasted forty days and forty nights (hard to miss the irony there), and her window for making the historic climb closed with the onset of an especially brutal winter in Grindelwald. Although her hopes were dashed, Cherie did later recognize how the fates had smiled upon her—and not just because she was gifted with a Mensa baby. Later examination revealed that *her* idea of "freebasing" entailed an activity quite ... *different* from rock climbing without equipment.

But that's a story for another book ...

Eternal thanks, finally, to my incredible mother and real life best friend, Dee Dee. You were my biggest champion and my harshest critic, wrapped up together in a super-sized bundle of love and contradiction. You taught me to read, to write, to love books, to ask hard questions, to tell the truth no matter how hard it was, to push myself to be better at whatever I chose to do, and to always fold my towels in thirds. It is intolerable to me that I cannot talk with you—even for two minutes. But I will always hear your voice, I will always remember the valuable things you taught me, and I will *never* not miss you. It pains me beyond reason that I've finally, sadly reached the place where I have written a book you never got to read. All that remains for me is to promise you that the *next* one I write will be better. Rest in peace, dear Dee Dee. I will always love you.

Books by Ann McMan

Dust
Hoosier Daddy
Festival Nurse
Backcast
Beowulf for Cretins: A Love Story

The Jericho Series
Jericho
Aftermath
Goldenrod

Story Collections
Sidecar
Three (plus one)

At Bywater Books we love good books about lesbians just like you do, and we're committed to bringing the best of contemporary lesbian writing to our avid readers. Our editorial team is dedicated to finding and developing outstanding writers who create books you won't want to put down.

We sponsor the Bywater Prize for Fiction to help with this quest. Each prize winner receives $1,000 and publication of their novel. We have already discovered amazing writers like Jill Malone, Sally Bellerose, and Hilary Sloin through the Bywater Prize. Which exciting new writer will we find next?

For more information about Bywater Books and the annual Bywater Prize for Fiction, please visit our website.

www.bywaterbooks.com